D1366607

ZEN AND THE ART OF VAMPIRES

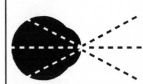

This Large Print Book carries the
Seal of Approval of N.A.V.H.

A DARK ONES NOVEL

ZEN AND THE ART OF VAMPIRES

KATIE MACALISTER

THORNDIKE PRESS

A part of Gale, Cengage Learning

GALE
CENGAGE Learning™

Detroit • New York • San Francisco • New Haven, Conn • Waterville, Maine • London

GALE
CENGAGE Learning™

The publisher does not have any control over and does not assume any responsibility for author or third-party Web sites or their content.
Thorndike Press® Large Print Romance.
The text of this Large Print edition is unabridged.
Other aspects of the book may vary from the original edition.
Set in 16 pt. Plantin.
Printed on permanent paper.

LIBRARY OF CONGRESS CATALOGING-IN-PUBLICATION DATA

MacAlister, Katie.
    Zen and the art of vampires : a dark ones novel / by Katie
MacAlister. — Large print ed.
        p. cm. — (Thorndike Press large print romance)
    Originally published: New York : Signet, 2008.
    ISBN-13: 978-1-4104-1443-4 (alk. paper)
    ISBN-10: 1-4104-1443-4 (alk. paper)
    1. Vampires—Fiction. 2. Large type books. I. Title.
PS3613.A227Z36 2009
813'.6—dc22   2009001656

Published in 2009 by arrangement with NAL Signet, a member of Penguin Group (USA) Inc.

Printed in the United States of America
1 2 3 4 5 6 7 13 12 11 10 09

This book is offered to the lovely ladies (and the few brave men) of my message forum, in gratitude for the hours of amusement, entertainment, and chuckles. You're too many to list here, but you know who you are. And don't think I haven't noticed that there is now a waiting list for people to get into the Corner of Shame — I told you guys that having buff, shirtless, kilt-clad men as waiters was just going to cause trouble. . . .

CHAPTER 1

"Experience the romance of Iceland under the starry summer night sky with a descendant of the Vikings of yore; that's what the brochure said."

Eyes a startling shade of unadulterated grey considered me seriously.

"Thus far, my starry summer nights have been trying to figure out why my hair-dryer adapter keeps blowing out the hotel lights. I don't suppose you are free tonight for a little stargazing?"

The grey eyes didn't blink, just continued to watch me cautiously, as if their owner expected me to suddenly leap onto the tiny round metal and glass table at which we sat, and start dancing the cancan. "Stargazing?"

"Yes, it means looking at the stars. Speaking of which, your English is remarkably good. But I assume your lack of enthusiasm means you'd rather pass on the idea." I

7

sighed. "I kind of thought so. It's par for the course, you know. Well, par for *my* course. A couple of ladies on the tour have done well for themselves thus far."

Three women danced by in progression. The first two were strangers, but the third one, Magda, was a decidedly plump, buxom lady of Spanish descent who had snapping black eyes and a wicked sense of humor.

"Pia, you're not dancing?" Magda called as her partner, Raymond, whirled her around to vaguely Germanic music, complete with accordion. It was the middle of June, and all of Iceland was celebrating their Independence Day with much abandon, even the tourists. Small booths of crafts and food vendors lined the square, filling the air with an intriguing mixture of smells that ranged from floral (a dried-lavender seller) to mouthwatering (a Mediterranean gyro stand). At the far end of the square a stage had been set up, and various bands ranging from country (who knew Iceland had country music?) to easy listening had played all day. I gathered that the more raucous bands were to grace the evening's stage.

"Not this time, no," I called back.

"You should!" she yelled, her deep, throaty voice carrying surprisingly well over the noise of the music and people. "The music is divine!"

I thought about pointing out the obvious, that thus far in the trip, no blond, blue-eyed descendant of Vikings had asked me to join the throng, but a small morsel of pride kept me from bellowing that out to Magda.

My tablemate swigged down the last of his beverage and belched, politely excusing himself.

I eyed him doubtfully for a moment, before deciding beggars couldn't be choosers. "Would it be forward of me if I asked you if you would care to dance?"

He looked thoughtful for a moment, then nodded and stood up. "Dance is good."

I was a bit surprised at his easy acquiescence, but determined to enjoy myself no matter what, I took his hand and wound my way through the crowds perched at café tables to the part of the square where the dancing was taking place.

"Do you two-step?" I asked my partner politely.

He glanced down at my shoes. "Two feet."

"Yes. It's a dance. I assume you don't know it?"

"No." He shook his head. "I like dance."

With careful deliberation, he put his faded-sandal-clad feet directly on top of my sturdy, if somewhat scruffy, leather walking shoes, and looked up with expectation.

"It's a good thing you're as small as you are, and I'm as big as I am," I told the boy, taking his hands and moving in gentle, vaguely dancelike motions that would keep him from being dislodged. "How old are you, exactly?"

The boy scrunched up his face for a moment as he sorted out the proper word. "Four."

"Really? Then your English is even more remarkable than I thought. I couldn't say squat in another language when I was your age, and here you are dancing with me and chatting away like crazy. Well, all right, I'm the one doing most of the chatting, but you seem to understand what I'm saying, and as I am probably the only person on Sgt. Patty's Lonely Heart's Club Tour who has yet to hook up with either a fellow tour mate or a handsome local, you're pretty much it as far as available conversationalists go. What's your name?"

His brows pulled together again for a moment. "Geirfinnur."

"What an interesting name. I'm Pia Thomason. I'm from Seattle. Do you know where that is?"

He shook his head.

"Let's see, what's Seattle known for . . .

10

Microsoft? Have you ever heard of Microsoft? Starbucks? Google?"

He shook his head again.

"Geirfinnur!" A man appeared from out of the dancers, gesticulating at my feet as he spoke in Icelandic. My dance partner reluctantly stepped off my shoes, shooting me a chastened look.

"Are you Geirfinnur's dad?" I asked, as the subject of his ire's eyes started to fill with contrite tears.

"You are English?" I could see the similarity in their faces, and the same clear grey eyes. "I am very sorry that he is behaved so poor with you."

"He wasn't behaving badly at all," I said quickly, ruffling the boy's hair. He rewarded me with a toothy grin. "In fact, just the opposite. He wandered past while I was sitting and watching everyone, and kindly kept me company and helped me eat ice cream. He speaks English so well, I'm really quite amazed at how young he is."

"My wife is from Scotland," the man explained, giving his son a fond look. "You say thank you to the English lady."

"American, not English. I'm from Seattle."

Geirfinnur's father adopted the same look of concentration his son had worn as he obviously tried to pinpoint Seattle.

11

"It's in the Pacific Northwest. Upper left-hand corner of the country. We have Boeing and Amazon."

"Seattle?" the man said, his brow clearing. "Nintendo!"

"Yes, we have that, too," I answered, smiling as my dance partner leaped around us shouting, "Nintendo, Nintendo! Super Mario Brothers!"

"You are here as a tourist? I am Jens Jakobsson. That is Geirfinnur."

"Yes, I'm with a . . . uh . . ." I waved a vague hand, suddenly shy about the fact that I was on a singles' tour. "It's a three-week tour of Europe."

"That is most excellent. You enjoy Island?" He pronounced the word "Iceland" with its native inflection.

"Very much. Dalkafjordhur is a lovely little town. We've been here two days and have three more to explore Reykjavík and the area before we move on to Holland."

"This is good," he said, grinning. "You are so kind to Geirfinnur, we will show you around tonight, show you places tourists don't normally see. We know a good place to see fireworks. You would like that?"

"I would love it," I said, sincerely pleased at the thought of meeting some local folk. My happiness was short-lived as I pulled up

12

a mental image of the tour itinerary. "Only . . . drat. I think our tour is going out into the countryside tonight, to see some ruins."

"Ruins are very pretty here," Jens said. "But not as pretty as fireworks, I think."

"Fireworks!" Geirfinnur parroted, suddenly rushing me and wrapping his arms around my waist as he looked up. "Fireworks are good!"

"Geir, do not annoy the lady. She has a tour to go with. What ruins are you going to visit?"

"It's some sort of protected forest with a ruin contained within. I'm afraid I don't remember the name, but evidently it has some tie-in to a cult that was supposed to be very prominent around midsummer, and since that's just a couple of days away —"

"Ilargi!" Jens gasped, his expression suddenly horror filled as he snatched his son from where he was bouncing up and down on my feet. "You are Ilargi?"

"Me? No, I'm Irish. Mostly. There's some German on my mom's side."

Jens eyed me warily. "If you are not Ilargi, are you from the Brotherhood?"

"I'm not overly religious," I said slowly, confused by his reaction. "I'm sorry, maybe we're having a communication issue, despite the fact that your English is exceptional. This Ilargi place that we're going to visit tonight isn't an abbey or a religious house; it's a stretch of untouched forest, which I gather is rare. It's supposed to have some sort of pagan meaning, but I'm afraid I kind of skimmed that section of the itinerary."

"Not pagan," Jens said, picking up his squirming son and backing away. "Not good. Stay away from Geirfinnur. Stay away from Ilargi."

Before I could ask him just what the dickens that meant, he turned and bolted, Geirfinnur's waving hand the last thing I saw before they were swallowed up by the dancing crowd.

"Well, how do you like that?" I asked no one in particular. I was answered by a brutal jab to the back, reminding me that there were better places for contemplation of confusing Icelanders than the middle of a dance floor.

I made my way back to my table and ordered another lemonade, nursing it as I watched the people swarm around me. What on earth was so wrong with the Ilargi forest that it triggered such a strong reaction in Jens? Did Audrey know about it? I wondered.

Before I could mull over what I wanted to

do next, a dark-haired woman plopped down in the chair that had previously been occupied by Geirfinnur. She shot a glare over her shoulder toward a very handsome blond man as he bumped her back while escorting two children wearing blue and white horns past us. "Hey, Pia. You look like I feel. Did you hear? The trip to the forest is off for tonight. And a good thing, too. I could do without being eaten alive by mosquitoes and god knows what other kinds of insects there are around here. I don't suppose you've seen Audrey? She disappeared right after she told me about the cancellation, and I didn't have time to have a word with her about the serious lack of men on this tour."

"Not since lunch, no," I answered, digging out my disposable camera to snap a picture of the behorned kids as they waved flags madly. "I think she said something about checking on the accommodations in Amsterdam."

Denise, the fourth woman on the tour, and my least favorite of all the members, curled a scornful lip at my answer. "Bah. We don't go there for three days. Not that I won't be glad to get out of this country. I've just been in the most appalling bookshop over there. Ugh. They didn't have anything

15

printed in the last hundred years. And the spiders! Who'd have thought that Iceland would have such big spiders? Positively tarantulas! Here, you! Diet Coke. Coca-Cola. You understand?" Denise grabbed a passing waitress and shook her arm. "Pia, you have a phrase book — how do you say that I want a Diet Coke?"

The waitress gave her a long-suffering look. "I speak English. We do not have Coke. I will bring you a Pepsi."

"Whatever, just so it's cold." Denise released the waitress and used my napkin to mop at the sweat that made her face sparkle in the bright afternoon sunshine. "Sorry I just sat down without asking you, but we big girls have to stick together. You weren't waiting for anyone, were you?"

Sharp, washed-out hazel eyes peered at me from beneath overplucked eyebrows, a gloating glint indicating that an answer in the affirmative would surprise her greatly. I adopted a polite smile and shook my head, my teeth grinding at both her expression and the big-girl comment. I had come to grips with the fact that I was what my mother euphemistically termed "big boned," but I didn't need to be reminded of it every few minutes, as Denise was wont to do.

"Didn't think so," she answered with sour

pleasure. "Women like us never get the guys. It's always the ones who put out who end up having all the fun. That Magda. Did you hear her last night? She was at it all night long. I asked Audrey to change my room, but she says the hotel is full and they can't. Honestly, why on earth did I spend two grand on a singles' tour of romantic Europe if the only men on the trip are old, perverts, or gay, and I have to spend every friggin' night listening to Magda get her jollies. 'Oh, Raymond! Harder! Harder, my stallion of love!' " she all but yelled in an obscene parody of Magda's Spanish-inflected voice.

"Shhh," I cautioned, frowning at the startled looks we received from people seated around us. "Others can hear you."

"So what?" She shrugged. "They can't understand us, and even if they could, I'm not saying anything that isn't true. Has Raymond hit on you yet? He tried me this morning, but I wouldn't have anything to do with him. I don't take her leftovers." She cast an acid glance toward the dancers.

I had no doubts at all — Magda and I shared a bathroom, and noises from her room were audible through it — that Raymond and she were actually hitting it off rather well, but it was almost impossible to believe that he'd want anything to do with

Denise. She was pretty enough, with dark brown hair that was carefully coiffed, a heart-shaped face, and an overall impression of neatness despite the trials of traveling out of one bag, but her personality did much to ruin the first impression.

"Sorry." She raked me over with a scathing look. "I didn't mean to rub it in that Raymond wants into my pants but not yours. Not that you're missing much, despite Magda's histrionics. Have you ever seen such a motley collection of men as the ones on this tour? We're expected to hit it off with Ray, the lounge lizard; Gary, who has to be right off the set of *Queer as Folk;* Ben, who is clearly sixty if he's a day; or Alphonse, the Mafia pervert. And we paid money for this? Audrey sure has some sort of a scam, and we're the suckers who fell for it. Romantic Europe, my ass."

I'd lived with Denise's negativity and overall nastiness for three days now, and was sorely tempted to tell her just what I thought, but I reminded myself that we had another eighteen days together, and it wouldn't actually kill me to turn the other cheek. Instead I indulged in a fantasy wherein she was left behind on a remote fjord.

"Have you dated much lately?" she asked,

obviously sharpening her claws for another attack.

I smiled and threw in a couple of hungry wolves prowling along the edge of the fjord. "I live outside of Seattle in a small town in the mountains. There aren't a lot of people there to begin with, so it's kind of hard to meet guys. That's why I decided to go on this tour, to open my horizons."

"At least you're not opening your legs for everything with a penis, unlike some people I could mention," she said with another waspish look toward Magda. "I think we've been had, though. The men on the tour are useless, and as for these Icelanders . . . they may be descended from Vikings, like Audrey says, but I don't see any of them panting over us. Mind you, if you said the words 'green card' to them, that would change things fast enough, but that's not going to happen."

"We've only had three days so far —" I started to object, but was cut short when she slammed her glass down on the little table.

"You don't get it, do you? Pia, look at yourself! You're, what, forty? Forty-five?"

"Thirty-nine. I won't be forty for another ten months," I said defensively, trying to keep a grip on my temper. I had spent every

19

cent I had to go on this tour, and I absolutely refused to let one sour woman ruin
what was sure to be the trip of a lifetime.

"Close enough to count. You're forty, with
no man, no looks, and a dead-end job in
some insignificant little town."

"Hey!" I objected. "You don't even know
what I do. My job is quite nice."

"You said at the orientation that you were
some sort of a secretary."

"I am the administrative manager for an
animal shelter that specializes in elderly pets
who have been displaced," I answered, my
fingers curling into fists beneath the table-
top. "It's a very rewarding job!"

"I'm sure it is," she answered with a half
sneer. "But there's hardly any room for
advancement, is there?"

I gritted my teeth and said nothing. I
didn't have to defend myself or my job to
this harpy.

"Face it," Denise said, grabbing my arm
as she leaned forward across the table.
"Women like us get the shaft our whole
lives. You may think that there is a man out
there for you, a Mr. Wonderful who will be
everything you want, but there isn't. Look
around you, Pia. Look at who has all the
handsome men — it's the pretty ones, the
skinny ones, the ones who don't give a fuck

about anything but getting what they want. They've got no morals and don't care who knows it."

"I don't buy that," I said, jerking my arm out of her grip. "I know a lot of nice women who get men. Sometimes it just takes a while; that's all."

"Something your mommy told you?" she asked, her words whipping me like a scorpion's tail.

"I really don't think —"

"No, of course you don't. That's because everyone is so politically correct these days. But let's cut the crap, shall we, and get real. We're the last pick on the volleyball team, Pia. We get the leftovers. I can tell you don't like to admit it, so I'll prove it to you." She scooted around in her chair, waving a hand toward the stage.

The music had stopped while one group of musicians was being replaced by another, leaving the dancers to catch their breath, and the square half empty. The sun was low in the sky now, little fiery orange and red tentacles streaking upward, long indigo shadows beginning to edge their way across the square. A few people strolled through the shadows, mostly families, the kids leaping about less enthusiastically as they started to wind down from the day's activities.

"That guy, that one there, the blond guy with the receding hairline. You think he'd like you?" Denise asked, pointing at a man who stood with his arm twined around a slender woman. "Or how about that one, the man with the beard. He looks like an accountant. Maybe he'd go for you."

My lips tightened. I refused to tell her that she was perfectly welcome to live in her misanthropic world, but I preferred a much happier place.

"Oh! Those two! Those two across the square, coming out of that building. Oh my god, they're gorgeous. That's what I'm talking about — perfect eye-candy specimens. Both tall, both dark haired, although I don't like long hair on a man, and both absolutely and completely out of our reach."

I looked where she was pointing. "Oh, I don't know."

She swiveled around in her chair to pin me back with a maliciously triumphant gaze. "You're never going to have a man like that, Pia. Neither will I. If we're lucky, we'll get some balding, paunchy couch potato, but the good ones are not for us."

"There's nothing wrong with a man who is balding and has a bit of a paunch," I protested.

"Oh, come on! They all end up that way, sure, but you don't want them to start out looking like that!"

"Not all men are alike," I pointed out. "Some men like more than just a perfect body, just as some women prefer men who aren't drop-dead gorgeous. There's no reason to assume that just because we aren't supermodel gorgeous, we'll never have a hunky guy like one of those eye-candy men."

A hard look settled on her face. "You just refuse to face reality, don't you? Well, let's put our money where our mouths are, OK? You go talk to those two hunks and see what happens."

"I didn't mean those two specifically," I said quickly, my palms suddenly sweating at the thought of the humiliation that would follow should I even think of approaching the two men in question. "I just meant eye candy in general."

She stood up and scanned the crowd for a second before sitting down. "I don't see anyone as gorgeous as those two who aren't with someone already. Mind you, they could be gay and a couple, in which case I will still win, but let's go on the supposition that they're not gay and not married. You go talk to them and see if one of them asks you out."

"This is not a contest, Denise."

"Sure it is. You think you're right, and I know I am. You think you can date someone as gorgeous as the two male model wannabes, and I say they won't even give you the time of the day. Prove me wrong; that's all I'm asking."

"They could have wives or girlfriends who aren't here," I protested, a slight feeling of panic making my stomach tighten. "Or maybe they just broke it off with someone and aren't looking for a relationship. There are any number of reasons that they wouldn't want to ask me out."

She flicked the wadded-up paper straw wrapper at me. "That's a cop-out, but I'm willing to give you the benefit of the doubt. How about this: you walk past the two guys — just walk past them — and see if one of them is interested enough to watch you."

I opened my mouth to protest that catching a man's eye wasn't going to prove anything, but the triumphant gleam in her eyes was too much for the tenuous grasp I had on my temper. If nothing else, I would be able to escape her presence. "All right, you're on. I'll walk past them."

"I'll be here, waiting, when you come

back. Alone," she said with a smile that made my palm itch with the need to smack her.

"I am not a violent person," I muttered as I gathered my things and shuffled my way around the people at the café. "It is illegal to kill a tour mate, no matter how provoked I am."

The square was still partially empty as people took the opportunity offered by the band switch to refresh themselves at the cafés and food stands that lined the area. I paused a moment at the edge of the square, having no trouble in finding my quarry.

The two men continued to stand in the shadows cast by a tall, sculpted stone building, evidently having some sort of a conversation, since one of them periodically nodded, while the other spoke, his hands gesturing quickly.

Glowing bluish white lights suddenly blinked on around the perimeter of the square, causing me to squint for a minute as my eyes adjusted to the brightness. The sun in this area of Iceland never quite set during midsummer, but it went far enough down on the horizon to bring on a sort of twilight, what was called "white night." The sky was a glorious palette that ranged from a gorgeous amber to deep blues, the glow enough to see by, but dark enough to leave everything a bit softened about the edges. A little ripple of excitement filtered over to me as people started to drift away from the square, heading to the nearby park that sat overlooking the waterfront, where the evening fireworks were to be held.

I eyed the two men who stood in conversation. They were both clad completely in black, one carrying a leather jacket, the other wearing one despite the heat of the day. The jacket wearer was farthest from me, his face too shadowed to see in detail, but I did notice he had short curly chestnut brown hair. The one turned slightly away from me, holding on to his jacket slung casually over his shoulder, had long black hair pulled back in a ponytail.

Despair welled in my gut as I edged my way around the square toward them, my mind frantically trying to find a way out of the untenable situation I'd managed to create. "What on earth are you thinking, you foolish woman? So Denise has stung your pride with her constant cracks about your appearance and likelihood of getting a man. Do you seriously think there's any way on this green earth that you will ever be able to garner even a momentary flash of interest from those two gorgeous men, let alone a second glance?"

I glanced back at Denise, hoping against hope that she might have given up on me and gone to see the fireworks, but doubting she'd miss the opportunity to do a little old-fashioned gloating when I failed at my goal.

"I hate being right," I said under my breath. Denise stood at the table, the café nearly empty now as more and more people headed to the park. She made shooing gestures toward me.

I edged my way past a tiny clothing shop and pretended interest in racks of dusty books that sat outside an even dustier bookseller. This must be the spider-filled shop Denise had mentioned. I glanced toward her. She had her back to me as one of the men on the tour stopped to talk, gesturing in the direction of the park. Excellent! She was distracted! Now was my chance.

I ducked into the spider-filled bookshop, scurrying to the back, grabbing a couple of books with English titles to pretend interest. "She's not likely to come looking in here for me if the spiders are as bad as she said. I'll just hide out for a little bit. There's no shame in hiding. She'll figure I skipped out, and go look elsewhere for me, right? Right."

My relief lasted about two minutes, after

which shame got the better of me. Being a coward wasn't my style. I started toward the front door, stopping when a tiny, wizened old man coughed at me, looking meaningfully at the books in my hands. Hastily I dug out a couple of bills and gave them to him with a word of apology.

A careful and covert survey of the square from inside the bookshop confirmed my hunch. Denise was disappearing down a street opposite, clearly on the hunt for me. "Yay for insight into human nature."

I strolled out of the bookshop, adopting a casual, not in the least bit stalkerlike air as I meandered toward the two men, eyeing them critically as I got closer. "Maybe I'm just too cynical. There's nothing wrong with me, other than there's a bit too much of me. I don't have any vices or bad habits other than talking to myself. I like animals. I am open to new experiences. Is it so out of the bounds of reason that one of those two guys might actually look at me?"

One of them gestured in my direction. The other turned to look. I spun around and feigned interest in a bakery window. When I glanced back, they were continuing their conversation.

Denise was still nowhere to be seen, but I was not about to chicken out now. This had gone beyond a silly dare. "My honor is at stake, dammit!"

Ignoring the fact that the very same sense of honor had been lacking a few minutes before, I squared my shoulders and turned to face the two men. "Just get it done, Pia. Think positive, and get it done."

The two men loomed closer as I strolled confidently toward them, my belly roiling with anticipation of what was sure to be a deflating experience. "Maybe I could bribe them. Maybe I could offer them a few bucks if one of them would walk back to the hotel with me . . . Ugh. Is this what it's coming to? Bribing men to pretend an interest in you? For shame, Pia. For sha — *oof!*"

A woman whumped into me with enough force that it sent us both reeling, my books and her large bag falling to the ground.

She excused herself in French.

"Do you speak English? I'm afraid my French is pretty rusty," I said, kneeling to help her gather up the things that had spilled out of her bag. I handed her back the usual assortment of items — keys, cell phone, compact, and a paperback — before gathering up the couple of books I'd pur-chased.

"Oh, thank you. Yes, I do speak English. I am so sorry, I am very late for an appoint-

29

ment and wasn't watching where I was going," the woman said in a delightful French accent, her delicate-boned face perfectly framed by fluffy blond hair. She had that air of fragility common to Frenchwomen, the one that screamed "gamine." That she plowed into me with the force of a Mack truck mattered little, I suspected, to the men who no doubt flung themselves daily at her feet. "Did I step on you? No? Good. I am very distressed, you see. I've lost the address where I'm supposed to go, and none of the bookshops seem to be the right one. Ah, there is another one. I will try there."

"Beware of spiders," I warned as she tucked her belongings away in her bag.

The smile she flashed me faded. "Spiders?"

"Yes, evidently some big hairy ones."

She shuddered. "I detest spiders! Perhaps that shop is not the one. . . ." She eyed the bookstore with obvious distaste.

"If you're looking for a current book, they probably aren't going to have it. It seemed to be mostly old and antique books."

"Antique," she said thoughtfully. "That does not sound correct. The Zenith was most specific it was an English book with the man and woman on the cover dancing . . . oh, la la! The time!" She had glanced

30

at her watch, hoisting her bag onto her shoulder. "I will try another one; that does not look like a shop to have the dancing books, does it?"

"Naw, the only thing I found there was an old Agatha Christie and some Regency romance," I said, gesturing at my books.

"*Bien.* It is good I run into you, I think!"

"No problem," I called after her as she started off. "Always happy to save a fellow tourist from death by dusty spiders. But you're not going to the fireworks? The park is that way."

She paused and looked at where I was pointing. If she was a tourist like me, perhaps she didn't know where the festivities were to take place.

"Fireworks?"

"They're supposed to be having some fabulous fireworks show that you won't want to miss. For the Independence Day stuff."

"I cannot, I'm afraid," she said over her shoulder as she hurried off across the square. "I'm so very late, you see, and I lost the name of the shop. The light be within you, sister."

Her voice trailed behind her even after she was gone from sight.

The light be within me? That was an odd

thing to say. "She must belong to one of those religious groups, like the celebrities are always touting," I said to no one.

I shrugged and turned back to the men, who were still standing in close conversation.

"Boy, I give you guys a chance to go away and cut me a little slack, and you refuse. Fine. Be that way. I might as well get this over with, not that Denise is here to witness it."

I clutched my books and took a deep breath, then without any further dillydallying, marched myself toward the two men, determined to . . . I didn't know exactly what I was determined to do. Maybe smile at them as I passed, and hope one of them smiled back? If I did that, at least I could face Denise with a clear conscience over the breakfast table.

"Well, hell," I said out loud, stopping abruptly as the two men split up, heading in two different directions, neither of which encouraged them to so much as glance my way.

Denise's crow of laughter rolled over the square. She had come from the side nearest the park, arriving at the perfect moment to see the two men walk away from me.

"Worst timing ever," I ground out through

my teeth as I forced a smile, waving a hand at Denise to show that I heard her and admitted defeat. "I don't have to take anything more than that, though," I added softly to myself, hoisting my bag, camera, and books higher.

With one last look at the nearest of the two gorgeous men as he melted into the shadows of a connecting street, I lifted my chin and took myself off to the park.

I was going to have a good time, dammit, even if it killed me.

CHAPTER 2

"Is she gone?"

"One sec." Audrey, our tour leader and co-owner of Sgt. Patty's Lonely Hearts Club Tours, peeked out from behind the statue of a Viking explorer to scan the immediate crowd. Most people were sitting on the grass, watching with appreciative oohs and aahs as fireworks etched brilliant paths into the equally colorful night sky. Children ran around with the usual array of sparklers, the fireworks spitting glitter as they trailed brief-lived images into the air. The acid smell of the smoke hung heavy around us, slowly dissipated by the breeze blowing in from the water.

"I think that's her over on the other side. She's been prowling around all night looking for me, no doubt to complain about one thing or another."

"She didn't seem too happy about missing the trip out to the ruins," I admitted.

"Happy?" Audrey snorted. "She bitched so much about missing the fireworks, I decided it just wasn't worth it, and canceled the trip just to suit her. She certainly ought to be happy. Oh, lord, she's spotted Magda and Ray. They haven't seen her, poor things, and she's making a beeline straight for them. I wish I could just refund her money and boot her from the tour, but Patty would have a hissy if I did anything to piss off a client."

I patted Audrey on the arm. "You have my sympathies, and I wish I could help you with the truculent one, but I'm pretty much Denised out. I think I'll toddle back to the hotel."

She turned a distraught face to me. "Oh, Pia, don't go! The fireworks aren't over yet, and after that there's more music. You don't want to miss your chance at having a romantic encounter with a handsome Viking, now, do you?"

I thought of the two men whom I couldn't quite steel myself up to approach, and gave her a grim little smile. "I think I'll pass for tonight. You have fun, though."

"I'm sorry if Denise has made you feel uncomfortable," she said, clearly upset.

"Don't be. It's not your problem. I'm a big girl and can handle myself, even with

Denise. I'm just a bit tired from seeing Reykjavík this morning, and then all the wandering around the town I did this afternoon. Happy Iceland Independence Day!"

"You, too," she said, watching me with a rueful look as I made a dash for the exit.

The town we were staying in wasn't large, but its city center was filled with narrow little streets that twisted and turned upon themselves. I got lost twice, trying to find my way to the top of the town, and had to backtrack to the still-brightly-lit main square to get my bearings before setting out again on a street I hoped led to the small hotel we called home.

I'd just left the lights of the square and was making my way down a narrow, dark street that I had a horrible suspicion I'd just been down, when a dark form loomed up out of a doorway, causing me to simultaneously jump and shriek. My jump was to the side, however, not straight up, causing me to crash into the stone wall of the building.

The man said something in an unfamiliar language while I clutched the heart that seemed to be leaping from my chest. "Oh dear god, you scared me. You shouldn't do that to people; you could give them a heart attack."

The shadowy figure was still for a moment, then moved out into the light. "My apologies, madam," he said in a voice heavy with an Icelandic accent. "I did not see you, either. Here are your things."

"No harm done," I said, scrabbling at my feet for the contents that had spilled out of my purse.

"You are a tourist, yes?" the man asked.

"Yes." He seemed nice enough, with a freckled face and the same open, cheerful countenance that I was becoming convinced was standard in Iceland. "Just here for a few days, unfortunately. Oh, thanks." I tucked my bag under my arm, taking the books from him.

He stooped once more and picked up something else at my feet, offering it to me a second before he froze. The light hit his palm, flashing off of something held there.

I looked in surprise at the object he held: a narrow silk cord from which a stone hung, a small oval stone somewhat milky in color, blue and green flashing from the depths.

"Oh, that's nice," I said, taking it to admire it better. "Is it an opal? It doesn't look quite like an opal."

"It is a moonstone," the man answered,

his voice kind of choked.

It looked like a bookmark, the kind you slid around the pages and cover of a book, but rather than a charm hanging from the end, as I'd seen before, this one had the moonstone.

"It's very pretty. Did it come from one of my books? I didn't know it was in there. I'll have to take it back to the bookseller. He probably didn't realize this was tucked away inside —"

The man suddenly broke into laughter. "You didn't tell me who you were," he said, chuckling a last couple of chuckles before he took my arm and steered me out of the alley in the opposite direction. "I thought you were just an ordinary tourist."

"Um . . ." I didn't quite know what to say to that. It seemed odd to insist that I was, in fact, perfectly ordinary, but I had a suspicion that the nice Icelander thought I was someone else. "I think maybe there's some sort of a mistake."

"No mistake," he said, smiling with genuine happiness. "We've been expecting you, you know. The Zenith said you'd arrive today, but we thought you'd be here earlier. I suppose you felt it necessary to maintain your cover as a tourist?"

"OK, now we really are talking at cross-purposes." I stopped, not willing to get myself any more lost than I had been. "My name is Pia Thomason, and I really am just an ordinary tourist."

"Pia? Heh-heh. You are very good," he said admiringly, taking my arm again and gently pushing me forward. "I am Mattias. I am the sacristan."

"Sorry?" I said, unfamiliar with the word. Would it make me a Bad American if I tore my arm from his grip and turned around to run back to the holiday crowds? With everyone down at the waterfront park enjoying the celebrations, the town was all but deserted.

"It means — let me see if I can translate it for you — keeper of the doors, yes? You understand?"

"A doorkeeper? Is that some sort of a doorman?" I asked, puffing a little since Mattias was hauling me gently but persistently up one of the steep stone roads. "Like at a hotel, you mean?"

"Doorman . . . that may not be the right word. Doorkeeper sounds better. I am doorkeeper of the Brotherhood of the Blessed Light."

I tried to remember what was the predominant religion of the area, but drew a blank. "Ah. I assume that's a religion?"

He chuckled again. "You wish to play? I will play. Yes, it is a religion, a very old one. Its origins are in the Basque region. We were once known as Ilargi, but now we are called by the name of the Brotherhood. We have been around since the beginning of the darkness."

"Ilargi?" I asked, startled at the familiar word. I peered up into the face of the man who continued to urge me up the street. "Isn't that the name of the woods outside of the town? The place with the ruins?"

"Woods?" His blond brows pulled together. "I do not understand. Are you testing me?"

I dug my heels in and stopped him a second time. He faced me with a puzzled expression, but I could see no signs of hostility or, worse, madness. He had to have me confused with someone else. "I'm sorry, Mattias, but I really do think you have the wrong person. I do not understand half of what you are saying."

"It is I who am sorry. My English is not very good."

"Your English is better than mine. I meant you're misinterpreting what I'm saying, and I haven't a clue about your responses. For example, I don't know where you're taking me."

40

"Here," he said, waving a hand at a building ahead of us. It was a small church made of grey stone that sat at the top of the street.

I relaxed a smidgen at the sight of it, feeling that Mattias was no threat despite his confusion. "Is that your church?"

"Yes. We will go in now."

I hesitated, trying to figure out how to get through to him that I wasn't the person he thought I was.

"It is all right," he said, taking my hand and tugging me up the steps to the church door. "I am the sacristan. I am the sun."

"The son of who?" I asked, eyeing the church carefully. It looked perfectly normal, not at all out of the ordinary.

"Not 'who' . . . the sun. You know, the sun in the sky?" he said, pointing upward.

"Oh, the sun. You . . . er . . . you think you're the sun?"

"Yes."

I switched my examination from the church to the man who was leading me into it. He still looked sane, but if he thought he was the sun, perhaps it would be wiser to let him think I was going along with his claims until I could slip away.

The church did much to reassure my nerves. It, too, looked perfectly ordinary, and was pretty much as I had expected from

41

my visits to other ancient Icelandic churches — a small anteroom that opened out into the main part of the church, narrow aisles running down the middle and on either side of two banks of pews. At the far end stood the altar. It wasn't until I was halfway down the aisle that I realized that something was wrong. The church was decorated with the usual crosses and symbols of Christianity, but over these had been thrown small black cloths embroidered with silver crescent moons.

"Uh-oh," I said, squirming out of Mattias's grip. Had I stumbled onto some strange cult? *Were* there strange cults in Iceland? I had thought they were pagans before Christianity swept through Scandinavia — perhaps this was a pagan cult? "I think this is far enough."

"Mattias?" A woman called out from the other end of the church, emerging from a room behind the altar. She was middle-aged, with salt-and-pepper hair, and eyes that practically snapped as she bustled down the aisle toward us. She continued in what I assumed was Icelandic.

"Kristjana, I bring the Zorya," Mattias interrupted her. "She is English."

"American, actually, although my name isn't Zorya. It's Pia, and I'm really terribly sorry to intrude, but I think Mattias has me mixed up with someone else," I explained to the woman. She looked perfectly normal, perfectly sane and unremarkable, kind of a plump grandmotherly figure. All but her eyes, that is.

Those intense dark eyes examined me for a moment before she asked Mattias a question.

"I am sure," he answered. "She bears the stone."

"You mean this?" I asked, holding up the silk bookmark.

Kristjana's eyes widened for a moment, then she nodded. "You are very welcome to our sanctuary, Zorya."

"Ahh, a light begins to dawn," I said slowly as my mental fog cleared. "It's this, isn't it?" I waved the bookmark around. The moonstone at the end of it glowed gently in the dim interior of the church. "That's where all the confusion comes from. I'm happy to tell you that this isn't mine."

"No, it isn't; it belongs to no one, but you are its keeper now, and you must guard it well. We have much work for you to do," Kristjana said primly. She gestured toward the back of the church. "You will come now and we prepare for the first ceremony. We were told you would be arriving earlier."

43

I glanced as casually as I could manage around the church. Relief filled me at the sight of the half-open front door. With an expression I hoped bore no indication of my intentions, I shuffled backward a few steps. "This is really a lovely church. I like the moons; they're pretty, as well. Is that something your group worships?"

Mattias frowned a little as Kristjana watched me, her face expressionless. I hoped neither of them noticed I was still moving backward, toward the door, in tiny little baby steps.

"The Brotherhood are children of the moon, although we do not worship it," she said carefully. "We are of the light. We spread the light. It is through the light that we cleanse the world."

Hairs on my arms started to prickle at her words. I had no doubt now that I had somehow managed to get myself mistaken for someone expected by this odd pagan cult. They didn't look dangerous, but I felt it was wiser to make as few waves as possible before I dashed for freedom. "You spread light? You mean you do good works?"

"Through us, the light cleanses darkness from the world," she answered, her voice almost singsong, as if she was speaking a catechism. "Through us, the light purges evil."

"We definitely need less evil in the world," I agreed, and shuffled a few feet closer to the door. If either of them had noticed that the distance between us was growing, they didn't comment on it.

"The Midnight Zorya focuses the light, using the power on behalf of us all."

"You said that word before," I said, slapping a pleasantly curious look on my face. I took another two steps backward, reaching out with a hand behind me to feel for the door. I was still too far away to touch it. "What exactly is a Zorya?"

Kristjana didn't even blink. Mattias shot me a puzzled glance before turning his gaze on his companion.

"There are three Zoryas who rule the skies — morning, evening, and midnight. Auroras, they are called by the Westerners, but the Brotherhood call them by their true names."

"Auroras. That's really interesting." This had to be some sort of a pagan cult. Who else would worship the northern lights and the moon?

"Tradition says that the sun dies in the Midnight Zorya's arms each night, and is reborn each morning. That is why you must wed tonight."

"Whoa!" I said, stumbling to a stop. "Wed? Excuse me?"

"You must wed the sacristan, the sun," the woman said. She nodded toward Mattias. "The Zorya has little power until she has taken a husband and been recognized by the Brotherhood."

"Wed as in marry?" I asked, wondering if perhaps their English was not as good as I had assumed.

"Yes, marry. Zoryas are always wed. It is the way."

A horrible suspicion dawned that both relieved and annoyed me. "This is part of the tour, isn't it? You're not some wacky cult after all — you're just doing a lot of hand waving and mystical mumbo jumbo to distract my attention away from the fact that this is a blind date, right?"

"The Brotherhood are earnest in their intent to cleanse the world of evil," Kristjana said, an annoyed look flitting across her face.

"I can see you are." I crossed my arms over my chest, my relief that they weren't wackos mingling with my own irritation. However much trouble they went to, I wasn't inclined to go along with their silly production. "You can tell Audrey from me that I don't find it very entertaining. I may be on a singles' tour, but I'm not so desperate I'm willing to do some sort of role-playing thing, no matter how handsome the participant is."

Mattias's frown cleared. He smiled. "You are plump, but I like that. We will be good together sexually."

"Uh-huh," I said, unsure of whether I should be offended or amused by the scenario. At least I didn't have to worry that they were strange cultists who would perform who knew what sorts of acts upon my person.

"I am a very fine lover," he continued, obviously feeling it was a point he needed to drive home. So to speak.

"Well, I'm flattered and all, but as I said, I'm not really that . . . er . . . desperate. Not that I'd have to be desperate to want to hook up with you, Mattias, but I'm sure you know what I mean."

"No, I don't think I do," he said, the frown having returned.

I ignored that, smiling brightly and taking a couple more steps backward. "Well, this has been fun, but I think I'm going to get going. I'll be sure to tell Audrey just how good you guys were, though. And thanks for the plump-but-still-attractive comment.

It's always nice to know that there are men out there who like women who aren't walking advertisements for anorexia. Night!"

Identical startled expressions manifested on their faces as I turned and walked out the door. Either they had believed their acting was enough to suck me in or, what was more likely, Audrey told them I'd be an easy mark, lonely enough that I'd agree to just about anything in order to have a date with a handsome man.

What stung was just how close to the truth that was. "After all, you're on a tour meant to pair people up. You can't get much more desperate than that," I told myself. My conversation was short-lived when I heard my name being called behind me.

Mattias stood at the door of the church. The older woman shoved him out of the way, pointed at me, and snapped out an order. He looked surprised for a moment, but ran down the steps with a set look on his face that triggered a sudden spurt of adrenaline.

What if they weren't set up by Audrey? What if they were, in actuality, a creepy cult that seriously believed I was going to marry a complete stranger simply because my book had an odd bookmark?

"Oh, crap," I swore, telling my brain to

stop thinking and start making my legs move. I bolted down the street, spinning around a corner into a darker street, hoping to lose Mattias despite the fact that he was much more fit than me, not to mention probably quite familiar with the town.

I dashed around tidy trash cans, emerging into a lit street, screaming at the sudden noise of an approaching car slamming on its brakes and squealing to a stop a few feet away. I didn't wait to apologize, just gathered my tattered wits and sped across the remainder of the street and into a twisty narrow passage that ran between two tall stone buildings.

A man's voice called out behind me. Damn that long-legged Mattias. I was already out of breath and had a suspicious pain in my side that warned of a stitch.

"Please let me get away, please let me get away," I chanted in time to my pounding footsteps as I ran blindly through the still empty town, my brain squirreling around frantically for some way to escape Mattias. I had to double back somehow. That would surely throw him.

As I emerged from behind a different church, I spied a narrow set of stairs that led down to a small landing beneath the entrance. I flung myself down it and hunkered beneath the cement bridge that spanned the area, my back plastered against the cold stone. I covered my mouth to silence the sounds of labored breathing.

A few seconds later, a shadow flashed on the ground next to me, paused for a moment, then flickered past me toward the main square. I counted to ten, holding my breath, until black spots threatened to dance before my eyes. Cautiously I crawled out of my hiding spot and peered over the edge of the railing toward the street, my lungs wheezily drawing in much-needed oxygen.

People were starting to appear from the direction of the park, some heading for cars, others going to the central square, where sounds of a band warming up could be heard. "The fireworks must be over," I mused aloud, "which means if I stay put, there will be a lot of people I can use as cover. That sounds smart."

"Excuse me, could you help us?"

At the soft voice behind me, I whirled around, clutching at the railing as my heart just about jumped out of my chest for the second time in an hour. "Holy cheese and crackers! You almost scared . . . me . . . to . . . uh . . ."

The two people who stood before me, at first glance, were nothing to make a mature, reasonably intelligent woman turn into a babbling fool, but that's just what happened. The man and woman were clearly a couple, because the woman, petite, with big, soulful eyes, clung to the man's arm as she peered up at me from under the low brim of a hat I vaguely remembered was called a cloche. She was wearing a low-waisted dress, while he was in an old-fashioned-looking suit and a fedora. But what had me stammering to a startled stop was the fact that the two of them were translucent, almost transparent, an odd bluish sort of glow about them as if they were made up of the ghostly images sometimes seen on old TVs.

The word "ghost" reverberated around in my head with growing intensity.

"We're lost. Can you help us?" the woman said, glancing up at her man.

"Uh." Hesitantly, I held out my hand, the hairs on my arm standing on end as my fingers reached the man's arm and passed right through it with only a tiny tingle.

"We were on a ship," the man said, looking around him. "We were going to Canada. But now we're lost, and we don't know where we're supposed to be going. You are the one who is supposed to help us, aren't you?" the man asked, a doubtful look on his translucent face.

"You're . . . not real," I said slowly, trying to understand what was going on. "Are you?"

"I am Karl. This is my wife, Marta. We were on a ship," the ghostly man said again. "What happened to it?"

"Karl, I'm afraid," the woman whimpered, pressing herself closer to her husband. "Maybe she is the other one."

I blinked in dumb astonishment. "I'm Pia, and frankly, I'm a bit confused."

"There's nothing to be afraid of," Karl told his wife, obviously trying to appear brave for her benefit. His expression continued to indicate that he was anything but calmly confident. "You are the reaper, aren't you? The old woman said there would be someone in town to show us the way. She said we'd know you by the light you carry." He gestured toward my hand.

I looked down in even more astonishment. The stone-bedecked bookmark that I'd looped around my wrist while I made my escape from Mattias had somehow morphed into a small lantern shaped like a crescent moon. It dangled like a charm from my wrist, and from it, a gentle glow illuminated the area immediately around me. "All right. This is going way beyond weird or possibly a mental condition, into the land of . . . well, I don't know quite what land it is. Maybe the unbelievable? Regardless, I'm not quite sure what to tell you. I don't think I'm the grim reaper — at least no one has informed me of anything like that," I said with a forced little laugh that sounded hollow.

"She doesn't seem to be anxious to help us," Marta said, a sob in her voice. "What are we going to do? What if the evil one comes?"

As if on cue, Mattias appeared briefly at the end of the street. I ducked down until I could just barely see him. He stood for a moment in indecision, quickly scanning the front of the church and the street before he made a right turn and hurried off down a cross street.

"I'm sorry. I don't quite understand what it is you want me to do for you. You say an old lady told you to find me? Did she say her name?" I asked, wondering if the woman at the church could have sent the pair after me.

"She was on the ship. She said she would stay there, where her son was, but that we should go ashore and the reaper would show us the way. She said we'd know you by your light, and that there might be another one, an evil one, who did not have a light. You *do* have a light," Karl pointed out.

"Yeah, and I'm not quite sure how that happened, but given the present situation, I think maybe I'll just move past that point. Where exactly did you need directions to? I'm a stranger here, myself, and don't know too many of the local spots, although I do have a good map."

The couple squatted down next to me as I pulled out the detailed map I had for the area.

"We were going to Canada. To Halifax, to be with Marta's brother and his family," Karl said as they peered at my map.

I glanced at their period clothing, and bit my lower lip for a moment. "Would you mind me asking you when you were on the ship? What . . . er . . . what year was it?"

"It was 1922," Karl answered quickly, looking puzzled. "Why?"

I reached out to touch the lapel of his coat. Just as before, my hand met no resistance and passed right through him. "I hate to tell you this, but I don't think your ship made it to Canada. I have a suspicion that it might have wrecked offshore of Iceland, and you're . . . well, you're ghosts."

"Karl," Marta said in a near wail, grabbing her husband's arm again. "She is not the good one. She is Ilargi!"

"Shhh!" I hissed, peeping over the edge of the railing to see if Mattias had come back. The street, luckily, was clear. "I'm not anything other than really confused."

"Now, love, don't panic," Karl said, patting her hand. "She is a reaper, not Ilargi. We just need to convince her we're worthy of her help."

"Oh, you don't have to convince me of that. I can see you're a very nice couple, and I'm really sorry to have to be the one to break it to you that you're . . . er . . . life challenged. And I would help you if I could, but I really don't think I'm the person you're looking for."

"You're not going to show us the way?" Karl asked with a nervous glance at his wife.

Marta stared at me with bleak, hopeless dark eyes that seemed to wring my heart. "You would not leave us to the other?"

"I'm not sure who you're talking about, but I'll tell you what I'll do — you explain to me exactly where it is you're trying to get to, and I'll find out how you get there, OK?"

"But . . . you know where we're going," Marta said, her eyes moving between her husband and me. She looked strained, somehow stretched, as if she was about to tear apart into a thousand wispy bits.

"All right, then, I'll find out where you're

going, and then we'll work on how to get you there," I said, trying to sound confident and calm. "Have you two been wandering around the town the whole time?"

They both stared silently at me.

"Let me put it this way — what's the last thing you remember?" I asked.

"We were on the ship," Karl said.

"Yes, I got that part. But what happened to the ship?"

The pair glanced at each other.

"I don't understand," Karl said. "We were on the ship. The old lady said to look for you, and we found you."

Clearly the trauma of their deaths had left them drifting, both figuratively and literally, and they didn't remember the transition between life and the afterlife.

I made a little face to myself at how quickly I'd become accustomed to the idea of ghosts and an afterlife, but I had to admit, the evidence was even now staring hopefully at me. "OK. We'll just let that go. While I'm looking, why don't you two go down to the café on the main square. I'll meet you there when I find out where it is you're supposed to go."

"Café?" Marta asked.

I gave them directions on where to find it, and reiterated that I would meet them there.

"I've got a few things to take care of first," I said, straightening slowly as I verified that the street was clear of Mattias. "But just as soon as I can, I'll try to find someone who knows what's going on. Sound good?"

"And if the other should come, the Ilargi?" Karl asked, clearly worried. "He will steal our souls!"

"That's not good." I made a little face as I thought. "Um . . . run away?"

That evidently satisfied them, because they nodded and thanked me, drifting off down the street until they disappeared into the night. I noted with interest that the second they disappeared from my view, the glowing silver moon dangling from my wrist changed back into a moonstone hanging on a silk cord.

"Too strange," I told the bookmark. "But right at this moment, I'm not going to try to figure you out. I've got to get myself out of this predicament with Mattias, and much as I'd like to hunker down, staying in one spot might be asking for trouble if he comes back to look closely at the church. Better get a move on now Pia."

There's really no use talking to yourself if you're not going to listen to your own advice, so I did as I was told, and crawled up the narrow stairs to the street, glancing around quickly to make sure the woman in charge of the cult hadn't been following us, before heading off in the direction opposite the one Mattias had taken.

The threat of a stitch in my side blossomed to full life a couple of blocks later, leaving me clutching my side and limping (for some reason, limping made me feel better). Holding the paperback books and my bag made it difficult to try to ease the pain in my side, so I dumped the books into the nearest trash can, hesitating for a moment over the pretty moonstone bookmark. Part of me wanted to dump it, as well, and wash my hands of anything to do with crazy moonstone cults, frightened ghosts, and lusty Icelanders, but the moral part of my brain pointed out that it wasn't really mine to throw away, and the least I could do was try to find its rightful owner. It was entirely within reason that whoever it belonged to could help Karl and Marta.

"Maybe the bookseller will know," I murmured as I reclaimed the bookmark from the top of the trash, but as I did so, a cold chill ran down my back.

The top book was, as I had told the Frenchwoman who had plowed into me earlier, a mystery, but beneath it lay the Regency romance I'd snatched up. I hadn't really looked at the cover, since I had a love of Regencies, but I saw now that the two people gracing the cover were depicted dancing. "Dancers on the cover . . . oh, no. Now what am I going to do?"

I grabbed the book and stuffed it into my bag, wondering if there was any chance I'd find the woman in the holiday crowd.

"What a mess," I murmured, and with a hand pressed to my side, I limped my way down the street toward the waterfront. Perhaps I would get a glimpse of the woman if she was still looking for bookstores.

I had just made it across the park when Mattias popped up out of nowhere. He didn't see me, but I knew that, exposed as I was, he soon would. I had to get away, but he was in a position that allowed him to look down the three streets that met at the park. I whirled around, scanning for anywhere I could hide, my gaze sharpening on a dark curve at the far edge of the park, where it butted up against a cliff. People were still streaming out of the park, but couples were using the darkness along the tree-lined end to engage in a little romantic snogging.

I hunched over and tried to use people to shield me as I made my way to the trees, intending to hide behind one of them until

Mattias left. But as I glanced over my shoulder toward him, he was looking in my direction; he started forward hesitantly, as if he wasn't sure he had seen me.

"Dammit," I muttered, excusing myself when the couple nearest me broke off what was surely a marathon lip-lock session to glare at my interruption. "Sorry. Go on with what you were doing."

The woman snorted and, grabbing her partner by the hand, dragged him off. Just beyond them, Mattias was heading straight in my direction.

Another couple left the security of the shadows, giggling and laughing about something as they passed. A shadow separated from the wall behind them, a male shadow who appeared to be alone.

"Pia?" I heard Mattias call as he approached.

"This is so cliché I can't believe it, but desperate times and all that," I muttered to myself as I gathered up my mental strength and stopped the man who was walking past me. "I sure hope you speak English, and I really hope you don't take this the wrong way, but here goes."

At my touch, the man stopped, turning toward me, his face deep in shadow. Eyes the shade of blue known as teal, like a

Siamese cat's, seemed to glow at me. I prayed I wasn't about to get tossed in jail for assault, grabbed his other arm, and more or less flung myself on him, chickening out at the last second and kissing the very edge of his cheek where it met the corner of his mouth.

"Please don't yell or anything like that," I murmured against his skin, my lips tingling at the sensation of soft stubble.

"Yar!" a man said next to my ear.

I jumped and stared with shock at the face that appeared just behind the man. Like Karl and Marta, he was nearly translucent.

"I likes a bit o' the cash, meself, but ye're missin' the dock there, lass," the ghost said. "Yer aim's off."

The victim of my pathetic but desperate plan stiffened in my arms but didn't shove me away or yell or even try to kiss me back (more's the pity — I've always been a sucker for blue eyes). He did, however, look a bit taken aback at what was surely an expression of utter and complete befuddlement visible on my face.

Mattias loomed up in my view, but he couldn't reach me, blocked as he was by the people between us. "Pia?"

I slunk down a few inches lower, shifting my grip on the man I held so that my fingers

61

clutched soft, curly hair. I threw in a rapturous moan as I kept my lips glued to his cheek, my attention moving from him, to Mattias, to the ghost who continued to leer at me.

Mattias peered at us for a moment, then gave a little shake of his head and moved off. At that moment, hands that felt like they were made of steel grabbed my wrists and pushed me backward.

"I appreciate the offer, but I am not interested," the man said, his voice deep and lyrical, with an Italian accent that seemed to skitter over my skin like electricity.

"I am," the ghost said, winking. "You can snog me any day."

"Um," I said, not sure how to respond to a lecherous ghost. "Are you a sailor, by any chance?"

"No," the blue-eyed man said, frowning.

"I'm sorry. I wasn't asking you; I was asking him," I said, nodding toward the ghost.

The man looked behind him, then narrowed his eyes at me. "Are you drunk?"

"Not in the least, although I'm really wishing I was at this point. You don't see him?"

"See who?" he asked.

"The ghost. I think he's a sailor from a

ship that went down in 1922."

"*The Rebecca*," the ghost said, nodding. "Went down in a bank o' fog the likes o' which I'd ne'er seen afore, and hope to ne'er again."

"There is no one there," Blue Eyes said slowly.

"You're bein' the reaper, then?" the sailor asked. He was a short man, somewhat squat, with a face that looked like it had been in more than one bar fight.

"I'm sorry, but I'm not. I just have this," I told the ghost, holding up my wrist to show him the moonstone, which had once again changed into a tiny crescent moon lantern. "But if you go to the café on the square, you'll find a couple of other people who were on the ship, and who are waiting for the person in question."

"What are you talking about?" asked the man.

"Café, you say?" the ghost said, looking hopeful. "Ye be thinkin' they'll have a tot o' rum there?"

"They might. You never know."

"Aye, that ye don't. I'll be on me way, then." He gave me a gap-toothed grin. "Ye might want to be practicin' yer aim while I'm gone. Looks like yer fella doesn't appreciate ye kissin' naught but his cheek."

63

I said nothing, not wanting the man whom I'd jumped on to think I was any crazier than he already did. Obviously the moonstone/lantern contained some sort of magic that allowed only its bearer to see ghosts.

"I'm so sorry; you must think I'm the worst sort of woman," I told Blue Eyes. "But there was a man chasing me, and I really didn't want him to find me."

He had continued to hold my wrist bearing the moonstone. While it was a lantern, he didn't glance at it, but the second the ghost left, it reverted to the stone, and he clutched my hand even tighter.

To my surprise, rather than release me, he took a few steps into a bluish white pool of light cast by a portable lantern. I gawked when the light revealed him to be one of the two eye-candy twins, the one with short hair. The light hit him only on one side, but the planes of his face were hard and angled, a cleft cutting deep into his chin, his nose narrow, but not straight, as if it had been broken and not set properly. And then there were those lovely eyes, shining from within, beautiful pure teal blue with little spiky black bits that seemed to seep from his pupils. Oh, yes, they were gorgeous eyes . . . and they were focused on me with a look that had my color rising.

"I know it sounds crazy," I stammered, "but it's true. There really was someone behind you, only you couldn't see him and I could. I think it's because of the moonstone, but that's really neither here nor there. But I've bothered you enough for one night, and clearly you feel the need to go get checked for scabies or something. I mean, I would if some strange guy suddenly swooped down and started kissing me. Not that I have scabies, you understand. I'm perfectly scabies free. In fact, I'm not quite sure what scabies is, although I know if you're not careful you can get it from sexual partners. Oh, lord. I'm babbling. I'm sorry. I do that when I'm nervous, or embarrassed, and wow, am I embarrassed now."

The man stared at me like I had just turned into a tap-dancing llama, complete with top hat and cane.

"Sorry," I said again, making a little gesture of vague apology.

His eyes narrowed as he looked again at my hand.

"I'll just go now," I finished lamely, jerking my hand from his and scurrying away toward the street, my face hot with embarrassment. "What on earth is wrong with you, Pia? You babbled at that poor man, positively babbled like a deranged person. Dear god, I can't take you anywhere, can I?"

A sleek red car purred up to the curb.

"I bet I'm even redder," I muttered to myself as I hurried by the car. "I should just go home. I can't get any lower than thieeeeeeeeee!"

Before I could pass by completely, one of the doors opened and I was shoved from behind. I grabbed at the roof to keep from falling into it, but another shove at my back more or less folded me in half, resulting in me collapsing inside the vehicle.

CHAPTER 3

"Hey!" I yelled as I was tossed halfway
across a leather seat, landing partly on it
and partly on the floor. The door slammed
behind me, and the car started off. "Hey!" I
yelled even louder, clawing myself into an
upright position. "What the hell is going on
here?"

The other eye-candy guy was driving, his
gaze meeting mine in the rearview mirror
for a moment before he said something in
what sounded like German to the Italian
guy. The latter answered with one word.
"Zorya."

"Oh, no, not you, too!" I said, goose
bumps crawling up my arms and legs.
"Look, you've made a big mistake!"

"I thought she was French," the driver
said, his voice a pleasant baritone with a
slight German hint to it. "She sounds
American."

"She is American, and she's not very

happy right at this moment, so if you would kindly pull over and let her out, she won't have to either scream, or go stark, staring insane, whichever comes first!" I said loudly, my temper finally frayed beyond repair.

"Kristoff —" the driving guy started to say, his eyes flashing from the road, to the mirror, to his buddy.

I grabbed for the door handle, so angry I was ready to throw myself out of the moving car to escape the two men. Quickly, the driver hit a button that locked all the car doors.

"Damned child locks," I cursed as I tried to pry the lock upward.

"She has the stone," the man identified as Kristoff said, his head jerking back toward me.

"It's not mine!" I yelled, shaking the stone at him. "I told the same thing to those other people, not to mention the ghosts."

"Ghosts?" the driver said, looking more interested than skeptical.

"Yes. People who drowned on a ship, I think. A long time ago, but I'm not whoever they're looking for, either. I've never seen this stone before. I think it came in a book I bought this afternoon, a book that a French-woman was trying to find."

The unnamed man driving slowed down

and pulled over in the parking lot of a darkened bank. "What is your name?"

"Pia Thomason. I'm from Seattle, here with a tour group." My cheeks flamed to life again. I didn't think I could stand the contempt that was sure to be in Kristoff's eyes if I mentioned what sort of group it was. "I bought a couple of used books this afternoon, and I think the bookmark must have been hidden in one of them, because I sure as shooting never saw anything like it before." Quickly I recounted the brief meeting with the woman in the square. "The bookmark is probably hers."

"Bookmark?" the driver asked.

"Yeah, it's a bookmark, see?" I pretended my hand was a book and slid the silken cord over it.

"I can assure you, Pia, it is *not* a bookmark," the man said, smiling at me in the mirror.

I couldn't help but smile back at him, charmed by the warmth in his expression. His face had a softer look to it than his harsh friend's, his green eyes slightly tilted up at the edges, with laugh lines radiating outward.

"That's as may be, but I assure you it's not mine. I was going to try to find the woman it belongs to, but there are so many people out, I doubt if I could spot her."

He watched me for a moment before turning to Kristoff, who regarded me with suspicious eyes. "She could be telling the truth."

"It's not likely," Kristoff answered. "She saw ghosts."

"That's probably to be due to the stone, since I've never seen anything weird before. Well, sometimes at the beach guys who think they are Speedo-worthy, but that's neither here nor there. And just an FYI — I hate being talked about as if I'm not here even more than I hate being stuffed into a car and driven off without my consent. I believe technically this a kidnapping, and I'm fairly certain it's illegal even in Iceland."

They both ignored me.

"She was running from the sacristan," the nice one said.

Kristoff's lips thinned. "It is an act, Alec, put on to make us think just what you're thinking."

Alec! Aha, a name at last.

"But —"

"If you would oblige me by not believing everything a woman tells you, we might live to see this task done," Kristoff said, rubbing a spot on his chest.

Contriteness filled Alec's face. I spent a moment musing just how much I liked his name, but dragged my mind back to the task of escaping the latest in what seemed to be an evening filled with strange episodes.

"You said the wound was healed. If it is still bothering you —"

"It has long since healed, but it reminds me of the folly of taking people for granted." Kristoff's eyes glowed in the darkness of the car as he glanced back at me. "It is said the blood of a Zorya can heal any injury."

"That's it!" I said, holding up my hands. "I'm officially through. I've been insulted, challenged, nearly brainwashed by some deranged cult, hunted, pleaded at by a pair of ghosts and leered at by a third, rejected, and now kidnapped, but when you start talking about using my blood, it's time for me to go to bed and pretend I never came on this trip. Since you're so determined to drive me somewhere, would you please drive to the Hotel Andersson? Thank you."

I sat back in the seat, determined to hang on to what was left of my shreds of reason. If I believed hard enough that these two handsome, but clearly unbalanced, men were just taking me to my hotel, and not about to commit some sort of ghastly blood sacrifice, perhaps I could escape with my sanity intact.

Alec considered me again with a not

71

unfriendly eye. "We could go to the book-seller, to see if it proves her story."

"That would just be a waste of time. The shop is sure to be closed at this time of night."

"If I was still talking to either of you, which I'm not because I no longer recognize your existence, I would point out that although the shop was closed, there might be some sort of clue there as to the origins of the bookmark," I said, calmly examining a fingernail.

"She has a point," Alec agreed.

I decided to unbend enough to give him a grateful smile. He returned it with a little wink. I started to feel a bit warm as another blush swept upward. Could it be possible he was flirting with me? A man as handsome as him? As unobtrusively as possible, I sat up a little straighter to maximize my good points (large boobs) and minimize the bad (rest of the body).

"Not really, but if you are going to insist on giving her the benefit of the doubt, we might as well get it over with quickly so we can take her before the council."

"Council?" I asked, grabbing the backs of their seats and hauling myself forward. "What council?"

Kristoff's face could have been made of

granite, so cold was it and the accompanying gaze he cast toward me. "I thought you weren't speaking to us."

"I have decided in the interests of avoiding an international incident that I will keep the lines of communication open. What council?"

"The Moravian Council," Alec said, hitting the gas and sending us shooting down a bumpy street, making a tight U-turn to head back into the heart of town. "Don't worry, Pia; if you're truly what you say you are, you have nothing to fear from the council."

I sat back, grasping the seat belts, unwilling to strap myself in just in case I needed to make a fast getaway. "Just out of morbid curiosity, what exactly is this Moravian Council? And what would happen if I wasn't telling the truth?"

"You will be taken before the council to answer for the seventy-three deaths your people have caused over the last three years," Kristoff answered in a deep, lyrical voice that would have sent shivers of delight up my back if he hadn't clearly been repulsed by me, and obviously under the delusion that I was someone bad.

"My people?" I asked, running my mind over my immediate family members. "They

73

run an apple orchard in eastern Washington. I don't think they've conducted any mass executions in, oh, geez, years and years. Although with my brother, you never can tell. He's a Microsoft yuppie."

My humor, sarcastic as it was, was not wasted on Alec. He chuckled and flashed me a quick grin in the mirror before returning his eyes to the road as we approached the square.

Kristoff grunted and looked out the window.

I figured it would take Alec forever to find a parking spot, but he solved the issue by simply parking sideways across a sidewalk. "That is the bookstore?" he asked, pointing to the end of the street, where it opened into the pedestrians-only square.

I nodded.

"Let me see the books," Alec said, opening the door for me and offering his hand to help me out of the car.

I was simultaneously charmed by the gesture and pleased by the warmth in his eyes. "I'm afraid I only have one of them. I dumped the other one when Mattias started after me."

"Mattias?" Alec asked, examining the book I held out for him. He riffled the pages but found nothing.

"The sacristan," Kristoff informed him. He turned a hard gaze on me. "Why, exactly, were you running from him?"

I was flummoxed for a moment when Alec tucked my hand in the crook of his arm, covering my fingers with his free hand as he led me down the street. It was a surprisingly intimate gesture, one that gave me more pleasure than I wanted to admit.

Part of me, the vindictive, evil part that I really liked to pretend didn't exist, wished that Denise would walk past us at that moment. I wouldn't gloat, I wouldn't preen, I'd simply smile and allow my two incredibly handsome escorts to accompany me.

Fortunately for my ego, she wasn't present in the crowd that now pulsed and bobbed in that odd throbbing fashion large groups of people packed into a small space have when they attempt to dance. The music hit us with the force of a brick wall, and it wasn't until we slipped around to the back of the row of buildings lining that side of the square that I could make myself heard above the noise.

"No answer?" Kristoff said, stopping at a metal door bearing a faded plaque with the name of the shop. One of his chocolatey brown eyebrows rose in mock surprise. I had the worst urge to yank it back down.

"I'm not avoiding the question. I just didn't want to bellow it out in front of everyone," I said with dignity. "I was running from him because he was just as mistaken as you two — he thought I was this Zorya person, and wanted to marry me."

Alec pulled out a large set of keys and started applying them to the door.

Kristoff eyed me from toes to nose. I flushed for the umpteenth time that night and, in order to forestall the obvious comment, said quickly, "You can stop looking at me like I'm a big, fat liar, because I'm not."

Kristoff blinked for a moment in surprise; then his face hardened into its familiar suspicious expression.

For some reason, that just seemed to irritate me more than if he'd come out and accused me of trying to pull his leg. "You can believe what you want, but it's the absolute truth. The lady . . . what's her name . . . Kristjana mentioned Mattias and me getting married so he could die in my arms or something like that. So you can just wipe that you're-so-insane-you're-barking look right off your face."

Behind me, Alec started laughing. Kristoff's eyes lit from within with anger, and for one horrible second, I thought he was going to hit me. But instead he took two steps forward, backing me into the wall of the shop. "Do you have any idea who I am, woman?"

"I know you don't like me, and I have to say that the feeling is reciprocated," I told him, my stomach quivering, but whether it was from fear or anger, I wasn't quite sure.

Kristoff wrapped the long fingers of one hand around my throat, tightening them with uncomfortable pressure. "I could kill you right now."

Fear won out over the anger, but I wasn't going to let him see that. I clutched the material of my skirt with both hands to keep from grabbing at his wrist. "If I'm who you say I am, that would defeat your purpose," I pointed out, ignoring the fact that my voice was quavering. "You'd have to explain my death to the Brotherhood."

A slow smile curled the very edges of his mouth, but didn't do much to warm up his icy gaze. "I believe I would enjoy that."

My eyes widened at the threat obvious in his voice, but before I could protest, Alec interrupted.

"Stop frightening her, Kris. It serves no purpose."

His gaze continued to bore into mine for another few seconds, and I felt swamped by the waves of anger and hostility that all but rolled off him. He snarled something under his breath and released me, turning on his heel and stomping off down the alleyway.

I collapsed against the wall, my legs feeling like they were made of tofu. Instantly, Alec was at my side, propping me up, peering down at me with a concerned look. "Are you all right, Pia?"

"Yeah. Your friend is a bit intense, isn't he? I'm thinking anger management classes might be in order," I answered, rubbing my neck as I watched the dark silhouette disappear into the shadows.

To my surprise, Alec defended his friend. "He has no love for the reapers."

"Reapers?" I pulled my gaze back to him. "That's what the ghosts kept calling me. Who are they?"

"Reapers were once Ilargi. That is, technically they still are, although they were divided into two types, sun and moon reapers. The former were called Ilargi before they were all but destroyed. The latter . . . well, that is a long story."

"Ah. The Brotherhood of the Blessed Light," I said, nodding.

Alec eyed me for a few minutes before answering. "You do know of the Brotherhood?"

"No. Not really. I ran into a couple earlier, but that's all."

I thought he was going to tell me about the organization he and his buddy belonged to, but instead he changed the subject. "Kristoff had a mate. Not a Beloved, you understand, but a woman whom he considered his mate. Angelica and Kristoff were together for many decades. She was killed three years ago. He has not forgotten her death. It haunts him still."

"Oh, how awful," I said, contrite at acting so rudely to a man who was mourning the loss of a loved one. "Poor man. I had no idea. . . . I'm so sorry."

"It is no excuse for Kristoff scaring you, but it does, I hope, explain something about his mental state," he said, opening the door, which he'd managed to get unlocked. He flicked on a tiny penlight, flashing it around the room. "Let us hope we find something here to explain the unusual situation you say has clasped you in its grip."

We made a fast search of the bookshop, but there wasn't much to be found. Alec went through the papers stuffed willy-nilly into the drawers of an old rolltop desk that served as the owner's filing cabinet, while I examined each book on the rack where I'd nabbed my two books, flipping through the remainder to see if anything had been tucked inside any of them.

Twenty-five minutes later we returned to the car to find Kristoff leaning against its side, his arms crossed, his expression hard but relatively neutral. He was silent as we approached.

"There was nothing," Alec admitted with defeat. "But I do not discount what Pia has told us. I think we should investigate the matter further."

Kristoff came close to rolling his eyes, I could tell. "We have wasted enough time, Alec. We have few enough hours before dawn to reach the council as it is —"

Alec interrupted him, speaking in German.

I gnawed on my lower lip for a moment as the two men argued. I had a decision of my own to make — did I want to stick around and try to make them see reason, or did I want to get far, far away from the scary Kristoff? There was nothing to guarantee that the next time he felt like throttling me, he would stop before actually killing me.

Unbidden, my eyes went to Alec. Although Kristoff had more of a stark, visceral physical appeal, Alec was certainly no slouch in the looks department. If anything, he could be thought the better-looking, since his expression was warmer and friendlier.

I thought back to the twenty-five minutes we'd spent together in the musty darkness of the bookshop. Twice he'd brushed against me as we searched, and once, as he leaned over to fetch a scrap of paper, his arm pressed against my breast. He'd apologized and moved away, but I could still feel the sensation.

My fingertips touched my neck. Then again, I could still feel the steely grip of Kristoff's fingers.

I shook my head sadly. Even if there was a spark of interest in Alec to be breathed to life, the whole situation had a bad feeling about it. The sane thing, my down-to-earth brain pointed out, would be to leave now and not look back.

I did just that, not stopping to say anything, just spinning around and racing down the alley to the lighted square filled with people who would keep me safe. There was a shout that followed me, but I made it to the crowd without being stopped, breathing a sigh of relief that had far too much regret in it to make me happy. "Second time lucky, I guess," I said to myself as I squirmed my way through the pulsing crowd to its center.

"Madam! Madam, please, you wait!"

A slight tug at the back of my shirt had

me looking over my shoulder. The tiny Frenchwoman whom I'd bumped into earlier was squeezing her way between couples, a worried look on her face.

"It is you; oh, I am so glad. I must speak to you. It is very important."

I was so relieved to see her I could have whooped. "Likewise! But maybe we should get out of here. I can barely hear you over the music."

"What?"

I bent toward her and repeated the suggestion. She nodded and pointed to the café where I'd sent the ghosts. It was still open, serving the late-night crowd. I hesitated a moment, not wanting to remain out in the open where Alec and Kristoff could find me, but at the same time not wanting to face the ghosts when I was no closer to helping them. In the end, I chose the latter as the least worrisome.

As I entered the café, I saw Karl and Marta in the corner, huddled together. They stood at the sight of me, but I waved them back and squeezed myself into a chair at a tiny table. The sailor ghost was nowhere to be seen.

"Coffee?" I asked the woman as she pulled out a mirror and checked her reflection.

"*Non.* Wine!"

"I like how you think," I said, smiling, and asked the waiter for two glasses of the house white wine.

"You must think I am very forward, but I assure you, it is most important that I speak to you."

"As a matter of fact, I was looking for you, too."

"You were?" she interrupted, taking the glass of wine the waiter offered. She took a small sip of it. "But you do not know why I sought you?"

"Oh, I think I do," I said, smiling as I held up a copy of the Regency paperback. "Dancing people."

She sagged in relief, reaching for it. "You did find it. I thought that you must have when I asked the book man and he said that an English lady with curly blond hair had just bought it."

"You have no idea of the evening I've had because of that thing," I said, dropping it into her hand. "I don't think you know just quite what you're getting into, though. I assume you're the Zorya?"

Her eyes widened. "You are of the light?"

"No." I shook my head. "But I had an introduction to the folks around here who subscribe to that religion, and I feel it only right to warn you about them."

"Warn me?" She surprised me by laughing. "Warn me about the Brotherhood of the Blessed Light?"

"They're the Ilargi, aren't they?"

Her smile faded. "No. Not anymore. It has been a millennium since that name was applied to us. We prefer the name Brotherhood."

"Then who, exactly, *are* the Ilargi? Every time I mention the name people start looking wary or scared."

She toyed with the stem of her glass for a few moments, her gaze avoiding mine. "The Ilargi were once brothers to my people. They were not of the light, but they served a purpose nonetheless. But they were corrupted and driven out, and now there are only a handful left. They have become tainted, you understand. They eat souls."

"That sounds pretty nasty," I said, the hairs on my arms standing on end. "No wonder everyone gets a bit weird when they're mentioned."

"My people are trying to track down those Ilargi who remain, but it is not easy. They are cunning, you know? And they hide in the mundane world. But the Brotherhood is strong, so they pose us no threat."

"Well, I don't know about that," I said slowly, picking my words with care so as to avoid insulting her. "I just know that the people I met tonight seemed to be under the impression that I was you, and that I was going to marry an Icelander named Mattias."

"The sacristan?" Her smile was back, albeit with a wry cast. "I have not met him, but yes, we are to marry. It was supposed to be tonight, but" — she glanced at her watch — "it is too late now. The ceremony will have to take place tomorrow instead. Oh, but here I am talking and talking and I have not even introduced myself. I am Anniki. You are . . . ?"

"Pia Thomason. And can I just say how glad I am that you found me? If I had to explain to any more people tonight that I'm not the Zorya, I think I'd probably need locking up in a padded room. The ghosts will be thrilled to see you, too, although one of them is apparently wandering around looking for rum. I understand they need help going somewhere."

"Spirits? You have seen some? Ah, but that is to be expected." She set down her glass of wine, her smile fading. "It is one of the jobs of a Zorya, you understand. We shine the light that illuminates the path of the dead."

"So I gathered. Better you than me,

although I have to say that Karl and Marta seem like nice enough people. Er . . . ghosts. But still, I'm sure they'll be delighted to know you can help them."

"It is the job of the Brotherhood. I will be the light the lost ones seek," she said simply.

I sipped my wine. "This is probably out of line for me to ask, but don't you find those Brotherhood people a little too . . . well, intense, for lack of a better word?"

She frowned a little frown. "Intense? What do you know of the Brotherhood?"

I shook my head. "Not much really, nothing other than some connection to northern lights and the moon."

"The light has its power in the moon," she said in all seriousness. "But I see it is not that which disturbs you most. You were *afraid* of the Brotherhood?"

"Not afraid, just a little uncomfortable," I hedged, not mentioning how Kristoff had threatened me.

She was silent for a moment, sipping her wine before she leaned forward. "You are mundane."

I was a bit taken aback by the comment. Did she just insult me?

"You are not of our world, but you have kind eyes, and you have seen much tonight that most people will never know exists. I will tell you about the Brotherhood so that you will understand why they are intense. There is darkness in the world. You have felt it, have you not?"

"You mean like terrorists and such?" I asked, confused.

"No, that is part of the mundane world. I speak of true darkness — Dark Ones, they are called, although they are better known as vampires."

"Vampires!" My urge to laugh died with a glance at her serious expression. Clearly she believed what she was saying. . . . That or she was a very good actress going to a whole lot of trouble to pull my leg.

"Yes. They do not like that term because people fear vampires, and they wish for the world to view them as victims, rather than as the evil murderers they are, but you must not let yourself be fooled. They are born of darkness, and carry it within them, spreading their evil like a disease. You know that they have no souls?"

I blinked a couple of times and shook my head.

"It is so. They are born without them, damned just as demons are damned, only they do not bear the stench of Abaddon on them so noticeably."

"Abaddon being . . . hell?" I guessed.

"More or less, yes. The vampires have existed since the beginning of man's time, hoping to dominate them, to infect them with their darkness until all the light is gone from the world. The Brotherhood seeks to destroy them, to wipe out their evil, to cleanse the world of the poison that they would use upon innocent people."

"Good god," I said, seeing the truth shining in her eyes. "How can this have been going on and no one in the — what did you call it? mundane world — knew it existed?"

"The Dark Ones are very clever," she said, sitting back. "They hide themselves with mortalkind, blending in so that their evil is not discovered until it is too late. But the children of the light have existed through the ages to find them, to cleanse them of their darkness."

"Wow," I said. "I'm just . . . I guess I'm flabbergasted that this has been going on around me and I had no idea. *Vampires!* We're talking about the same thing, right? Wait — are we talking about the sexy Frank Langella type of vampires who seduce women, or the Gary Oldman–scary bun-head guys who kill people?"

Anniki frowned. "I do not know of this scary bun-head people you speak of, but I assure you, there is nothing romantic about the Dark Ones. They are heartless, soulless fiends who want only their own domination over the mortal world. And they are nearly impossible to kill."

"Really? So the old stake through the heart is just a fallacy?" I asked, fascinated despite the horrible subject matter.

"It would slow one down considerably, yes, but not necessarily kill him unless it was done using the power of the light."

"Sunlight?" I asked, thinking back to the stash of *Buffy* and *Angel* DVDs that sat next to my TV.

"They burn much easier than mortals, but it would take a long time exposed to sunlight to do more than cause them discomfort. They do not burn up in a flash as seen in movies."

"Huh. What do you know about that. Holy water?"

She shook her head. "The Brotherhood has over the centuries worked out the best ways to destroy their evil. But we are not callous, heartless killers as they are — we call upon the light to cleanse the Dark Ones, to purify them in a ritual that allows them redemption rather than damnation."

"Holy Jehoshaphat," I said, shivering a little. I rubbed my goose-bumpy arms. "I had no idea. No wonder the Brotherhood folk were so grimly determined. Where exactly do you fit in with all of this?"

Tears welled up in her eyes. "My sister Sara . . . she was the last Zorya. She . . . she was killed two weeks ago, probably by a Dark One. They found her with . . ."

She slumped against the wall, digging through her bag for a tissue.

"I'm so sorry. I had no idea. Please don't distress yourself by telling me any more," I said, feeling horribly gauche.

"No, it is all right. Sara would have wanted people to know how bravely she gave her life to the cause of the light." She gave a harsh little laugh. "Some people call us reapers, you know. Reapers. As if that is all we do."

"I'm sorry," I said again, not knowing what else I could say.

She dabbed at her nose and eyes and made an effort to gather her control. "When I heard that Sara had been killed, I was destroyed, you know? But then the Zenith told me that I was to take her place."

"The who?"

"Zenith. It is a title, the name of the person who heads our order. Since I was not with Sara when she died, I could not take the stone from her. The Zenith told me to pick it up here before I went to marry the sacristan, but me, I am horrible with the directions, and I lost the information where to find the stone. But now you have found it for me, so I can take up the battle where Sara left it."

"That's really amazing of you," I said, still rubbing my arms. "I don't know that I'd be able to do something so selfless."

She gave me a tremulous smile. "You are not an ordinary mortal, Pia Thomason. I sense that about you. I have no doubt that you would do just fine as a Zorya."

"Well, luckily, we don't have to put such a generous assessment to the test."

Anniki murmured an agreement as she glanced at her watch.

"You must be wanting to go meet with your people and see your hubby-to-be," I said, putting a couple of coins on the table before gathering up my things and standing.

"Yes, it is late, but I hope to find them before the sun rises." She pressed my hand. "Thank you for guarding the stone so carefully, Pia. You are truly blessed by the light."

"Thank you," I said, wondering if that qualified as doing my good deed for the day. Somehow, casting my mind back over my actions of the evening, I had a feeling it wouldn't. "Good luck with your battle. Oh, the ghosts! There are two of them in the corner over there. Karl and Marta. Want me to introduce you to them?"

"Not yet. I will tend to them as soon as I have seen the Brotherhood. May the light continue to shine upon you," she said, waving good-bye as she hurried off into the dusky twilight.

I glanced at the corner where the ghosts had been when we entered the café, but they were gone. I wondered if they'd given up finding their way, but decided it was Anniki's problem now.

I made my way out of the café at a slower pace, mulling over everything she'd said to me. I glanced around at the people strolling around the edges of the square, the center still being packed with dancers. Vampires! Wandering around pretending they were human! Who knew!

"Pia! What luck!"

Startled, I spun around, but it was a familiar voice that shouted out my name.

"Over here!"

My heart fell when Denise clawed her way over to me, one hand firmly on the sleeve of a balding man with a handlebar mustache. There was a look of desperation in his eyes that I wholly sympathized with. "This is

Sven. Or Lars. Or something like that."

"Oskar," the man said, giving me a faint smile.

"Nice to meet you."

"Still alone?" Denise asked, pretending to look around. "Aww. That's too bad, it really is."

I bit back any number of retorts and just smiled a little smile. "I'm so tired, it's probably for the best. I think I'll go back to the hotel."

"Night's young yet," Denise said, grabbing Oskar with both hands and hauling herself up to him. "But suit yourself. I suppose if I was in your shoes I'd rather be by myself, too."

I gave her victim a sympathetic smile and left Denise to her gloating, thinking with pleasure how her expression would change if she'd known about the two men with whom I'd spent the last hour, not to mention the odd, but now seemingly genuine, offer of marriage by Mattias.

"There you are! We've looked all over for you. Are you going to the hotel?" A hand descended on my arm, but it wasn't the hard, unyielding grip of Kristoff.

Magda emerged from the crowd, her face flushed, her black eyes dancing. Immediately behind her our fellow tourist Raymond followed, his look of anticipation a clear indicator of how he expected his evening to end.

"I am. I'm a bit tired, to be honest."

"We can get a taxi together. If there's a taxi to be had," Magda said, laughing as we wove in and out of the crowd toward the busiest of the streets. "I think everyone in all of Iceland is here tonight!"

"Certainly everyone in this town is," Raymond agreed. "I'll see if I can find you ladies some transportation."

Magda blew him a noisy kiss, taking my arm and walking slowly with me to the edge of the square. I listened with only half an ear to her giddy talk about how much fun she and Ray had during the celebrations, most of my attention being spent on scanning the people wandering around, but I didn't see anyone who resembled a fanged, murderous vampire.

I sat in silent contemplation of the evening as the taxi that Ray had found whizzed us up the hill to the top of the town, where our hotel resided. I thought we passed the street that led to the church I'd been to earlier, but was too distracted to pay much attention. Not to mention the fact that my brain was starting to feel fuzzy around the edges. Magda kept up a non-stop conversation that luckily required only the briefest of responses to keep going.

". . . so outstanding, I never could have imagined anything so beautiful in a country that sounds like it's nothing but ice and snow. This is definitely the best money I've ever spent," Magda said, shooting Raymond a mischievous look. "I hope you're having a good time despite that bitchy Denise. She's just horrible, isn't she? And did you see that poor soul she got her clutches into? That man had no idea what he was in for when she spotted him alone. I wanted to warn him, but eh. He is a grown man, and certainly should be capable of telling her he's not interested in what she has to offer."

The memory of nearly identical words directed at me made me squirm uncomfortably on the seat. Is that what I had appeared like to Kristoff? A desperate, man-hungry woman who lacked self-control? I would have rolled up into a mortified ball, but the thought of Alec's smile and the warmth in his eyes gave me a little courage. So his friend thought I was the worst sort of hussy — what did that matter when Alec had a better impression of me?

What foolish thoughts. "It doesn't matter at all what they think," I lectured myself as I got out of the taxi.

"No, of course it doesn't," Magda said, calmly climbing the stairs to the hotel's entrance. She paused to shoot me a conspiratorial smile as Ray paid off the taxi. "You have something on your mind, dear Pia. Or should I say some*one?*"

My cheeks grew hot again, and I damned my Irish genes that allowed everyone to see my every blush. "It's been an interesting evening. Eye-opening, in fact."

"Ah, like that, is it? Well, I don't doubt it'll improve. Ready for a little nightcap, Ray?"

I left them giggling and stealing kisses and made my way up to my room, emotionally exhausted by the evening's adventures.

CHAPTER 4

"Could this day get any longer?" I asked my empty room as I closed the door and leaned against it, sagging with the aftermath of far too many emotions felt in a very short space of time.

"Is that a rhetorical question, or an indication you're too tired to feature in the starring role of my fantasies?" a male voice asked, causing me to shriek and clutch the door in fright.

Alec emerged from the bathroom. A naked Alec. A *very* naked Alec. I stared in utter and complete surprise.

He paused for a moment, striking a pose of which I couldn't help but approve. "Did I startle you? It seemed much more discreet to let myself in and wait for you rather than alert everyone in the hotel to the fact that I sought your company."

I stared some more.

"Pia?" An amused expression flitted across

his face.

"Hmm?" My eyes wandered over his body. I felt a bit dirty ogling the man so obviously, but then, he came out of my bathroom that way. Surely he intended for me to ogle?

"You're staring."

I swallowed a couple of times before I could speak. "I know. I'm sorry. I can't seem to stop. I'm trying, but you're naked. All of you. I mean, really naked."

"Yes, I am. I . . . er . . . realize that we parted in a less than satisfactory manner. I hope you won't hold Kristoff's determination to seek justice against me."

"Justice? Is he looking for vampires, too?"

Alec smiled. It was really a very nice smile, one I greatly enjoyed. "We are working together, but I can assure you that I mean you no harm. Quite the opposite, actually," he said with a little waggle of his eyebrows.

"Well . . . I did kind of think you didn't intend for me to get away when we were at the bookstore," I said, trying hard to keep my eyes from wandering. It wasn't easy. "I rather thought Kristoff was going to drag me off despite the fact that I'm not the person you're looking for."

"Ah, but how do you know you're not?" He took a few steps toward me, with a glint in his eyes that had my palms suddenly sweating. His hands cupped my breasts. "How do you know that you're not exactly what I'm looking for?"

I opened my mouth to tell him I wasn't that sort of a girl, wasn't interested in him, and he could just take his extremely gorgeous body to hell, but the thought of saying anything so obviously ludicrous left me with the urge to break into hysterical laughter.

"You have a really impressive penis," I heard myself saying, and immediately slapped my hand over my mouth, appalled that I could speak without thinking.

His hips rubbed against me. "I'm glad you think so. I'm fond of it, myself, but I am naturally biased. Would you like to touch it?"

"I'd be lying if I said that wasn't suddenly at the top of my to-do list. Um . . . would you mind if I asked how you found me? And is Kristoff going to burst in here at any moment in order to drag me off to be a Zorya?"

His thumbs flicked across my breasts, leaving me gasping. "Let us leave discussions of all that for later, shall we? As for your first question, I followed your scent, your sweet, feminine scent."

I stared at him in complete befuddlement.

"I didn't think you'd buy that," he said with a wry smile and a faux sigh. "Actually, I took this while we were searching the shop."

He held out the hotel pamphlet with a map of the area that I'd received when the tour group checked in.

"Oh. So you really want to be here?" I asked, having a hard time believing that idea.

A look of doubt crossed his face. "Did I misread the signs? I thought you were just as interested in me as I am in you."

He couldn't be serious, could he? He didn't actually mean what I thought he meant, did he? I banged the back of my head on the door a couple of times, just to clear the cobwebs that so were clearly muddling my brain.

"Pia? Are you so distraught that you are trying to beat yourself senseless?" he asked, eyeing me in a manner that was definitely not of the romantic ilk.

"No, just trying to unscramble my brains. Alec, I'm . . . I'm . . . oh, hell." I gave up trying to reason, and flung myself on him. As I've mentioned, I'm not insubstantial by any stretch of the imagination, and the force of me plowing into him sent us both sprawling backward until we hit the bed, the two of us going down in a tangle of arms and legs, and one extremely naked penis.

He laughed as I stammered out an apology, his arms coming around hard behind me to hold me in place.

"I'm so sorry! Did I hurt you? Am I squashing you? Can you breathe? Oh dear god, I've killed you!"

"You didn't hurt me, and I can breathe just fine. It takes a great deal to harm me, you know," he answered, his voice once again warm and filled with sensual promise.

I pushed myself off his chest so I could look down at him, well aware that I was straddling him in a manner that would have probably constituted the definition of actual sex if I hadn't been fully clothed. "I'm dreaming, aren't I? I hit my head on the door when I came in, and I'm dreaming all this."

"I assure you, I'm very real." He laughed again, and suddenly, I was on my back, his chest warm against my hands as he leaned down and kissed the tip of my nose. "I take it you don't have objections after all, despite my friend's rather determined efforts to coerce you?"

He slid off me. I couldn't help giving a self-conscious grimace. "I told you before that I'm not the Zorya —"

"Hush." He stopped me by putting a finger over my mouth. "You need not protest your innocence with me, my love."

My eyebrows rose at both his words and the endearment.

"I believe you are who you say you are, Pia. That Kristoff still harbors suspicions to the contrary pains me, but you need not have any fear that I will allow him to act against you. You are too honest — as sweet as the honey you taste of — to mislead us as he believes."

I heaved a sigh of relief. "I'm so glad you see the truth, but I have to say that I met the Zorya earlier —"

He stopped me talking again, this time with his lips in a much longer, much hotter kiss. "We decided not to speak of Kristoff or the Zorya. This night is for us."

My brain was squirreling all around with any number of thoughts, not the least of which was an appreciation for his ability to kiss. "That sounds like a good idea, although I have to say that I don't generally fling myself on a man I've just met."

"Ah," he said, rising. "I thought that might be the issue. That's why I brought with me a little libation."

He padded off to the bathroom. I admired the scenery of his backside as he did so, then scrambled off the bed and ran to the mirror next to the door.

"You like champagne?" His voice drifted out of the bathroom, along with the sounds of a cork being popped.

"Love it!" I said, snatching up my brush and quickly brushing my hair. I grimaced at my reflection, then dug quickly through my bag for a stick of cinnamon gum, chewing it at warp speed while I mentally ran over the list of important issues. Thank god I had bought all new undies for the trip, not wanting to have to launder the worn-out and somewhat tattered things I habitually wore. But the thought of my underwear brought up a whole new horror — I couldn't let him see me in it, let alone naked.

"Good. I also have strawberries, but I think we'll leave those until later. Ah, nicely chilled." A clinking sound accompanied a slightly metallic clang as Alec put the bottle back in what I assumed was a wine bucket. I spat out the gum into the wastebasket, praying my cinnamon breath wouldn't be too obvious, then pulled up my shirt to stick my nose in and take a few worried whiffs. I couldn't smell anything offensive, but I'd done a lot of walking, not to mention running away from various folks. Perhaps I was just oblivious to less than savory odors? A quick dab from my perfume bottle took care of any problem therein.

"Should I bring some ice, as well?" Alec asked, still in the bathroom.

"Ice?" It was too bright in here, far too bright. Although I'd flipped on only one light when I entered the room, Alec had turned on all the others, leaving the large room lit in such a way that every bulge, every bit of pudge, would be starkly high-lighted. I dashed around the room and turned off all the lights but the one by the bed, and that I'd take care of as soon as he had a few glasses of champagne in him. "What do you mean, ice?"

"Ah. Don't care for it? Some women don't. We'll proceed along more traditional lines, then, shall we?" There was a tinkle of ice cubes hitting the sink as he dumped them out.

"That's breath, pits, underwear, flabby bits . . . oh dear god, birth control!" I raced across the room to my purse, dumping out everything onto a chair, frantically sorting through the contents until I found the small packet I'd made up that contained birth control pills, and more condoms that I thought possible to use on a three-week trip. The condom packages were connected in one long strip, intended for each individual one to be separated, but there was no time for such niceties. Clutching the strip, I hesitated, worrying about my underwear.

"Would you like me to light some candles? I see there are some in here."

Should I leave my panties on? Although I didn't have a lot of experience being seduced, I did have the occasional relationship, and I remembered distinctly one time when it was downright embarrassing to have my partner attempt to wrestle my undies off. Maybe I should take them off now, to save Alec the trouble. But surely he'd notice, and then what sort of an image would he have of me?

The picture rose in my mind of Kristoff's startled expression when I accosted him in the park. I knew exactly what Alec would think: Only shameless hussies strolled around without their underwear in foreign cities, flinging themselves on unsuspecting men. "I'm fine without candles, thank you."

I dashed back to the bed and stuffed the condoms under the pillow while arranging myself in what I hoped was the same position I'd just occupied.

Alec appeared at the door with a sweating bottle in one hand, two glasses in another, and a smile that promised much. "There you are, my goddess. How fetching you look, although don't you think you're a little overdressed for the occasion? After all, I have adopted an informal mode of dress; don't you think it's right that you do the same?"

"Definitely. But . . . er . . . after we've had a little champagne, don't you think?" I said, scooting back so he could sit next to me.

He frowned, looking from the bottle and glasses to me. "I think perhaps we'll save that for after," he said, setting them down before suddenly pulling me to my feet. "I'm hungry, lovely Pia, and only you can feed me."

I defy any woman to be in my shoes and not melt at those words. And melt I did, all over him, sagging against him, too overwhelmed with my good luck to do much of anything. Alec's hands were everywhere as I pressed an awkward kiss to his collarbone, his mouth busily nibbling my neck, and somehow, my hands found their way down to his penis, which had gone from a dormant to an active state in the last few seconds.

"That's it, my darling, touch me, do not be shy. I am yours to enjoy, just as you are mine."

His hands were on my breasts, my back, coaxing my thighs apart so I could straddle the leg he thrust through mine, and all the while his mouth was as hot as fire on my neck. My fingers explored the equally hot flesh between my hands, leaving me marveling that such a mundane-looking bit of skin and tissue could bring us both so much pleasure.

"Sins of the saints," Alec groaned, his hips moving as I stroked him a bit more boldly. "Yes, just like that, my love. You drive me to distraction, Pia. I'm afraid I must . . . I must . . ."

He bit me then, bit me hard as he climaxed. I winced at the pain for a moment, but he must have realized he was going a bit too rough with the love bites, for the pain eased almost immediately. His groan trailed off as he clutched me tight, his fingers digging into my arms, his hips thrusting three more times before he stopped.

"By the saints, woman," he murmured into my hair as he deftly backed me up toward the bed. "If I said I've never had it better, you'd probably laugh, but it is the truth. And now, dear Pia, you must allow me to reciprocate."

I was oddly elated and deflated at the same time. There was, I admitted to myself as Alec carefully pulled my cream-colored linen blouse over my head, a certain amount of pride to be had in being told one gave a good hand job, but there was also a distinct lack of . . . well, a lack. I puzzled over my dissatisfaction with the way the events were proceeding until I realized with horror that Alec was tugging my now-soiled skirt upward.

"No, I'll do it. It's a bit . . . er . . . ooky. Why don't you get in bed and I'll just pop into the bathroom and get this off without making any more of a mess."

Alec's eyes were filled with contrite hurt. "You wound me, darling. But I see your point — I was rather more excited than I thought. I will naturally replace your ruined skirt. Let me take it off you and we will proceed."

Embarrassment flooded me, leaving my face hot. "You know, that's not really necessary. I'll just —"

"It is very necessary, I assure you," he said with a wolfish grin. "I will greatly enjoy undressing you."

I wanted to die right there on the spot, but equally, I wanted to experience all the pleasure that was promised in his eyes. Desire won out over shame. "All right, but you have to turn out the lights first."

"Turn out the lights?" A little frown appeared between his brows.

"You're going to make me say it, aren't you? Fine. I can stand a little more humbling. I don't want you to see me naked, OK?"

He glanced down toward my breasts, shameless hussies that were barely restrained by my bra. "Ah. I begin to understand. You are self-conscious about your body and think that I will find fault with it."

"Well, you have to admit there's a lot of me to find fault with," I said frankly, nodding toward the light. "If you could just turn that off, I'll go dump the skirt and we can proceed from there."

To my utter and complete relief, he did as I asked, his laughter filling the suddenly darkened room as he switched off the light. There was a rustle of sheets followed by, "You have nothing to fear, I assure you, but if it will make you feel better, I will satisfy myself with feasting my other senses on you."

While in the bathroom shucking the remainder of my clothing as quickly as possible, I had another quick check that everything was as it should be, wished I had time to brush my teeth quickly, and prayed that I wouldn't do anything to screw up what was surely going to be the best evening of my life.

Alec chuckled as I blindly groped my way to the bed, pausing to hop on one foot for a moment when I stubbed my toe on the bedstead. "You are a tease, Pia Thomason. But such a delightful tease, I can't find fault with your decision to drive me insane with desire. Ah, there you are."

He was warm and male and pretty much fit the description of every fantasy man I'd ever imagined. I slid into bed beside him, crossing my fingers that he wouldn't insist on feeling all the pudgy parts of me. Men liked breasts — maybe if I could keep him interested in those, he wouldn't notice my stomach and thighs and just exactly how big my butt was.

"What have we here? Nipples? How delightful." Before I could point him to the appropriate spots, he dived at my chest, his hands tweaking and touching and generally getting right to business.

"Do you like this?" he asked, and I about jumped off the bed when he took one nipple in his mouth and scraped his teeth against it.

"Dear god in heaven!" I yelled, clutching his head.

"I will take that as a yes." Laughter was in

his voice as he turned his attention to my other breast, one hand starting to move downward. I sucked in my stomach, but needn't have worried — his hand kept drifting lower until he reached points south.

"I'm sorry, I don't wax," I blurted out, suddenly mortified. What if all European women were naked down there, or at least trimmed? "I tried a bikini wax once, when my girlfriend was getting married, and she begged me to try it with her, but I almost passed out from the pain, and swore I'd never do anything like that again."

His hand, which had paused a moment as I babbled, nudged my legs apart. "You make the most interesting bed talk, Pia. I assure you, I am not shocked or horrified. And please relax, my love. Your legs are as tense as a tightrope walker's."

I made an effort to relax and just enjoy the ride, wondering if I should bring up the subject of condoms now, or wait until things got a bit more heated. I assumed it would take Alec a while to regain his stamina, so it probably could wait.

That was my last coherent thought as his fingers dipped down into sensitive areas, his tongue swirling at the same time across one tender nipple. His fingers danced as I writhed on the bed, my hands clutching his shoulders as he spun me higher and higher. It didn't take long to send me flying, and I had a horrible feeling I shouted out something completely inappropriate as my body burst into a nova of pleasure.

His laughter wrapped around me in a cocoon as I regained my senses. "You are so very responsive, my adorable one. That does wonders for my ego."

I was about to tell him that there was no need for his ego to doubt his abilities when he rolled me onto my side and snuggled up behind me, his breath brushing my ear as he spoke. "I am delighted to have found you, Pia. More delighted than you can ever know."

I lay for a bit in confusion, listening as his breathing evened out and eventually fell into a sleepy rhythm. My emotions were in a tangle, disappointment raising its ugly head. Despite the orgasm, I felt as if the whole experience had ended too abruptly, as if it was unfinished.

"Don't be ridiculous," I whispered to myself. "Just because you didn't need the condoms doesn't mean anything. He's a man, and they can't do these things as frequently as women can. Be happy he didn't just roll over and go to sleep as soon as he got his jollies."

The words made sense but felt hollow nonetheless. Perhaps Alec had intimacy issues. Perhaps he was tired, and just didn't have a lot of stamina that evening. Perhaps he was one of those once-a-night guys, and that was that.

"Stop finding fault with the poor man," I murmured, and snuggled back against him, enjoying the feeling of a warm body spooned up behind me.

Besides, I had two more days in Iceland. There would be other opportunities.

CHAPTER 5

Mindful of the horrors of morning breath, I kept my mouth firmly closed as I rolled over to see if Alec was awake. To my utter disappointment — and, if I was strictly honest, a lot of relief, since I'd been wondering how to make it to the bathroom without him getting a good look at my butt — the bed was empty of insanely handsome, green-eyed men.

"Crap," I said aloud, then cocked an ear to listen for sounds of occupation in the bathroom. There were none, but the bathroom door was closed.

"Good morning," I called out brightly as I snagged my bathrobe from a nearby chair and pulled it on, adjusting it so that it left some cleavage showing while covering less savory parts. "I hope you don't mind that I'm one of those annoying morning people. I've tried to be a little less chipper in the morning, but I'm afraid there's nothing I can do about it. I'll just order us some breakfast, OK?"

There was no dissenting comment, so I dialed the number for room service and placed an order for a breakfast for two.

"Coffee or tea for breakfast, Alec?" I asked, one hand over the phone.

I frowned after another moment of silence.

"Madam?" the room service person prodded.

"Um . . . how about one coffee and one tea," I said to cover both bases, then hung up and went to the bathroom door. "Alec? Do you prefer coffee or tea?"

No sound of running water greeted me. There was a faint scrabbling sound, however, a sort of odd rustle that had me suddenly panicked. What if he'd slipped and hit his head on the counter? "Alec, are you OK in there?"

Silence met my question, silence that was broken only by what sounded like a whimper.

"I'm coming in. I hope you don't mind, but if you're hurt or stuck or something, I can help."

The bathroom faced southeast, and I knew from previous mornings would be filled with morning sunlight diffused through the privacy glass. I opened the door slowly, relieved to see that there was no man hunched over the toilet injured or being sick. That relief immediately turned to horror as the door swung all the way open.

"Oh dear god!" My skin crawled as I ran forward at the sight of the bloodied body that lay slumped up against the cupboard beneath the sink, the handle of a knife protruding from the chest. "Oh my god!"

It wasn't a man's body — it was a woman. A woman whose eyes opened slightly as I squatted next to her, unsure of what I should do. There was so much blood, sprayed on the wall and door opposite, splattered on the floor and sink and shower glass. "Don't move. I'll call the aid unit," I told the woman, then did a double take when I realized I knew her. "Anniki?"

She made a horrible mewing noise, her hands fluttering toward the knife as I spoke. "Take . . . it."

I stared in horror at the bloody knife. Only the handle was visible, the blade having clearly been sunk deep into her chest cavity. "Take . . ."

I touched the hilt, giving it the slightest of tugs. If it wasn't in as far as I thought, perhaps she just didn't have the strength to yank it out.

It didn't budge.

"I'm sorry, Anniki, but I don't think that's a good idea. On the cop shows I've seen, they always leave things in people when they take them to the hospital."

"Take . . ." She gasped, her eyes opening wide suddenly. Her hands grabbed me with a strength that startled me, her fingernails digging into the soft flesh of my palm.

I bit back a yelp as pain laced my hand.

"Let justice roll down like waters," she said, her voice taking on a strange, distant timbre, "and righteousness like an ever-flowing stream."

"What . . . ? I don't . . ."

"You must right the wrongs," Anniki begged. "Promise me!"

"I promise!" I said hastily, trying to pull my hand back, more than a little sickened at the sight of all the blood. The way her fingernails dug into my flesh, I assumed some of it was going to be mine. "I swear to you that I'll do anything you want, only let me go call for some help first."

A horrible gurgling noise rose from deep in her chest as she released my hand, reaching for her neck, her hands so slick with her own blood that her fingers fumbled with the clothing. "Take it. Follow the light. Make things . . . right. Be the stream."

The gurgling noise grew as she whimpered

with frustration, her hands finally closing around a thin chain worn around her neck. She pulled it off slowly, the chain cutting into her flesh for a second before it snapped. "Remember the light. Always remember . . ."

Her hands closed around mine, cold and wet with blood. I stared in horror that seemed to have no end as her eyes rolled back in her head. Her hands dropped limply to the floor, and I knew with absolute conviction that she had just died.

Every atom in my body recoiled with revulsion, my brain screaming at me to get away from the dead person. I don't know how long I stared with dumb incomprehension at her slackened face before my gaze finally drifted to my hands. They were covered in blood now, deep, crimson, crescent-shaped welts on my palm indicative of just how hard she'd gripped my hands. My blood mingled with hers as I stared in horror down at myself — it wasn't just my hands that were bloody; my arms and much of the front of my bathrobe were soaked red.

The moonstone from the bookmark I'd seen earlier was now hung on the bloody chain that lay across my bleeding palm. It was the stone that Anniki had pressed into my hands, and my brain, numb with shock, slowly brought itself back to life and realized what had just happened.

Let justice roll down like waters, she'd said. I recognized that from childhood Sunday school classes — it was from the Bible. Anniki had begged me to follow the light, to right the wrong done to her. She wanted me to be Zorya. And I had sworn I would.

Minutes seemed to crawl by as I knelt next to the mortal remains of Anniki, too stunned to sort through my wild thoughts. Why was she in my bathroom? Who killed her? What was I going to do about the deathbed promise I'd just given? And most importantly, where was Alec?

"Get a grip, Pia," I said aloud, and was shocked to hear how shaky my voice was. Somehow, I'd also been crying without knowing it. Bracing myself, I reached out a tentative hand to Anniki's wrist, gently taking it in hope of feeling a pulse.

There was none, of course. I hadn't really expected one, not since I was so certain she was dead, but I had to make sure. I stared at the body and blood-splattered bathroom, hoping against hope there would be some answer to all the questions that spun around in my mind, but there was nothing. Anniki had somehow magically appeared in my bathroom and been nearly murdered and left to die — all without me being aware of anything. I glanced quickly over to the door leading to Madga's room. Perhaps she or Ray . . . I shook my head even as I thought it. The door was locked from this side. I knew I had left it unlocked, which meant someone else had locked it.

That thought chilled me like no other, and had the benefit of sending me flying from the bathroom. I stared at the bloodied stone in my hand, throwing it on the bed as I thought furiously. "I'll have to call the police. They'll want me to leave everything just as it is, but what am I going to do about the stone? Think, Pia, think!"

Clothing. I needed to get dressed. That was the first priority — not even the police could expect me to wait around in a bloody bathrobe for them to arrive. With shaking hands I yanked off the robe, and quickly grabbed my clothing.

"Ick." My hands were still damp with blood. I glanced toward the bathroom, unwilling to go back in there, but having no other choice. I averted my eyes from Anniki's still body, using a damp towel to wash the blood off of me. I was about to leave when I realized I was being heartless beyond belief, and forced myself to go back into the room. I knelt on the towel, and with tears streaming down my face, took Anniki's hand in mine. "I'm not a religious person, but I understand what you asked. I don't know if I can bring about justice, but I'll do the best I can," I told her, and closing my eyes, said a prayer for the passage of her soul.

Grief washed over me, grief for the loss of a woman who had been so vibrant only a few hours before. I might not have known her well or long, but she deserved better than this. She deserved justice.

And righteousness like an ever-flowing stream.

"I'll do what you asked," I said, my voice thick with tears as I pressed her fingers. "I don't know how, but I will right the wrong done to you. You can rest easy on that account."

It didn't take long for me to mop the tears from my face and hurry into my clothing. I was next to Anniki, unsure of whether or not I should cover her with a blanket before calling the police, when a knock sounded at my door.

I froze for a second, terrified the killer had come back, but realized after a moment of incoherent thought that it must be the breakfast I'd ordered.

"Pia, can I borrow some ibuprofen? I've got the world's worst head—"

A familiar voice had me spinning around.

Denise stood in the doorway of the bathroom, her eyes and mouth making little *O*s of horror as she stared at the body on the floor.

"I didn't kill her," I blurted out, seeing the accusation in her eyes. I made a gesture of innocence, but Denise's eyes bugged out a bit more as she stared at my hand. It was red with blood. "Oh, that. That came from the stone she gave me. I really didn't kill her," I repeated. "I found her like that. Well, she was alive, but she died right away."

Denise started to back away slowly.

"Do I look like I'm the sort of person to stab another person in the heart?" I asked, following her out of the bathroom.

She paused for a moment, then flung back her head and screamed in the most unearthly way. *"Murder!"*

"Hell's bells, Denise, I just told you —"

"Murderer!" she screamed again, raising her hand to point at me.

It's an old adage that your life passes before your eyes when you're about to die. I'm living proof that such an idea is completely false. Not only did a speedy vision of all my life's high and low points zip through my mind at that moment, but a vision of the immediate future followed, one in which I tried to explain to the police about such things as Zoryas, handsome men who apparently indulged in one-night stands before disappearing into the blue, a group devoted to ridding the world of evil, and just how a dead woman I'd seen a few hours before happened to be murdered literally right next to me.

In my bathroom.

With my fingerprints on the murder weapon.

And a precious gem belonging to her now in my possession. All that zipped through my brain in the time it took for Denise to scream out one word. By the time she sucked in the air needed to fuel another scream, I'd come to a decision — there was no way I was going to be able to explain any of the happenings of the previous day. I'd have to seek help from people who wouldn't think I was crazy.

I didn't say anything more to Denise; I simply grabbed the moonstone, flung open the French doors that led to a small balcony, and climbed over the railing, praying I wouldn't break a leg in the fall to the grassy lawn one floor below.

I hit the ground hard, but not so hard that

I injured myself. Denise's scream wafted out of the open doors, which set me to running out of the tiny garden at the back of the hotel. I raced around to the front of the building, pausing for a moment to get my bearings. In front of the hotel sat a familiar-looking car, the passenger door of which opened almost immediately.

"Alec," I cried gratefully, and ran for the haven he offered.

The startled look in Kristoff's blues eyes told me he wasn't waiting outside the hotel for me.

"Where's Alec?" he asked, frowning as he peered over my shoulder.

Behind me, a woman screamed. I hesitated, unwilling to trust him, but equally unsure whether I would stand a better chance with the authorities.

The memory of the glow of pleasure in Denise's eyes as she screamed at me was the deciding point.

"I don't know," I answered, hopping into the car, slamming closed the door, and slumping down in the seat. "But we're about to have company, so unless you want to explain to the police why your buddy disappeared, leaving a murdered woman in my bathroom, I'd suggest you get moving."

I'll say this for the harsh Kristoff — he

didn't need to be told twice. He just slammed his foot on the accelerator and peeled off.

"Stay down," he commanded, using one hand to shove me onto the floor.

I wasn't about to argue the point. I curled up in as small a ball as I could and tried to keep from banging my head on the door or dashboard as he zoomed through the streets.

"We're out of the town. You can get up now. Who's been killed?" he asked after a few minutes.

"The Zorya." I winced when he took a corner too quickly, slamming me back against the car door. "Are we being followed?"

"You are the Zorya," he insisted, his face grim as I hauled myself into the seat, quickly grabbing for the seat belt.

"I am now, but I wasn't as of an hour ago. That job was held by a woman named Anniki."

"No," he said, his eyes on the road as he sped out of town. I glanced around. The car had darkly tinted windows, which gave everything a dull blue-black flavor, but I thought I recognized the road leading to a quaint little fishing village to the south that my group had visited on our first day in Iceland.

"Look, I know you didn't believe me before when I said that I wasn't the Zorya, but I really wasn't. Then."

"No, we're not being followed," he said, casting me a curious glance. "You knew the Zorya."

"It turns out I did, although I wasn't aware of it." I pulled off my necklace with its modest little garnet rose, and slipped the moonstone onto the chain, wrapping it around my wrist a couple of times before securing it. Did Kristoff know that Alec spent the night with me? If he was waiting outside the hotel for his friend, it would appear he did. "You don't know where Alec is?"

"He said he was going to be with you." Kristoff's jaw tightened. Obviously, he didn't approve of Alec's interest in me.

"He was. At least, he was there when I fell asleep. He wasn't there when I woke up. What were you doing outside the hotel?"

If he heard the suspicion in my voice, he didn't comment on it. "Alec told me to pick him up in the morning. Tell me about the Zorya."

I hesitated, unsure of whether or not it would be wise to tell him.

He slid me another glance. "Afraid?" he asked, one eyebrow quirking.

126

"Honestly? Right now you're tops on my list of suspects," I answered. "Despite the fact that you're about to swear up one side and down the other that you would never harm poor Anniki."

"On the contrary, I would quite happily dispatch a reaper if it was within my means."

A cold sweat started on my palms, but the memory of Anniki begging for justice was too fresh in my mind to ignore. "Did you kill her?"

The words came out stark and bold.

He glanced at me, his eyes unreadable. "Would you believe me if I said I didn't?"

"That's not an answer."

Silence filled the car for a few minutes. "Answering is a moot point if you don't believe I speak the truth."

"I think you do whatever serves you best," I said baldly.

To my surprise, he nodded. "Yes."

"Including killing the Zorya?"

His lips thinned. "As a matter of fact, I didn't kill her."

I relaxed against the side of the car, relieved.

Kristoff sent me a puzzled glance. "You believe me?"

"Stranger things have happened," I said, trying to gather my wits.

"That's not to say I wouldn't kill a Zorya if given the opportunity."

I stared at him. He looked in deadly earnest.

"I suppose, then, given the fact that I just promised Anniki I'd do her job, I should be very worried."

Amusement flickered momentarily on his face. "I have a different plan in mind for you."

"Oh, *that* makes me feel better," I said, my stomach turning over at the thought of what sorts of evil things he might do to me. I shook my head at my folly — surely the police would have been a better choice than a madman? "Why would you kill one of your own people?"

"I wouldn't."

"But you just said —" The penny dropped with an almost audible clang. "Wait a second — you're not part of the Brotherhood?"

"Would that I were so I could see them pay for their crimes," he said, biting off each word.

"Pay for what?" I was feeling more and more like we were talking in circles.

His knuckles went white on the steering wheel. "They killed Angelica."

"Your girlfriend?"

128

He nodded.

"I'm sorry. Alec said something about you losing a loved one a few years ago." Against my better judgment, a small well of sympathy opened up. Having lost both of my parents to a drunk driver some eight years before, I knew how long the grief of sudden, tragic death could remain. If he was on a vendetta against a murderer, I could understand his desire to see someone pay. "I assume the person responsible was never caught?"

He shot me a quick, unreadable look.

"I'm not asking just to be nosy — my parents were killed by a drunk driver with a long record and no license. It took my brother and me four years of legal wrangling before we finally got a vehicular homicide charge to stick, but I remember how consumed we were to see justice done."

"I killed the reaper who conducted the ritual upon her," he said flatly, his voice as hard as flint.

Horror stirred the hair on the back of my neck at the way he spat out the word "ritual." I remembered Anniki saying something about how the Brotherhood performed rituals on vampires. . . .

That last word echoed in my head with a terrifying enlightenment, one that left me gaping openmouthed for a moment. "You're . . . you're . . . you're one of those vampires, aren't you? The ones Anniki was telling me about. The whatchamacallits . . . Black Ones?"

"We prefer the term 'Dark One,' " he said without the slightest sign of concern that he had just admitted he was a vampire.

"Holy Jehoshaphat and the Wizard of Oz," I swore, fear skittering up my back. "A vampire. A real vampire. Oh my god. Does . . . does Alec know?"

He bent a look upon me that implied I was a moron, which at that moment was probably deserved. "Alec is older than me."

I stared at him, my brain trying to come to grips with the fact that the man sitting next to me, the perfectly normal-looking man, was, in fact, the evil undead. "What does that have to do with anything?"

He spun the wheel, sending us careening off the main road and down a winding track that led into the small fishing town. "You can't expect me to believe you're that na-ive."

I gasped, really gasped as his meaning struck me. "You're not saying Alec is one, too?"

"I just told you he's older than I am. I was born in 1623. He has at least eighty years on me."

My jaw dropped again, so stunned was I that it only dimly filtered through my brain that Kristoff had stopped the car in the shade of a squat stone building that was perched on top of a cliff that overlooked the small fishing village. "But . . . a vampire? Alec? No. I don't believe it. You're just trying to scare me."

"If I wanted to scare you, I'd tell you what I was thinking at this moment," he said dryly.

"Alec is no more a vampire than I am," I told him, absolutely confident in what I said.

Kristoff raised an eyebrow.

"Answer me this, then, Mr. Fangs — vampires drink blood, right? So if Alec is a vampire, why didn't he drink my blood?" I asked in tones of indisputable reason.

"I have no doubt that he did."

"A feeble answer at best," I said smugly. "I'd know if someone was drinking my blood."

Kristoff suddenly leaned over me, turning my head to examine the side of my neck farthest from him. "I thought so," he said after a moment's silence, releasing my chin and sitting back in his seat. "You are mistaken. You bear a mark."

"What?" I pulled down the overhead

sunshade, examining myself in the mirror contained on its back. Sure enough, there was a small bruising on the side of my neck, right where I remembered Alec nuzzling me. "That's not vampire teeth marks. It's a hickey."

I could swear that Kristoff was having to fight to keep from rolling his eyes. "It is the same thing."

I touched the spot gingerly, eyeing it before turning to him. "I always thought vampires left two little teeth marks."

"You watch too much TV."

"Are you saying you always leave a mark when you bite someone?"

"Not always. It takes much concentration, however, and generally we're . . . distracted."

"By what?" I couldn't help but ask. "Garlic?"

He did roll his eyes now. "Hardly. The act of taking blood can be very . . . intimate."

"Oh, that sort of distracted." I touched the spot again. It didn't hurt, just felt somewhat numb. "So drinking someone's blood is sexually arousing?"

"It can be, yes. Not always, but it can be so, depending on the subject."

I flinched at his term, casting my mind back to the events of the evening. There had been a moment when Alec was nibbling my neck, and I thought he'd bitten me a smidgen too hard, but that had eased up almost immediately. "And the person you're biting doesn't know you're doing it?"

"That depends," he said, consulting his watch.

"On what?"

"On whether or not there is a shared sexual attraction."

Well, there had definitely been that last night. So perhaps the hickey wasn't so much a hickey as it was an indicator that Alec was more than he seemed. But if that was true, then he'd be no better than Kristoff.

"No," I said, shaking my head. "I don't believe it. Alec is good. He's not evil, like you."

Kristoff turned his teal eyes on me, the look of scorn in them so strong it stung. "Your people kill mine ruthlessly, without prejudice, conducting the most obscene rituals they can think of, and you call me evil?"

I clawed at the seat belt, ripping it off as I jerked open the car door, desperate to escape the dangerous Kristoff.

He snarled something and leaped after me, slamming me up against the stone wall of the building. We were on the shaded side, the sun not having yet warmed the stone, but it was not for that reason that I shivered against the cold wall.

"The Brotherhood purifies people —" I started to say, grabbing at my memory of what Anniki had told me the evening before.

"Purifies." He spat the word out like it was poison, leaning close to me, so close I could feel the warmth of his body, but it was the rage and hatred in his eyes that left me paralyzed with fear. "Do you know how your precious reapers purified Angelica? They started with a crucifixion, draining almost all of her blood, leaving her racked with pain and almost unbearable hunger. After that, they called down their cleansing light. Do you know what that is, Zorya?"

I shook my head, tears blurring my vision.

"Complete immolation. They used to simply burn people at the stake, but now they use their damned light to burn a body from the inside out."

My stomach lurched, a horrible vision rising in my mind. I closed my eyes, tears burning paths down my cheeks.

"They didn't burn her to death then. That would have been too easy a death for her. Their last rite of purification was a beheading . . . slowly, taking several strokes, with the spinal cord severed last."

I shoved him away, racing to a small

scrubby bush and falling to my knees, wanting to vomit, but my stomach was too revolted to do even that.

"They left her head with her body so I could see the expression on her face," he said from behind me. "They wanted me to know what torment she suffered before she died. Those are the people you represent, Pia. And you wonder that I hunt them."

"If that's true, I wouldn't blame you in the least," I started to say, but before I could finish he yanked me to my feet.

"*If* it is true?" His furious gaze searched my face. "You doubt me?"

"I don't know what to think," I wailed, too overwhelmed with confusion to try to sort things out. "I don't think you're lying, no. I know grief when I see it. But Anniki wasn't that sort of person. At least I don't think she was — she seemed compassionate, as if she really cared about people."

"People, but not Dark Ones."

I opened my mouth to dispute that statement, but didn't know what to say.

"It doesn't matter," he said, his expression going hard as he wrapped a hand around my arm and hauled me to the front of the building. "Believe what you want. I'm going to ensure that you, at least, will not allow the reapers to kill any more of my people."

"Oh dear god, you're going to kill me!" I screamed, panicking as he jerked open a wooden door and hauled me inside the building.

"If I wanted to do that, I'd have broken your neck last night. Be quiet, woman!" he yelled, startling me into silence, the last few echoes of my screeches fading away. "The priest here doesn't speak English, so it's no use begging him for help."

"Priest!" I squawked, clawing at his hand in an attempt to get free. My entire body was riddled with fear and the knowledge that I was about to be killed by a vampire. "For last rites?"

A small, wrinkled man shuffled forward out of the gloom, and I realized with a start that I was in a tiny church. For some reason, that scared me even more. What if the vampires had their own horrible cult, some-place to conduct their dark doings?

"What I am about to do is much, much worse than death," Kristoff said, pulling me so close I could see the tiny black lines that flared out from his pupils. Suddenly, he smiled, but it wasn't a nice smile, not nice at all. It was the sort of smile a panther would give a particularly juicy-looking rabbit just before it pounced. "We're going to be married, Zorya."

I thought my eyes were going to pop out of my head. "You're not going to kill me?"

His smile grew. "No."

I sagged with relief until his next words hit me.

"But you're going to wish you were dead before I'm done with you."

CHAPTER 6

"Sign."

"No. I'm not going to do it."

Kristoff's hand tightened around my throat. "Sign it or I will break your neck."

It wasn't easy to swallow with him half throttling me like that, but I finally managed it. "Look, I don't know why you want to marry me —"

"I'd as soon as marry a viper," he interrupted. "Alec agreed to do it, but since he conveniently disappeared last night when I went to arrange for the license, I am the sacrifice instead."

I bristled a little at the word "sacrifice." "Well, I don't particularly like you, either! Alec is much, much nicer than you. He actually smiles."

"Sign the damned things so we can get out of here," Kristoff growled, indicating the two copies of marriage forms he'd produced.

I had discovered he'd spoken the truth about the elderly clergyman. Not only was he deaf to all pleas to save me, he performed what I had a horrible feeling was a marriage ceremony while I tried to reason with the insane man next to me. "This is ridiculous. This is 2008. You can't force someone to get married. There are laws."

"There are also bribes, and as I spent the night getting the correct documents and asking my old friend here to conduct the official ceremony, it will be completely legal and binding. As soon as you sign."

"But we're in Iceland! I'm not a citizen. Surely it can't be legal for noncitizens to be married without a ton of paperwork. And don't I have to be present to get a license? Surely I have to have been present!"

"There are ways to make it possible," he said grimly. "Sign the damned things."

"No," I said, folding my hands. "And you can't make me. Kill me if you want, but I'm not signing."

Kristoff snarled something rude that I chose to ignore, yanking a small blue object from his pocket.

"Hey! Where did you get that?" I tried to grab my passport back from him, but he held it out of reach, flipping through the pages until he came to the one with my signature.

"Your precious Alec gave it to me last night, when you were asleep," he said, snatching up the pen and thrusting it into my hand. Before I could throw it away he yanked me backward against his body, one hand clamping down on mine as he consulted the passport.

"Stop it!" I yelled, struggling as he forced my hand to write a scraggly version of my name. "This isn't legal! You can't do it!"

"It's done," he snapped, forcing me to sign the second form before releasing me. I jumped away and rubbed my abused hand.

"You don't have witnesses, Mr. Smarty-Pants," I pointed out. "You may have your buddy there falsely conduct the ceremony, and you may have a version of my signature, but there were no witnesses to the ceremony, and I'm sure that even in Iceland you have to have witnesses."

Kristoff put two fingers to his mouth and blew a piercing whistle that seemed earsplitting in the confined space of the small church.

Two men emerged from what I assumed was a back room. They both eyed me as they came forward, speaking in a language that I didn't understand.

"Do either of you speak English?" I asked sweetly.

"The one on the left is my brother Andreas. The other is my cousin Rowan," Kristoff said, almost smirking at my look of consternation. "They both speak a dozen languages, English included."

My hand itched to slap that look off his face, but I hung on to my temper.

"I don't suppose it would do any good to tell you that your brother is insane?" I asked the man named Andreas. There wasn't a lot of family resemblance, although he, too, was the sort of man who made women stop and stare.

"No more so than any one of us," Andreas answered, then signed the forms.

My heart sank as the second man did the same. The three of them spoke quietly for a few minutes while I contemplated my choices. I'd run for it, except Kristoff retained a hold on my arm, not to mention the fact that I wouldn't stand a chance of outrunning any one of the men present — other than the priest, and even he looked unusually spry for someone his age, laughing at something that the vampire named Rowan said.

That thought struck me oddly, somehow.

"Do you have . . . you know . . . fangs?" I

asked Kristoff, making a little fangy gesture with my fingers. "Like Dracula fangs?"

The three men all stared at me as if I'd just turned into a giant ice-skating sloth.

"You don't, then? So the whole fang thing is a myth?"

The look of disbelief on Kristoff's face was almost worth the experience of being there.

Rowan burst into laughter. Andreas frowned, saying something in what sounded to me like Italian.

"You know, I'm normally a pretty circumspect person," I told Andreas. "But since I woke up this morning, I've found a murdered woman in my bathroom, run away from the police, been kidnapped by a vampire, and been forced to participate in a pretend wedding, so what inhibitions I normally hold are pretty much gone. I'm sure you'll excuse me if I say that it's very rude to speak in a language that not everyone can understand."

Rowan laughed even harder.

Andreas's frown darkened for a moment, then he suddenly smiled. Although his face wasn't nearly as hard as Kristoff's, his smile was just as chilling. "I told my brother that he should have simply killed you rather than wed you."

"We're not married," I said, crossing my arms over my chest in a show of what I hoped looked like bravado. Surrounded as I was by three tall, extremely handsome bloodsucking fiends, I certainly felt anything but brave, but it wouldn't do to let them know that. "It wasn't a legal ceremony."

The two men looked inquiringly at Kristoff.

He gave me a bitter look. "It was entirely legal."

"It was not! I didn't understand anything that priest said, let alone agree to it! He could have been performing the last rites for all I know!"

"No, but I can arrange for that, if you like," Kristoff said with smooth menace.

I raised my chin. I may not be the bravest of women, but I hate being bullied. "You didn't even kiss me. Weddings always end in a kiss. So there!"

Silence filled the church for a moment before Kristoff made a low noise deep in his chest and yanked me toward him.

"Are you *growling* at me — ?" I just had time to say before he kissed me.

My mind, never the most reliable of organs in times of stress, shut down and left me flailing in Kristoff's arms. This was not the same sort of kiss that Alec had pressed all over me the night before — this was a kiss of aggression, a punishment, an invasion. He didn't even wait for me to invite him in, his tongue was there, inside my mouth, sweeping around as if it owned the place. Not even Alec had kissed me so intimately!

I shoved hard on Kristoff's chest and jerked out of his grip, wiping my mouth with the back of my hand. "If you ever do that again, so help me god, I'll . . . I'll . . . I don't know what I'll do, but you can bet your butt it'll be horrible!"

"The marriage is legal," Kristoff said, shoving one of the signed sheets into my hands. His eyes glowed from within, looking oddly lighter than I remembered them. "Complete with kiss. Tell that to your reaper friends."

I opened my mouth to tell him that they weren't necessarily my friends, but he didn't wait around for me to answer. He just turned on his heel and marched out of the church. I stared in surprise for a few moments before I turned to the other two vamps. They watched me with eyes filled with malice and suspicion.

"He left," I said, too surprised to care that I was stating the obvious.

"If you even think of using your powers

against him, I guarantee that you will pay in ways you cannot imagine," Andreas threatened before he, too, marched out.

Rowan said nothing, just gave me a long, hard look, shoved me aside, and left, as well.

"Good riddance!" I yelled after them, going to the door to watch as two cars backed out and sped off up the winding road. It was at that moment that I realized I was stranded, alone, without money, identification, or even a clear knowledge of the name of the town in which I'd been dumped. "Hey? Anyone? I don't have a car. Hello?"

I turned back to the clergyman, but he'd disappeared, as well, leaving me standing on a windy cliff, outside of a cold, dank little stone church, clutching a marriage certificate that I knew was false . . . but I had a horrible suspicion no one else would see it that way.

"Married to a vampire," I said out loud, the words whipped away on the wind. "Oh, joy. Now what am I going to do?"

"I don't suppose you know the way to Ostri?"

I turned my head and stared with absolutely no surprise at the translucent figure that stood there. I raised an eyebrow at the spectral horse next to him, but I didn't say one word about the fact that yet another ghost had descended upon me. "I'm afraid I'm new around here. You're . . . er . . . dead?"

"As you can see." The man, who was dressed in what looked to be Victorian wear, frowned. "You're the reaper and you don't know where Ostri is?"

"Afraid not, but since I'm evidently now the ghostly information office, I guess I'd better find out. What's your name?"

"Ulfur."

"How do you do? I'm Pia, and yes, I'm the Zorya." I held up my hand. The moonstone had once again converted itself into a small lantern. "But I'm afraid I'm new to the job, and don't know all the ins and outs of the whole thing yet. So you'll have to join the others while you wait for me to figure out what's what."

"Others?" he asked.

"Three other ghosts. They're back in town. I don't suppose you have a magical way of transporting us there?"

He pursed his lips and eyed me curiously.

"No? I didn't think so. Well, I guess we'd better go see if there's a bus or something. You can come with me."

"And the others?" Ulfur asked, falling into step with me as I started to pick my way

146

down the rocky hillside to the fishing village below.

"I told you — they're back in town. I think. I didn't actually see them when I left them, but that could be because Anniki had the stone."

"No, I meant the others here." He waved toward the shore.

I cautiously moved over to the edge of the cliff and looked down. Along the craggy shoreline, a group of about twelve ghosts roamed aimlessly. They looked up as I stood staring down in increasing despair. More ghosts. Just what I needed to complicate things.

"This is the reaper," Ulfur bellowed down to them.

They waved.

I lifted a wan hand and waved back.

"You're all ghosts?" I asked Ulfur.

He nodded and patted his horse's head. "Landslide. Wiped out half the village. I had been in college in Reykjavík but came home for my father's birthday."

"Ouch. You speak English really well," I said, curious about that fact.

Ulfur smiled. "There is not much to do with our time but watch and listen to people. A company runs tours from here to local fjords, so we get lots of tourists. It provides us all with an excellent means of learning other languages. English was the first we learned, and now that the Japanese tours have started, we're hoping to learn that language next."

"I suppose it would provide for entertainment." I thought for a moment. "Maybe you'd all better stay here until I can figure out how to get you to heaven. Er . . . Ostri. Whichever."

"I don't know that we're safe staying here," he said, his face becoming serious. "An Ilargi has been seen."

"One of those bad-reaper, soul-eater guys?" A little shiver zipped down my back. "They don't sound good at all. Well, I guess you'll all have to come with me."

He nodded and bellowed out orders to the folks below.

I looked out at the sea, bluey grey and wind tossed, and wondered what on earth I was going to do now. "Could my life get any stranger?"

The sound of the wind and the mournful cry of gulls wheeling overhead were the only answer to my question. I took one last look at the sea, then gestured to the waiting ghosts below and pointed to the village. A faint hurrahing cry met my ears as I jammed my hands in my pockets and started down the path into the village, Ulfur and his horse on my heels.

What on earth had I gotten myself into? And more importantly, how was I going to get out of it?

It took the better part of the day to get back to Dalkafjordhur. I didn't want to encounter the police, so I took the only bus that ran from the fishing village, praying the police wouldn't stop people going into town. There was a bit of a tussle when the driver found out I didn't have the fare, but I succeeded in returning to Dalkafjordhur by dint of clinging with desperate stubbornness to the railing on the back of one of the seats. Since none of the five passengers on the bus spoke English — or wanted to get involved — I don't quite know what threats the driver was using, but in the end he gave up trying to root me out, and let me ride without further harassment.

Ulfur, his horse, and the twelve other ghosts didn't raise a single complaint, but that's only because no one but me saw them. The ghosts were all polite, however, men, women, and children dressed in clothing from a hundred and fifty years before, all of them pathetically grateful I was taking them under my wing.

"I can't guarantee anything, but I suppose there's safety in numbers," I told them after the bus driver, giving up on me, drove us up the track to the main road.

A woman who was seated near me gave me an odd look from the corner of her eye. I smiled at her but didn't have the energy to try to explain that there was, at that moment, a ghost sitting in her lap, while a horse nosed her bag on the ground beside her.

"You are the reaper," an elderly male ghost said, nodding at Ulfur. "He says you will take us to Ostri."

"That's the idea," I said, gnawing on my lower lip.

The woman shot me another look, then got up and took a seat closer to the driver.

I mulled over my options on what ended up being an hour-long drive into town. I didn't have the faintest idea how to help the ghosts, but the Brotherhood people at the church must know something about it. Clearly, I'd have to go to them to get specifics. Maybe one of them could even take over and lead all the ghosts on to their reward.

Cheered by that thought, I sat back and tried to think positively.

The sight of a police car slowly patrolling the streets of the town as we approached ended that happy mood. Wary of being caught in a police cordon, I got out at the first stop, taking a good twenty minutes to carefully make my way through as many backstreets and alleys as I could find, a parade of ghosts trailing after me.

"Where are we going?" one of the ghosts, a petulant-looking teenage girl, asked in a grating, whiny voice. "Are we going to have to walk all the way to Ostri?"

An older woman shushed her with an anxious glance my way. "Do not speak so to the reaper. She will show us the way."

"So we hope," I muttered. The sun was low in the sky, sending long, inky shadows from the buildings, making the alleyways particularly dim.

I kept an eye peeled for any tour members who might suddenly spot me and set up a hue and cry, but the streets were bare of lonely American tourists.

"And a good thing, too," I said as I cut behind a row of buildings to avoid a busy intersection. "All we need now is to run into someone I kno— *oof!*"

A dark shape loomed up out of nowhere, as hard as brick, and a million times scarier.

Teal blue eyes glowed at me from the depths of the darkness.

"What are you doing here?" I asked, too

annoyed at having been dumped without a ride to be frightened of Kristoff. Behind me, the ghosts gathered. Ulfur's horse whinnied.

"Who's he?" the elderly male ghost asked.

"I don't know. I think she knows him, though," Ulfur answered.

"I do, not that it's here nor there," I answered.

Kristoff's eyebrows rose.

"Sorry. Talking to my ghosts."

He narrowed his eyes. "Ghosts, plural?"

"Yes. Thirteen of them. Fourteen if you count the horse."

Kristoff was silent for the count of ten. "Where's Alec?"

I put my hands on my hips, more than a little peeved. "Do you seriously think I'd be skulking around back alleys with a herd of ghosts if he was with me?"

"He said he was going to find you. He hasn't?"

"No." I glared at Kristoff as he emerged from the shadows, taking care to avoid the dim patch of sunlight that filtered down through the buildings. I hesitated, feeling unsure of what my emotions were with regard to Alec. I had a whole lot of questions to ask him, starting with Anniki and working down to why he had skipped out, leaving me alone without a word. "You spoke to him, then? Did he say anything about Anniki?"

"Oh! It's a Dark One!" Ulfur said behind me. There was a murmur of agreement.

"He's ever so handsome. He can bite me any day," the whiny girl said. I shot her a look. She smirked at me.

"What is there to say?" Kristoff answered, his scowl truly world-class. "I suppose I will have to take you to him."

"You don't have to sound so disgusted," I snapped, my pride stung yet again by the fact that he obviously disliked me intensely. "It's not like I have cooties or anything! And just for the record, I don't like you very much, either. You're not at all what a vampire should be like."

That took him aback for a few seconds. "And just what do you think a Dark One should be like?"

"Sexy! Like Angel and those guys in the vampire movies. Well, except the bun-head version, but that wasn't meant to be sexy."

"You don't think I'm attractive?" he asked, an odd expression flickering across his face.

"I do!" the teen ghost said.

I ignored her and made a big show of examining Kristoff from head to foot. If I thought he had been eye candy before, he definitely improved with nearness. His hair was sort of a chestnut reddish brown, with curls that looked as soft as satin. His face was hard, as I've noted, but it was a hard beauty, with a cleft chin that somehow kept drawing my eye. Like Alec, he was several inches taller than me, but where Alec was bulky with heavy muscles, Kristoff possessed a leaner frame that reminded me somehow of a big cat, like a lion or panther. I ignored the breadth of his chest, telling myself that Alec's was just as broad. His legs were longer, however, and filled out his faded jeans in a manner that left me admiring his obviously muscled thighs. I had a sudden urge to go peek at his behind, but quickly squelched that. The ghosts, I had a feeling, would never let me hear the end of it.

"Attractive?" I gave a little nonchalant laugh that sounded awfully strained. "No, not at all. Not in the least. That dead rat over there exudes more sexual attraction than you do."

"Is she blind?" I heard the girl ask someone else. "Or just stupid?"

"Hush, child, and let the reaper alone," the older woman answered.

"That's right, miss, you let him have it," another ghostly woman spoke up. "Don't do to let your man think as he can speak to you like that."

"He's not my —" I stopped before I said anything more.

Kristoff just stood there and looked at me with those uncanny eyes, making me squirm a little.

"Oh, all right, I'm lying like hell. Yes, you're very attractive, the kind of sexy that makes women want to rip off their underwear and throw themselves on you. Happy now?"

He didn't even blink, just stared at me for a second or two. "You mean as you did last night in the park?"

My cheeks burned at the memory. I glanced behind me. The ghosts were all gathered together in a half circle, watching me with interest. Even the horse seemed to be waiting to see what I'd say next. "That was a different situation entirely. And I had my undies on, thank you! Regardless of your god-amongst-men status, I don't like you. You have insulted me, deliberately intimidated me, and tried to make me feel guilty about something that is not my fault."

His eyes darkened. I swear to god, the teal color darkened a couple of shades. I watched in fascination as the black spikes from the pupils seemed to elongate and fill the iris. "When have I insulted you?"

The words snapped me back from a reverie about how bad men so often had such pretty eyes. "What? Oh. When *haven't* you insulted me? You wanted to kill me last night."

"If I wanted you dead, you'd be dead," he said in an even tone. That scared me more than anything else.

"Oooh," one of the ghosts said as there was a general intake of breath.

"Yes, well . . . that aside, you told me you'd rather marry a viper than me," I told Kristoff, incensed enough that I didn't care if I was arguing in front of an audience or not.

His lips tightened. "You didn't want to marry me, either."

"They're married?" the teen asked in a sulky voice. "That just isn't right."

"No, of course I didn't want to marry you, and still don't. I don't know you, let alone have those sorts of emotions for you that usually end up in a marriage. And there's the little fact that you're an evil vampire, and I'm evidently one of the good guys, so this whole Romeo-and-Juliet scenario isn't going to work."

He took a couple of steps closer to me, his glare menacing. "If you think I harbor romantic illusions about a mere legal convenience, I urge you to rethink. I am not Romeo."

The ghosts forgotten in my ire, I took a step toward him, the toes of my shoes just a hairsbreadth from his as I leveled him a look that told him I wasn't the fool he took me for. "With the implication, I suppose, that I'm no Juliet? Well, thank you, you don't need to point that out any more than you do the fact that you don't like that Alec and I spent the night together."

A bluish fire flared to life in his eyes as he leaned in toward me. "Don't like it? Are you implying I'm jealous?"

"Of course not," I said, gathering up my tattered shreds of dignity. "I'm no stranger to the mirror, and you've made it quite clear you not only think I'm physically repulsive, but that Alec is crazy for not having the same taste as you do."

"What are you talking about?" he asked, his eyes narrowing. "I did not say you were repulsive, and I don't give a damn who Alec sleeps with. His personal life is no business of mine."

"Who's Alec?" I heard whispered behind me.

"Shhh! I think they're just getting to the good part."

"You didn't actually say the word 'repulsive,' no, but you implied that just looking at me sickens you," I said, suddenly feeling like crying. Why did I care that he thought I was a frumpy, overweight hussy? "You can't deny that the only reason you kissed me is because I made you."

"Of course I deny it." He leaned even closer until I could feel his breath. "No one can make me do anything against my will. No one."

I ignored the fact that I couldn't seem to get enough breath into my lungs and gave him a cool look. "Oh, really? So you *did* want to marry me?"

"I said I was willing to do whatever it took to keep you from gaining the full powers of a Zorya, and I meant it," he answered, his voice low and gritty.

The air seemed to heat up several degrees in the alleyway. "That would imply that you did want to kiss me," I said, having to clear my throat a couple of times before I could speak.

His gaze dropped to my mouth, and I was suddenly aware of a most appalling fact — I wanted him to kiss me. Right then, right there, in front of the ghosts and anyone else who wandered by. I wanted to feel his mouth on mine, and taste him again, and

158

rub myself against him in a wholly foreign manner. But worst of all, I wanted him to force me into a kiss so that I could pretend to myself that I didn't want it at all.

Shame and disgust tumbled around with confusion and indecision inside me. How could I sleep with one man, and the next day be wanting to kiss his evil friend? What was wrong with me?

"I've never been adverse to kissing mortals," Kristoff said in his deep, unusually sexy voice. I shivered a little despite the sudden heat that was making me very aware of the clothing binding my skin. "And I don't find you repulsive."

"Oh," I said, my brain giving up any attempt at sanity and settling down to providing my mouth with really insipid things to say. "Good. You're not repulsive, either."

I swear his eyes darkened then. They went from teal blue to a dark navy, the black flares from his pupils seeping outward. I took a deep breath at his nearness, wondering why I could feel air going into my lungs, but still felt light-headed and breathless. My breasts rubbed against the soft leather of his jacket, the sensation making me shiver again.

"I'm glad you think so." His lips brushed mine, just the lightest of touches, more a little bump than a kiss, but with it, I finally came to my senses.

"I'm not a harlot," I yelled, grabbing two fistfuls of his jacket and shaking them. "I do not sleep with a man one day, and kiss the living daylights out of his friend the next, no matter how much I want to. I'm not that sort of girl! You're bad. You're evil. You're a vampire, dammit! But you're no Angel, and I'm no Buffy, and you can just stop making me confused about everything!"

A puzzled look was followed by a quick spike of anger in his eyes, and then he was kissing me, really kissing me, with his lips and tongue and his hands in my hair, and I lost it all again. His tongue twined around mine in an erotic, sinuous dance that made me aware of all sorts of suddenly erogenous spots on my body. I rubbed my breasts into him, allowing him to taste me, savoring the sensation of his body so hard and hot and utterly masculine.

It's a good thing he was holding on to me, because my legs started to go weak under the effect of that kiss. By the time he pulled back, I was gasping for breath, stunned with the intensity of emotions that seemed to spring from him, but which I unaccountably shared. I stared up at him in unadulterated amazement, not sure what to make of anything anymore.

His eyes were the deep blue of midnight. "The discussion of which of us is truly evil will have to wait for another time. You are not safe here. The mundane police are looking for you, and a number of reapers live here."

I stepped back, my face red with embarrassment at his words. I'd become my worst nightmare — a pushy, shameless woman. What must he think of me? I all but seduced him in an alleyway, for god's sake, right in front of a gaggle of ghosts, the very day after I'd spent the night with his buddy. I lifted my chin and tried to regain my composure. "I figured the police would be looking for me. I'm not afraid of the Brotherhood people, though. I know you have issues with them, but they don't pose me any threat."

"Don't they?" The faintest hint of a smile showed on his damned lips. I dragged my gaze up from them and gave myself a mental lecture about morality. "What do you think they're going to do when they find out their precious Zorya is married to a Dark One?"

I frowned. "If the Zorya has to marry one of their own people, as you say, they aren't going to be happy, but they're hardly going to do anything to me other than take away the stone and make someone else Zorya."

"That's not how it works," he said, his face hard and unyielding. Even as I marveled that I had wanted so badly to kiss him, the desire to do the same welled up inside me. I squashed it down mercilessly. "In their eyes, you have been tainted by your marriage to me. The only way they can have a new Zorya is by the elimination of the old one."

I stared at him in growing comprehension. "You mean they'd *kill* me to get a new Zorya?"

"Uh-oh," Ulfur said. "That doesn't sound good."

"You are wed to me," Kristoff said evenly, his face unreadable. "You cannot assume the full powers of a Zorya now, and thus you are useless to their purpose. It will be for Alec to keep you safe so that they cannot name a new one."

"I don't believe you," I told him, trying to convince myself that he was lying. To be honest, I wasn't sure he was, but something didn't ring true. I just didn't know what was what anymore.

He shrugged. "That's Alec's problem. He'll deal with you now. I've done my part."

"I'm not something to be dealt with, although I would appreciate talking to him," I said with as much dignity as I could muster. Which, given that I had just been sucking on his tongue, wasn't a whole lot. "As it is, I have a few questions for — look out!"

Three shadows rose up behind Kristoff, shadows that quickly resolved themselves into figures. It was a faint flicker of light off a long blade that had caught my eye. Kristoff slammed his hand into my chest, sending me crashing backward into a large stack of wooden crates. I hit my head hard on the wood, but by the time my vision cleared, I realized that he wasn't assaulting me; he had merely shoved me out of the way while he dealt with the attackers.

And deal with them he did. I had no idea where he carried the twin daggers that now flashed in his hands, but he whirled and attacked with incredible grace and power, sending two of the three men flying in opposite directions. One of them crashed at my feet. I snatched up an empty crate and brought it down on his head as he was about to rise, feeling immense satisfaction as the man collapsed unconscious to the ground.

The ghosts leaped around, yelling and calling advice, unable to interact with anything, their ghostly forms adding just another level of surreality to the situation.

Kristoff's fight with the other two men was over almost as quickly, increasing my respect for his prowess. One man he sent slamming into the nearest wall, which was enough to send the attacker sliding uselessly to the ground, where he lay in a motionless blob. The last man, the one wielding a sword, screamed something at Kristoff, and slashed at him with rhythmic strokes of the blade.

Kristoff parried them all, kicking out with one leg, catching the man square in the chest, which sent him, too, slamming against the wall. I was just about to cheer when suddenly I was yanked painfully backward by my hair, a burning sensation at my throat. The man I'd hit with the crate snarled obscenities as he dragged me backward, toward the other end of the alley.

"Touch me and she dies," he spat out, then gave as obscene a laugh as I'd ever heard, and continued in a foreign language.

"He can't kill our reaper, can he?" the elderly ghost asked.

"I don't think so," Ulfur said hesitantly.

"What'll happen to us if he does? The Il-argi will get us!" the teen wailed.

I squirmed, trying to get a purchase on the ground so I could twist out of my attacker's grip, but he kept me too much off balance.

Kristoff said nothing, just stalked toward us, his eyes as pale as ice. I shivered at the sight, understanding now what Anniki had said about the vampires. Kristoff wasn't human. He was something foreign, something dark and dangerous, and every instinct I possessed told me to get away before he caught me.

I screamed, my voice abruptly stopping when my captor wrapped his hand tighter in my hair before jerking me sideways into the brick wall. I saw stars again as pain burst out in red waves that left me nauseous and nearly unconscious. I grasped for something to keep me from falling into a deep, dark pit where I seemed to teeter at the edge, my fingers closing around a cold metal rim.

Air moved past me as my eyes slowly cleared, leaving me with a clear vision of Kristoff calmly wiping a bloodied dagger blade on the prone form that lay at my feet. I clutched the trash bin with all my strength, staring in horror at the body. Although my attacker had fallen facedown, I knew without a doubt that he was dead.

And Kristoff had killed him.

Right there in front of me.

If I needed any proof that what Anniki had said was the real version of what was going on, this was definitely it.

I looked into Kristoff's now smoky eyes and saw the rage he felt, saw fury and menace and triumphant victory. I was up and running down the alley away from him before I even knew my legs would still work.

Voices called out my name, one of them his, but I ran even faster, blindly careening off of walls and obstructions and even cars as I dashed madly through the city, sure of only one thing — Kristoff was a killer. Alec couldn't be like him. Could he?

CHAPTER 7

A light breeze ruffled my hair. "Pia? Are you all right?"

I looked up from where I'd been hunkered over, sobbing into my knees, right into the nostrils of a ghostly horse. I fought back the startled scream that threatened to burst out of me, sniffling instead and hunting desperately in my pockets for a tissue. "Ulfur?"

"Yes, it's me." His horse smelled my hair, then snorted into it with a shake of his head. "Ragnar, leave her be. She does not wish to pet you."

"I don't think I could if I wanted to," I said, giving up the search and dabbing at my damp nose with my sleeve. I pushed away the trash cans that hid me and got to my feet, a little wobbly, but not entirely surprised to find that the space behind the library where I'd collapsed was now filled with ghostly entities. "Oh, good, you found Karl and Marta."

"Yes, they were hiding near the park. There was another man, a sailor, I think, but he said he was going to search for rum and would find us later. You are hurt?" Ulfur's face was filled with concern, as were, in varying degrees, those of the other ghosts crowded around me. All except the smart-mouthed teen, and she was busy picking her nails until the woman I assumed was her mother cuffed her upside the head. "Did your husband harm you?"

"He's not my husband," I said, dusting off my clothing. "Well, that's to say, he might be, but if he is, he's neither legal nor wanted."

"You kissed him," one of the male ghosts said.

"That was . . . um . . . unintentional," I lied.

"It looked like you were enjoying it," Ulfur pointed out.

"I didn't say it was unpleasant, just that it was unintentional." I don't know why I felt quite so defensive about the kiss Kristoff and I had shared, unless it was over the immense guilt I felt at betraying his friend. "He's not really my husband. I may be married to him, but he's not a husband in the true sense of the word."

"Ah," the older ghost said, waggling his

eyebrows at the teen's mom. "He hasn't bedded her yet."

A chorus of comprehending *aah*s followed that statement.

"You'd best be seeing to that right away," snarky teen's mom said with a knowing look. "Men like that have an appetite for women, and you'll not be wanting him to stray."

"I'm not trying to keep him," I told her, waving my hands around vaguely as if that would help explain the situation. "He's not really mine."

"Not yet, but just you bed him a few times, and he'll be yours for life," an elderly, creaking voice said. There was a flurry of movement behind the ghosts, and a tiny, incredibly old woman appeared. "I've had five husbands, I have, and if there's anyone who knows how to keep a man, it's me."

Everyone nodded their heads, the teen's mom saying, "Aye, Old Agda knows. You listen to her, reaper."

"*Five* husbands?" I couldn't help but ask.

"They all died young, all but the last one, and he were thirty year younger'n me. Died happy they did, too." She cackled, elbowing the mom beside her. Mom smiled indulgently.

I gave myself a mental shake. I needed to

make plans, and standing around here talking about Kristoff and husbands was not going to help matters. "Well, that's nice, but —"

"I like the young ones," another woman called out from the back, a woman around whom three children were clustered, clutching her long skirts. "They've got stamina. Maybe our reaper ought to look for someone a bit younger."

"Bah," the first woman said. "What good is stamina if they don't know what to do with it? It's all about what god gifted them with, if you want my opinion."

"I don't need anyone with more stamina," I protested. "Besides, Kristoff is a vampire and is who knows how many hundreds of years old. Just about anyone is going to be younger than him."

"The younger ones lack experience," the teen's mom argued with the size-matters woman. "And it doesn't matter how long a man's member is if he hasn't the experience to use it properly. The young ones don't know how to please a woman, and the ones without experience just leave you wishing they'd be done so you can bring in the wash and tend to supper. Now, the reaper's man, he looks like he knows what he's about."

"I'll say he does," her daughter purred.

I narrowed a look on her that by rights should have turned her to stone before realizing what I was doing. I was not jealous of Kristoff! I did not want him! It was Alec I was interested in. Alec who smiled, and was happy to turn off the lights, and left me with a dead body . . . oy.

"That's all women's talk," the middle-aged ghost interrupted. "What our reaper wants is someone who can protect her. The true measure of a man is how he provides for his family."

"You're just saying that because you'd just built Ingveldur a new cabin," one of the other men called out. "Two rooms! Who has need of a separate sleeping room, I ask you? That's just flaunting your wealth in the face of god, that is."

"Ha! Thus speaks the man with three — *three* — milk cows, when one would do. If you want to talk about setting yourself above the rest of the village, Hallur Hallsson, then you'd best look to yourself first."

"I needed those cows," the man named Hallur yelled, storming forward to confront his neighbor. "I had six children to feed! Unlike Agda and her hundred chickens. All those chickens for just one old woman. Bah! That was flaunting wealth if there ever was flaunting."

The elderly lady shot him a nasty glare. "I'd quite a few less chickens than when I started out, and I know just whose pot they ended up in, don't I?"

An argument broke out amongst the ghosts about the merits of one-room versus two-room housing, cows, chickens, and, inexplicably, a pig named Freyja. I was about to yell for attention when timid little Marta came forward and put a ghostly hand on my arm, making my skin tingle a little where she touched me.

"Don't listen to them," she said softly, a little smile on her lips as she glanced at Karl. "I've been married a whole year, and what they're saying isn't that important. None of it really matters so long as you are fond of your husband."

"But I'm not," I told her, wishing like the dickens that someone, anyone, would just listen to me without forming their own assumptions. "I don't even like him. He murdered a man in cold blood, right in front of me."

"He was defending you," Karl said, raising his voice a little as the argument continued behind him. "He saved your life."

"Possibly, but we don't know that. The man who grabbed me could have killed me easily if he wanted to, but he didn't. He was simply using me as a shield to protect himself from Kristoff. Oh, it doesn't matter," I said, rubbing my temples. A headache had come in the aftermath of my tears, leaving my head pounding. "None of this really matters. What I have to do is decide what steps to take to get myself and all of you to safety. People. *People!*"

The arguing stopped as I yelled and banged the lid of a garbage can.

". . . told you that pig was barren, but would you listen to me? No, you wouldn't; you just had to . . . oh." The man who bore a strong resemblance to Ulfur stopped arguing and turned to look at me. "Sorry."

"Thank you." I eyed them all carefully for a few seconds. "Before we proceed, I'd like to know if any of you have any idea whatsoever of the whereabouts of this Ostri place I'm supposed to take you. Anyone?"

Fifteen blank faces regarded me.

"Hmm." I bit my lip and tried to think through the dull waves of pain that ebbed and flowed against my brain like molasses. "Kristoff said the Brotherhood will kill me, so I can't go to them. Anniki is dead, and I don't know any other Zoryas, assuming there are others to know, so I can't ask one of them where you're supposed to be taken. If I was home, I could look it up online and see if there's some clue as to where Ostri is located, but Kristoff has my passport. And besides, Audrey has all our tickets. I don't even have any money."

At that, my stomach rumbled, and I realized it had been at least twelve hours since I'd last eaten.

"Oh, man," I said, wrapping my arms around myself. "No money means no food, or a way out of here, or even a place to stay. I've got to get some money."

Ulfur pursed his lips and looked thoughtful. "I'd give you my coins, but they washed out to sea with the rest of the village."

I shook my head, thinking over my options. Wire home for money? That would probably require identification to pick up the funds, and my wallet had no doubt been confiscated. Steal it?

"Does anyone here have any thieving experience?" I asked my little gaggle of ghosts.

"Aye, Hallur does," the old lady named Agda called out. "He can take a chicken out of its nest without ruffling a feather."

"That's a lie!" he yelled, rounding on her.

"Anyone else?" I interrupted before they got started.

Everyone shook their heads. "Great. Me, either. I wouldn't know how to go about stealing money in this day and age of high-tech security." I chewed on my lip a bit more.

"Can you borrow some coins from a friend?" Ulfur asked, stroking Ragnar's head.

"I don't have any friends here —" I started to say, then remembered Magda. She wasn't a friend per se, but she was very friendly, and seemed an understanding sort of woman. The question was, would she help me, or turn me over to the police?

I shook my head at the notion of trusting my life to someone I didn't really know. Magda may seem like a nice person, but what proof did I have that I could trust her in a time of need?

I'd just have to find someone else.

"There's your husband," Marta said. "You could ask him for money."

"I'll ask Magda," I told the ghosts, coming to a snap decision. "But I can't go traipsing around with you all on my heels. We'd better find somewhere to park you that you'll be safe from the soul-sucking Ilargi person."

I contemplated trying to make my way around town without being spotted by police, fellow tour members, Kristoff, or the Brotherhood folk, but a few moments' consideration left me shrugging at the building in front of me. Why not? I hustled my little group into the library and told them to vanish. The library was due to close almost immediately thereafter, but with a cunning that was heretofore unknown to me, I managed to hide myself beneath a stack of beanbag chairs in the children's area, and remain there until the building was closed.

I lay there for another two hours while the employees puttered around, alternately listening to my stomach growl, dozing, and wondering what the hell I was going to do if Magda wouldn't help me.

An idea started to form. It wasn't anything I was proud of, and it definitely went against my better judgment, but if push came to shove, there might be a way out of the situation. I felt a little bit better when, two hours later, I crawled out from my beanbag cocoon and rallied my troops.

"Right, I'm going to go see my friend and pray she won't turn me over to the police. You guys stay here. If this bad reaper is human, like I am, he shouldn't be able to get in to the building to get you guys." I glanced around the darkened library, only a couple of security lights illuminating the interior. "I sure wish ghosts could read books and use the computer terminals. A little research into reapers and Ostri might be very helpful."

Karl looked from his wife to me. "But we can read books. I don't know about this computer terminal you mentioned, but I can read."

"I'm sure you can, but what I meant was more I wish you guys had the ability to interact with physical things."

"We can," Ulfur said. Ragnar nodded his head and snorted before munching the fabric of the nearest beanbag chair.

"Really?" I reached out to touch him, my hand passing right through his arm. "Um . . ."

Ulfur smiled and the air around him shimmered. His body slowly solidified, going from its bluish translucent state to that of a solid form.

"Holy Jehoshaphat," I said, reaching out with a tentative fingertip. It met solid cloth. "I didn't know you could do that!"

"We can't for very long. It takes a lot of energy to have a physical presence, but if it will help you, we can try looking for some information."

"That would be immensely helpful," I said, relieved. "I don't suppose any of you can operate a computer?"

I wasn't surprised when no one offered to use the nearby computer. I suspected that drifting around aimlessly for a hundred years or more didn't lend itself to techno-savvy.

"Oh, all right, I'll do it," the snarky teen said when her mother, the woman named Ingveldur, gave her a none-too-gentle shove forward.

"You know about computers?" I asked the girl dubiously.

She *tch*ed and plunked herself down in that boneless way teen girls have. "I'm not stupid, you know. People do come to the village with laptops and mobile phones and Game Boys. What am I looking for?"

"Does that computer have Internet access?" I asked peering over her shoulder. She solidified and tapped on the keyboard. "Oh, excellent. Google Ostri, would you? And maybe reapers. And the Brotherhood of the Blessed Light. And while you're at it —"

She gave me a look that told me I was trying her nerves.

"Just Google whatever you can and print out anything that looks important. Will the rest of you be all right?"

My words were spoken to an empty room. Ulfur and Karl had taken charge of the villagers and spread them out to search the library for any books that might help.

"I'll be back as soon as I can," I told Marta as she came with me to the window. It didn't show any signs of being wired for an alarm, which I took as an indication of the low crime rate of this area. "Close the window after me, and don't let anyone in who isn't me. OK?"

"All right. But, Pia, the old sailor is still out there," she said worriedly.

"If I see him, I'll send him this way. Don't look so glum," I said, swinging my legs out the window and jumping down to the well-tended flower bed below. "I think our luck is about to change."

That seemed to pacify her. She smiled and waved as I glanced down the street, muttering softly to myself, "And I just pray it's not going from bad to worse."

Dalkafjordhur at night was surprisingly busy. I didn't know if it was the white-night phenomenon of twenty-four hours of sunlight, or if the town was just like that normally, but there were a lot of people out. Luckily, I knew where I would find the tour group — we were supposed to be attending a reenactment group's dinner in a Viking longhouse, complete with Old Norse poetry readings, and scenes enacted from historical sagas of the period.

I didn't have any trouble finding the fake longhouse, since it was a popular tourist site located near the park. I didn't even have any problem slipping in the back way, through what I assumed was the employees' entrance. But as I peeked out from behind a curtain marking the stage, I faced nothing but trouble. The longhouse center was taken up with long tables, at which my tour mates sat stuffing their faces with delicious-smelling salmon, fresh bread, and at least a half dozen other dishes.

My stomach growled with increasing loudness.

I ducked into a small room at the sound of voices coming out of the area I figured was the kitchen, a slow smile emerging as I eyed the various bits of Viking period costume.

"Well, you're not going to fool anyone knowledgeable," I told my reflection a short while later as I examined the ensemble I'd cobbled together from bits and pieces of costumes that would fit my abundant self. "But with the lights out, and everyone focused on the stage, you may get by with it."

I grabbed a wig of long black hair and

clapped it onto my head, gave the wrap-around linen apron dress that I'd pulled over my own gauze sundress a tug to hide as much of the modern flowery print beneath as possible, and grabbed a box filled with small bottles of water, hefting it to my shoulder to hide my face.

When I emerged from the back depths, the stage show was just starting, and the lights, as I had surmised, were lowered to highlight the actors. I scurried around the back of the tour group, pulling the long black hair around my face as I sidled forward with a murmur of "Water?" to the nearest members.

No one sent me a second glance. Denise sat tapping with irritated fingers on the table, looking sourly at the actors as they demonstrated a Viking ritual. Audrey was next to her, looking tired and miserable. I had a pang of remorse for that, feeling certain she'd been through hell after I had run off.

Magda was at the far end with Ray. I hunched over and offered water to him first, then to her.

"Water?"

"No, thank you," Magda said without looking.

"I think you are going to want some," I

181

said softly, leaning a bit closer to her while keeping an eye on everyone else.

"No, thanks," she repeated, still not looking at me.

I sighed to myself and nudged her on the back with the box. "Water is good for you. Take some."

She turned around with a slight frown, her eyes growing huge when I pulled the hair away from my face enough so she could see who I was.

"Take the water," I said softly, braced for flight. If she shouted and screamed, I'd throw the bottles at everyone and make a fast retreat back to the safety of the library.

She did neither, however, simply took the bottle of water I held out and watched me with huge eyes.

"The bathroom is in the back. You may need it after drinking all that," I said softly, with a meaning I was sure was clear.

She nodded and I slipped backward, into the shadows of the room, quietly making my way out to the rear rooms.

I didn't have long to wait. Magda entered the bathroom with a backward glance, carefully closing the door before turning on me. "Pia, what on earth is going on? What are you doing in that atrocious black wig? Why is Denise saying you murdered someone?

And why were the police questioning everyone about you and a man you were with last night?"

I blinked at that last bit, irrationally focusing on the least important thing. "They know I was with a man last night? Who said so?"

"Who do you think? Miss Nosy-Pants Denise, that's who. She said she saw a man stealing away from your room in the early hours of the morning."

"Just what was she doing hanging around my room, watching for men?" I asked, suddenly outraged at the invasion of my privacy.

Magda crossed her arms. "There's a dead woman in your bathroom, and all you can do is get pissed at Denise's nosiness? What happened, Pia? I don't believe for one minute that you killed the woman, like Denise said. You're not a murderer. You don't have that sort of an aura."

I slumped against the sink in relief, pulling off the itchy black wig, ruffling my hand through my hair to fluff it back up. "Oh, thank god. You don't know how many horrible things I envisioned you saying to me. No, I didn't murder her, although I do know who she is, and I have a suspicion —"
I bit off what I was going to say, not wanting to put my worst thoughts into words.

183

"You have a suspicion you know who it was?"

I nodded.

Magda came over to me and put a hand on mine. "Pia, sweetie, who was that man you were with? Do you think it was him?"

"I don't know," I said miserably, wanting nothing more than to pour the whole story out to her, but knowing she wouldn't believe half of it. "His name is Alec, and it's possible he killed her, although he didn't seem at all like the violent sort of person."

Not until I knew he was a vampire, that is. Not until I learned how much the vampires hated the Brotherhood, and then it made all too much sense.

"Then again, Kristoff said he didn't kill her, but can I really trust him now? I just don't know!"

"Who's Kristoff?" Magda asked.

"Another guy. Alec's friend."

"You haven't gone to the police? I really think you should. If that guy you hooked up with is bad news, you don't know what he will do next. He might come after you."

I shook my head. "I wish I could, but it's . . . complicated."

"Complicated how? Pia, are you in love with this Alec? Because if you are, I'm here to tell you —"

"No, no, it's nothing like that," I said, blushing at the memory of the kiss I had shared with Kristoff. "He's a nice enough man, and I really don't think he murdered Anniki, although he might have. . . . Oh, it's so muddled, Magda. There are other people involved, a religious group, for lack of a better description, and Kristoff said he didn't, but what if he was lying? But if he did, how could I want to kiss him? I mean, wouldn't you know if someone was capable of murdering someone else?"

She blinked at me in incomprehension. "Just by kissing him? I don't know. I haven't kissed any murderers. Wait a minute — you kissed your lover's friend? Oh, honey, we *really* need to have a talk."

"No, it's not like that. At least . . . No, it's not. I'm married to him, but I don't like him."

Her mouth dropped open a little bit. "Whoa, back up a few steps. You're married? Since when?"

"This morning. I was forced into it. Kristoff bribed some people and had his friends witness it falsely. But I don't like him at all. He murdered a man in front of me, for heaven's sake!"

"Another murder?" she asked, incredulous.

"Yes, although Karl says that Kristoff was just trying to protect me from him."

"Who's Karl?" she asked, a puzzled frown wrinkling her forehead. "A third lover?"

"No, he has a wife," I said, not wanting to get into the issue of just exactly what he was. "And Kristoff isn't a lover. He's just my husband, that's all."

"Then, who did this unwanted husband kill?"

"The man with the knife." I ran my hands through my hair again. "I told you it was complicated."

"Honey, that's not even close to the word I'd use for it."

There was a knock at the door and an inquiry.

"Occupied! Be out in just a minute!" Magda shouted at it, then turned back to me. "What can I do to help?"

"Oh, god love you," I said, filled with appreciation. I gave her a swift hug. "Bless you for not pestering me with a thousand and one questions. I need money, mostly. I don't have anywhere to stay and haven't eaten since yesterday —"

"Say no more," she said, digging out a money belt. She handed me a handful of cash. "I'm afraid that's all I have. I was going to cash a traveler's check in the morn-

186

ing. Is that enough?"

I counted it quickly. It was about a hundred dollars in euros. "It's more than enough," I lied. "Thank you so much."

"Husbands and lovers and Karls with their wives aside, I think you really should go to the police," she counseled. "If people are being murdered in front of you, you have to do something about it. You can't just run away."

"I am going to do something," I said, mentally girding my loins. "I'm going to go to the only person who can help me."

"Karl?" Magda guessed. "Alec?"

"No. Kristjana."

"Is she a lover, too?" she asked hesitantly.

I smiled. "No, she's a woman who runs the religious cult I mentioned earlier. Kristoff said she'd try to kill me, but I think I know a way around that."

She opened her mouth to say something, but pounding on the door halted her.

"Magda? Are you in there?"

"Denise!" Magda hissed.

I spun around in the tiny bathroom. It consisted of a sink, toilet, and mirror, with a tiny window that would be impossible for more than one of my legs to fit through. "Crap! I have to hide!"

"Here. Put this on and hide your face,"

Magda said, shoving the wig at me before turning to bellow at the door. "Just a second! Give a girl a chance, for cripe's sake."

"Are you all right?" Denise called, her voice filled with suspicion. "Who are you talking to?"

"I popped my zipper, if you must know, and this lady is helping me get decent."

I hurriedly stuffed my hair back under the wig and draped the long tresses around my face.

"You ready?" Magda asked, her hand on the door lock.

I nodded and dipped my head.

Magda unlocked the door and shoved her way out, pushing herself directly in front of Denise, acting as a human screen for me. "Just the person I need. I think I have something in my eye. Do you see anything?"

Through the wall of hair hanging over my face, I could see Denise trying to get a look at me over Magda's shoulder, but the latter adroitly stepped to the side and blocked her view. I hurried into the little room I'd used before, counting to twenty before poking my head out. I just caught the sight of Magda whisking Denise back into the main room. I sent her another mental thanks and shucked my flimsy outfit.

Someone spoke as I left the room.

"What? Sorry? I'm . . . a bit light-headed. Do you speak English?"

The man, who wore a reproduction Viking outfit of leather and wool, carrying a huge tub of ice cream, nodded. "English, yes. You sick?"

"Just need a breath of fresh air. Is that the way out? Great. I'll just get a little air and then get back to the show. It's great so far," I said as I hurried out the door to freedom.

I was about a block away when I was grabbed from behind.

"Gotcha!" Magda said, laughing when I clutched my chest. I seemed to be doing a lot of that lately.

"What are you doing here?" I asked, looking around for anyone else.

"I'm coming with you. You don't think I'd miss meeting Alec and Karl and your murderous husband, do you?" She grinned. "This is the most exciting thing that's ever happened to me, and I'm not going to miss one single moment of it!"

CHAPTER 8

"You're insane."

"I know, but it's better than being bored, don't you think? Where are we going?"

"The library." I gave Magda a very stern look. "You really should not be getting involved in this."

She whapped me on the arm with the bottle of water I'd given her earlier. "I already am involved. You're wanted by the police, you know. And I helped you escape. That's aiding and abetting or something like that, so I figured as long as I'm in it for that, I might as well have some fun out of the whole thing. Why are we going to the library? Is that where the murderer is? I've never seen a murderer up close. Are you sure it's safe?"

"I don't know where Kristoff is," I said, somewhat bemused by her enthusiasm for something that seemed so horrible to me. "And honestly, I don't want to know. There are some . . . er . . . people in the library. Magda . . ."

I stopped outside the window that I had used to leave the library, biting my lip as I considered the woman standing beside me. I didn't quite know how I was going to explain the ghosts and the whole bit about being a Zorya.

"What? If it's about me being here, don't worry. I told Raymond that I needed some time to myself, and that I'd see him tomorrow." Dimples burst forth on her cheeks as she grinned. "Since we've been going at it rather fast and furious the last few days, I think he was only too happy to get a decent night's rest."

"It's not that I'm worried about. It's . . . well . . . do you believe in life after death?"

Her eyebrows rose in surprise. "Do I believe in what?"

"Ghosts. You know, spirits of people who have died but, for whatever reason, haven't made it to heaven or hell or whatever afterlife you believe in. That sort of thing." I watched her closely, worried she'd regret helping me.

To my surprise, she didn't scoff at the question. "As a matter of fact, I do believe in it. When my grandmother died, I knew the exact moment even though I was all the way over in California, and she was in Maine. She woke me up in the middle of the night, and said she loved me, and she wanted me to be happy. In the morning, when I woke up, I thought I'd had a dream, but later my mom called to say Grandma had died at the same exact time I saw her. So yes, I believe in spirits."

"That's going to make things a whole lot easier," I said, and tapped on the window. Marta appeared. I gestured toward the lock, watching Magda.

Marta transformed herself into a solid figure and flipped open the lock. Magda's jaw dropped.

"Did she . . . is that . . . ," she stammered, pointing at Marta.

"You can see her? Oh, good. I wondered if other people can see them in their solid form. I guess only Zoryas can see them in their normal state. Come on, I don't want anyone to see us loitering out here."

Magda followed me into the window, watching with complete astonishment as Marta, smiling, faded back to her normal translucent self.

"Where'd she go?" Magda asked in a whisper.

"She's here, but in a low-energy state. You can't see her without this," I said, holding up my wrist. The stone had switched into lantern form and was glowing with a gentle silvery light. "I'm a Zorya. They're someone who takes dead people to their final resting places. Or some dead people — I'm not quite sure about all the details. But the upshot is that there are fifteen ghosts here, sixteen if you count the horse, and I'm supposed to take them to Ostri. I don't suppose you've ever heard of it?"

Magda, uncharacteristically silent, just shook her head, her mouth slightly ajar as she looked around the main room of the library. Several of the ghosts were seated at a table, bent over books, alternating between solid and transparent modes in order, I assumed, to save energy.

"Who are they?"

"That's Karl and his wife, Marta. They're the first ghosts I met. Ulfur is over there at the computer with a young woman whose name I don't know. That's his horse eating the potted plant. The rest of the people are from Ulfur's village. Their village was wiped out by a natural disaster sometime in the mid-1800s, from what I can tell. Don't bring up the subject of pigs or chicken."

She pursed her lips for a moment, then nodded. "What are they doing?"

"Researching, hopefully. Hello, everyone!"

I raised my voice in order to cut through the murmur of conversation. "I'm back, and I've brought a friend. This is Magda. She's new to all this, like me. Have you found anything out about Ostri?"

"Ulfur did," Ingveldur said with pride, beaming at him. "In a book about mythology. Show the reaper, Ulfur."

"I don't know how helpful it will be," Ulfur said, gesturing to a distant table where a thick book had been placed. He escorted us over to it. I glanced at the book, but it was in Icelandic. "This is an entry for Ostri. It includes alternate spellings, and the etymology of the word, but has little about the meaning. It just says that in Basque and Iberian religions, Ostri was used to refer to heaven. The word changed over time, and later came to mean the Christians' concept of God."

"Hmm. It doesn't say anything about where it is?"

He shook his head.

"Crap. Was there anything about it online?"

"Not much more than what's in the book," he answered, going back to the terminal. "Dagrun found similar references to Ostri, but no specifics about how you get there. The information on the Brotherhood, however, is very interesting."

"Oh, really?" Magda and I crowded around the computer terminal.

"What's the Brotherhood?" Magda asked as I scanned the screen.

"The religious group who maintains the Zoryas. Is this their Web site?"

"Yes." Ulfur watched me as I read the page.

"That is interesting," I said.

"What's interesting?" Magda asked. "All I see is Brotherhood of the Blessed Light, a list of cities, and a Web page counter. There's not much there to be interesting."

"I find it interesting to know that the Brotherhood evidently has branches or churches or whatever they call gatherings of their members in all of the major cities of the world, including seven U.S. cities. And I don't think that's a Web page counter," I said, a chill feeling gripping my stomach.

She looked again. "Then what's it counting? People it's helped? Spirits, I mean?"

I shook my head slowly. "I think it's the number of vampires they've . . . er . . . cleansed over the centuries."

"Vampires!" Magda said, plopping herself down in a chair. "All right, spill. I want to hear everything, right from the start."

I gave her an abridged version of recent

happenings while puzzling over the starkness of the Brotherhood Web site. As Magda noted, there was nothing there other than a symbolic moon, the name, a list of major cities, and a somber number.

"You're married to a vampire," she said, looking a bit stunned.

"Yup."

"And the other man, the one you said didn't kill the other Zorya, he is also a vampire."

"So Kristoff says, and I really don't know why he'd lie about Alec."

She thought about that for a few minutes. "You slept with a vampire. Did he . . . you know . . . dine?"

I blinked in surprise at the question. "Kristoff says yes, and I suppose he'd know, but I'm not convinced, not absolutely. There was nibbling going on, but I don't recall anything out of the ordinary."

"Wow," she said, looking at me with something akin to awe. "That's just . . . wow. I really want to meet this Alec. Not that I'll take him from you, because one, you're a friend, and I wouldn't do that to a friend, but mostly because it's clear you guys have some sort of a connection."

I dropped my gaze, unwilling to follow that thread.

"One thousand, one hundred and eighteen," Magda said, her attention returned to the screen. She let out a low whistle. "That's a lot of vampires."

I thought of Kristoff's girlfriend. That, too, was an uncomfortable line of thought. "Yeah. Did you find out anything about the history of the Brotherhood?" I asked the young woman named Dagrun.

"Not much." She tapped a few keys and pulled up a Web page that appeared to focus on mystical societies. There was a brief description of the Brotherhood, with reference to reapers lighting the way of the dead, but nothing specific or even helpful.

"Well, pooh." I gnawed my lip for a few seconds, then sighed and said, "I guess we're going to have to go to the source for information."

"The Brotherhood people you ran away from?" Magda asked, smiling at Ulfur.

Interest sparked in his eyes as he smiled back.

"Yes." I straightened up and realized just how exhausted I was. No food and no sleep were quickly taking their toll.

"But you said that your vampire husband told you that they'd kill you when they find out you married him."

"That's why I'm not going to tell them.

All right, everyone, thank you for your hard work. I don't believe we're going to find out anything else here, however. I think it would be best if you all went into low-watt mode and stayed here in the library where you're safe."

"Stay here?" Karl strode toward us, Marta at his side. "Shouldn't we go with you? In case you need us?"

There was an assenting murmur from all the other ghosts.

"No, I think you'll be safer here than with the Brotherhood people, at least until I know what sort of a reception I'll receive."

"But —" Karl looked around at the others. "The Ilargi could find us. He could steal our souls while you're gone."

"You've all managed to hang on to your souls for eighty years or more," I pointed out gently. "I think you can handle one more night on your own."

"I don't know, Pia," Magda said, frowning at the computer screen. She'd taken Dagrun's place and was, I could see, conducting several Web searches. She pointed at a page containing a message forum. "This person here says that the soul eaters are attracted to an area by the light of the Aurora. Didn't you say that's another name for Zorya?"

"Yes," I said slowly. "But that doesn't necessarily mean anything. I only just took the job. I haven't had time to send out whatever cosmic Zorya signals there are."

Magda eyed me for a moment before turning to Ulfur. "When did you first see the soul eater?"

"Three nights ago," Old Agda answered. "He came to our village, sniffing around, but we were hidden in the cave and he didn't find us."

"Three nights," Magda repeated, her gaze back on me. "That's when we landed in Reykjavík."

"Purest coincidence," I said. "I wasn't Zorya then."

"No, but you said the woman who was killed had a sister who was Zorya. When was she killed?"

"I don't know," I said, suddenly uncomfortable. "She just said that her sister died recently, and she was called in to be the replacement Zorya."

"Hmm," Magda said, tapping her lip as she thought. "The Brotherhood people and the vampires hate each other. The Brotherhood killed your husband's girlfriend."

"He's not really my husband," I started to protest, but was shushed to silence.

"For all intents and purposes he is. They

killed his girlfriend a couple of years ago, right? I'm sorry, but it's looking more and more like he, or your lover Alec, probably killed your Zorya friend." She paused for a moment, then looked up at me. "Is there anything to say they didn't take out the previous Zorya as well? Anniki's sister, that is?"

I shook my head, my gut tight at the thought of Alec being involved in anything so heinous.

"So let's assume that just as the Brotherhood are picking off the vamps, so your hubby and his buddy are picking off the Zoryas. First your friend's sister — do we know where she was killed?"

"Here, I assume."

"Gotcha. So Anniki arrives to take over as Zorya, and then your husband-to-be and his handsome friend show up. You don't think they're from here, either?"

"No, I'm pretty sure they're not. Their car was a rental — I saw the tag on the key chain."

"So they show up, probably hot on the trail of the new Zorya, and at the same time, a whatchamacallit, Ilarki?"

"Ilargi."

"Ilargi is seen sniffing around the local dead people." Her eyes met mine, her gaze serious. "Pia, I hate to tell you this, but I think your husband is doing more than sucking blood."

I stared at her in growing horror. "You think *Kristoff* is an Ilargi?"

Gasps reverberated off the walls of the library. A low murmur of concern started up as I tried to process that thought.

"Look at the facts. One, he wants to stop the Brotherhood. What better way to make them obsolete than to destroy the reason for their existence?"

"But they don't just exist to guide the dead. There's the whole thing about cleansing the world of evil."

"That is recent," she said, pointing to the screen. "According to the person here, the Brotherhood existed first solely to help dead people find their destination. It wasn't until the last five hundred years that they branched out to vampire killing."

"But the latter seems to be their focus now. More so, I got the feeling from Anniki, than tending the dead."

"Apples and oranges. If they don't have any dead to take care of, there's no reason for there to be Zoryas. And didn't you say something about the Zorya focusing their power?"

"Yes," I said slowly, remembering the

conversation with Kristjana. "The Zorya acts as a focal point. I didn't pay it much attention because I thought it was all a bunch of hogwash, but you may be on to something. Kristoff could have killed me if he wanted to, but another Zorya would simply take my place."

Magda nodded. "This way, he takes you out of the running, thereby hamstringing the local group. It makes sense, especially if you couple it with him sucking down all the souls of the dead around here so there's nothing for you to do."

"It's all conjecture," I protested, although I had to admit I wanted to believe it. I wanted Kristoff to be the bad guy. "And it doesn't explain why they would want to kill Anniki rather than simply marry her."

Magda sucked on her lower lip for a second. "What if she refused?"

"I refused. That did no good."

"Exactly." She pointed a finger at me. "What if Kristoff tried to get her to marry him, but she refused to the point that they felt there was no other option but killing her? When it came time to try the same thing on you, he was ready — you said he had friends waiting, and that he'd bribed someone."

"Yes," I said slowly.

"That makes sense. He learned via Anniki that he'd have to pull off some illegalities in order to get the marriage pushed through. Say what you will; he gets full credit for not wanting to kill you."

"Thank you," I said with a little grimace. "But we don't know that this is anything but guesswork."

"Unfortunately, that's true. We won't know until we can find out more about Anniki and the Brotherhood."

"Well, I'm about to do that," I said, straightening my clothing and squaring my shoulders. "I fully intend to get some answers from the local Brotherhood group."

"Brava, sister," Magda said, standing.

"You really shouldn't come with me. I know you want to help, but we don't know how they're going to take my reappearance. If worse came to worst and they went ballistic, I wouldn't want you to get hurt."

She patted me on the arm and gave me a cheerful smile. "I'm not a vampire, am I? So I'm perfectly safe. Lead on, Macduff."

I smiled at her misquotation as we left the library, but my stomach was wadded up into a leaden ball. Magda might not be a vampire, but I was married to one.

Would I be able to get the help I needed without them finding out that fact?

CHAPTER 9

". . . and so you see, I just needed a little time to myself to sort things out. I wasn't so much running away from Mattias as I was sending out a desperate plea for a little me time." The sentence ended lamely, about as lame as the excuse Magda and I had come up with while we walked to the north end of town, where the Brotherhood's church was located. "But I'm here now, and ready to take on my full Zorya duties. Assuming, that is, you still want me?"

Kristjana looked at me with suspicion. Mattias, behind her, had a similar look on his face, although that was gradually replaced with a relieved smile. The two were joined by a third person, a man of indeterminate years with a soft French accent, who had been introduced simply as Frederic Robert.

"I don't think they're buying it," Magda murmured softly.

Kristjana looked even more suspicious.

I sighed. "All right, that was a big pack of lies. I'm not Anniki, and I didn't run from Mattias because I needed some time to cope with my sister's death and the awesome responsibility of becoming the new Zorya. The truth is that I really am Pia Thomason, a tourist, just like I told you before, only Anniki and I bumped into each other, and I inadvertently got the moonstone thingie that becomes a lamp, although I later returned it to her. She said she was going to see you guys. I take it she didn't?"

Mattias shook his head.

Kristjana's eyes narrowed. Frederic looked faintly bored.

"I'm sorry to have to tell you, but she was discovered dead in my bathroom."

"Dead?" Kristjana looked instantly suspicious.

"Yes. I didn't kill her, and I don't know who did. I promised her I would find out, though, and I mean to do just that." I gave all the Brotherhood people a long look to let them know I meant business.

"But why would someone kill her in your bathroom?" Kristjana asked.

"I don't know that," I admitted. "The only thing I can think of is that she wanted to see me because we'd talked earlier."

Frederic nodded after a moment's thought. "There might be something in that. We will, naturally, wish to conduct our own inquiries."

"I figured you would. I'm trying to stay off the local police's radar, though," I said, hesitant to put myself in their power.

"Naturally. The Brotherhood protects its own . . . just as it takes responsibility for seeing wrongdoers punished."

There was a warning in his voice, but I simply gave him a quick nod. "Thank you."

"So you took the moonstone from her body?" Kristjana asked, her expression darkening.

"No. She wasn't quite dead, and before she died, she gave me the moonstone and told me I was the next Zorya, and begged me to make everything right. Since then, I've gathered up a few ghosts who want me to take them to Ostri, not that I know where that is, so I figured I'd better come here to get some help and try to do what Anniki wanted. Magda is my friend, and she came along to provide support."

"You really are a tourist?" Mattias asked, his face scrunched up in confusion.

"Yes. I swore to Anniki that I would take over her job, and unless you have someone else to do it, I guess I'm it."

"It does not work that way," Kristjana said, her voice as cold as the icy waters surrounding the island.

"That's what someone else said, but the ghosts seem to think I'm a Zorya. And the moonstone turns into a little glowy moon when I'm around them."

"There must be a blood tie between Zoryas in order for one to succeed another." Her words were clipped and abrupt. I definitely had the feeling she was not happy to see me in place of Anniki. "One cannot simply don the stone and become Zorya."

"Well, I'm not related to her in any way," I said, feeling oddly deflated. For some reason I couldn't pinpoint, I was a bit disappointed at the thought of no longer being Zorya. I was becoming fond of my little pack of ghosts, and looked forward to helping them.

"You will give me the stone," Kristjana snapped, holding out her hand. "I will take charge of it until another Zorya can be found."

I stared at her hand with growing dismay.

"Pia," Magda said, nudging me with her elbow.

I nodded, knowing exactly what she wasn't putting into words. If another Zorya was chosen, Kristoff and Alec would simply go after her, possibly even killing her if she put up a fight, as Anniki apparently did.

That wasn't the only reason I was hesitant. "I might not be the most honest and moral person in the world," I said slowly. "But Anniki asked *me* to make things right, and I promised her I would. I don't think she'd view me handing over the job to someone else as righting the wrongs done to her."

"That is not your decision to make —" Kristjana started to say when she was interrupted by Frederic.

"You said Anniki was bleeding when you found her. Did she — this sounds strange, I'm sure — did she touch your mouth at any point?"

I stared at him in surprise. "No."

"Hmm." He was silent another few moments. "She did not harm you in any way? Cut you? Scratch you?"

"Anniki? She was dying!"

"Yes, and she must have known that, so she would make every effort to pass on to you the mantle of her responsibility. She would have instigated a blood exchange."

"Well, she didn't do anything like that," I said, shuddering slightly. I remembered the grip she had maintained on my hand and held up my palm. "Other than dig her nails into me."

Everyone looked with interest at the three faint crescent markings on my palm. Although the wounds weren't deep and had closed almost immediately, faint marks could still be seen.

"Ah, I thought it must be something like that. Very good."

"It may be good to you, but frankly, I'm more worried about her transmitting some horrible disease because I had her blood all over me."

He smiled. "I can assure you that you will not receive a disease. What you witnessed firsthand was simply the passing of the light from one Zorya to another."

"That does not apply here," Kristjana protested. "She is not of the Brotherhood."

"Nonetheless, she has been chosen," Frederic told her.

"Maybe you need to explain that a little more to me," I said, still wary.

"There is normally a blood tie between Zoryas, as our learned sister says. But in the cases where there is not, one can be created by the exchange of blood between two individuals."

"Is that the only way a new Zorya can be made?" I asked, rubbing my palm.

"No," Frederic admitted. "The stone itself can choose a Zorya."

"The stone can?" Magda asked, clearly disbelieving such a thing.

"Yes. It does not happen frequently, but it can happen in cases where a blood relationship is not possible."

Magda looked thoughtful. "So Anniki was putting her seal of approval on Pia by digging her nails into her hand and making her bleed? That sounds painful, but pretty definitive."

"It is indeed." Frederic made one of those European bows that men here seemed to do so well. "Welcome to the Brotherhood, Zorya Pia."

"Thank you," I said, heaving a sigh of relief. So far, so good.

"Now, perhaps you will tell me again what happened to Zorya Anniki," he added smoothly, taking my elbow and steering me toward a back room.

"Again? I thought I went over it well enough already." I glanced back over my shoulder at Magda, who was following close behind. "There's really not a lot more I can tell you."

Beyond Magda, Kristjana marched with a determined set to her jaw. I had a feeling she wasn't buying my tale. Mattias, on the other hand, looked positively sunny in comparison.

Frederic escorted me into a tiny, dimly lit office, holding out a chair for me before seating himself behind a thick Victorian desk. Magda took the chair next to mine. Mattias leaned against the wall, shooting me an anticipatory smile every now and again. Kristjana stood next to Frederic, her eyes veiled.

"Perhaps you would take notes?" Frederic asked her.

"Notes? There're going to be notes taken? Really, I don't know that I have that much to tell you —"

"It's just a formality," Frederic interrupted, giving me a bland smile that made me more than a smidgen uncomfortable.

I glanced at Magda. She gave an almost imperceptible shrug.

"You may proceed," Kristjana said, pulling over a chair from the wall so she could write at the end of the desk.

I briefly went over my actions upon finding Anniki.

"I find it . . . interesting . . . that you were sleeping so soundly that you were not aware of someone entering your room, let alone stabbing the Zorya. Do you, perhaps, suffer from a sleeping disorder?"

"No," I answered hesitantly. I really did not want to tell them I'd been with a man, not through any prudishness, but more a desire to avoid the repercussions that would be sure to follow if they found out just what Alec was.

"Ah?" Frederic's mild brown eyes considered me with an unusually perceptive glint. "Do you have a reason accounting for the fact that you slept through the attack on the Zorya?"

"Is all this really important?" Magda asked before I could answer him. "I mean, so she slept through two people creeping through her room into the bathroom. It's not really so out of the bounds of reality to imagine that she was just tired and didn't wake up."

"I do not imply that it is," Frederic countered. "However, you must grant that the Brotherhood has a right to be interested in the circumstances of the death of one of our most esteemed members. More than a right — we have a duty to ensure that the guilty person is punished for the murder."

"I want the person caught, naturally," I said slowly. The question was, did I really? It couldn't have been Alec. It just couldn't have been. I couldn't have slept with a man who possessed the ability to mercilessly slaughter a woman while I slept in the next room. I would have sensed that sort of evil. Wouldn't I?

But if the killer wasn't Alec, then it had to be Kristoff, and much as I knew him to be capable of killing someone, I had a hard time resolving the image of him stabbing Anniki in the chest and running away. Kristoff wasn't the sort of man to run — if he killed a Zorya, I imagined he'd take full credit for the act, feeling it a point of pride.

I bit my lower lip while those thoughts chased each other around. Alec or Kristoff . . . it had to be one of those two who had killed Anniki. And yet my instincts told me that neither had. But what motive would anyone but a vampire have to want the Zorya dead?

"You wish to tell me something but are afraid we will think poorly of you for it." Frederic's voice cut through my murky thoughts. I glanced up to find him smiling benignly at me. "I can assure you that will not be the case."

Would it matter if I told them I was with a man, so long as I kept Alec's nature from them? It was clear they knew I was keeping something back, and I was a horrible liar, as was proven a few minutes earlier. If I tried to lie about what it was I was hesitant to say, they'd know, and perhaps keep after me until the truth came out. And then surely they'd wonder why I felt it necessary to keep mum about something so innocuous as spending the night with a man.

"You're right, of course," I said, taking a deep breath. I would hedge my bets a bit by mixing most of the truth with a little bit of a red herring. "I come from a small town where old-fashioned values are still held, and I forgot that Scandinavians are more open to such things. The reason I slept so heavily is because I had been up into the wee hours of the morning with a man. He was gone by the time I woke up, an unflattering reflection on my charms that I hoped to avoid dwelling upon."

"A man?" Mattias said suddenly, frowning. "You are *my* Zorya, and yet you slept with another man? Who is he?"

"I really don't think his name is pertinent," I said, striving for a lofty tone. "He didn't kill Anniki."

"You have known this man for some length of time?" Frederic asked, his expression shrewd.

I gave a little embarrassed laugh that was entirely heartfelt. "Now you really are making me bare my sins. As a matter of fact, I just met him last night."

"If you just met him, then how do you know he did not murder the Zorya?" Kristjana asked, looking up from her sheets of paper.

That was the question, wasn't it?

"I don't make a habit of sleeping with murderers," I said, manufacturing an outraged expression.

"But you don't know for sure that he didn't kill her."

"No more so than I know any one of you didn't creep into my room and stab Anniki, but I certainly don't think that's likely," I pointed out.

"I wish to know more about this man," Mattias demanded. "Is he a tourist? American?"

"I think he's a tourist," I said, not wanting to get into too many details, "although he's not American. He has a slight German accent."

"German. *Tch*," Mattias said with a frown.

"How exactly did you meet him?" Frederic asked.

"Look, I've answered your questions no matter how embarrassing I've found them, but I am not going to subject myself to a third degree!" I said with a quick glance at Magda. She gave me a discreet thumbs-up at my indignant attitude. "The details of my night with him are neither here nor there. I've told you that he didn't murder Anniki.

He was with me for part of the night, and after that he left. I don't know anything other than that."

Frederic was silent for a few moments before he rose and went to the lone window in the room, pulling back a faded gold curtain to glance outside. It was starting to get late, and I was beginning to feel the full effects of a day of stress and no food. "You do not seem to understand the full ramifications of the death of the previous Zorya, Pia. She was a blameless member of the Brotherhood, and had no enemies that we know of — save one. You are aware of the existence of Dark Ones, yes?"

"Dark One what?" Magda asked, clearly confused.

My fingers tightened around the armrests of the chair. I forced myself to relax. "Anniki told me about them, yes."

"Who are they?" Magda asked.

The three people in the room all watched me, clearly expecting me to provide the answer.

"They're the vampires I told you about earlier," I said, picking my words carefully. "They have a long history of animosity with the Brotherhood people."

"Animosity?" Kristjana snorted, jabbing her pen into the paper. "That is a deceptively mild term. It is our goal to cleanse the world of the evil the Dark Ones possess."

"Oh, *those* vampires," Magda said thoughtfully. She nodded after a few moments' reflection. "The ones you do the Buffy number on, right?"

"Buffy number?" Frederic looked confused for a moment.

"It is a reference to an American television show," Kristjana explained.

"Ah. Buffy! Yes, I remember that now. It is not quite the same thing, mademoiselle. In reality, Dark Ones are merciless, soulless monsters intent on corrupting our world until no light at all exists."

I sat silent, thinking of Alec. He wasn't evil. Kristoff certainly had a harder edge, but even he wasn't a monster. He could have killed me easily, but opted not to.

"I had no idea," Magda said, shaking her head at her folly. "Well. That's certainly an eye-opener, but what has that to do with Pia? You don't suspect her of being a vampire, surely."

"No, of course not," Frederic said quickly, making a vague gesture. "We would know if she was, but there is the fact that the only people who would desire a Zorya dead are Dark Ones. Thus it must be one of them who killed Anniki. And it is entirely within the bounds of reality, as you so charmingly put it, that your friend here was used by one."

"You think she slept with a vampire?" Magda asked, with obvious incredulity.

I arranged my face to look surprised at such an idea. "I think that's stretching things a little, don't you?"

"Perhaps," Frederic said, moving quickly to my side. Before I could object, he swept back my hair and examined the side of my neck. "But not so unlikely as you might imagine. You are aware of the mark you bear here, Zorya Pia?"

"A mark? She bears a mark?" Kristjana said, half standing.

"It's just a hickey," I protested, pushing Frederic back and getting to my feet. "A love bite, if you will. Not a vampire bite."

"She does! She bears the mark," Kristjana said, throwing down her pen and starting toward me.

Suddenly worried, I backed up, holding out my hands as if to ward them off. "You people are blowing a little bite way out of proportion —"

"Pia Thomason," Frederic said, cutting across my protest as the three of them closed in around me. There was something

218

in his voice, some indefinable note that held a compulsion with it. Despite my desire, I found myself meeting his gaze, my eyes locked to his as he stalked toward me. "You will answer my questions truthfully."

"I . . . I . . ." I reached out behind me, part of my mind screaming for me to run, the other part calmly agreeing that whatever Frederic wanted was for the best.

The three people stopped in a semicircle around me. Out of the corner of my eye I could see Magda beyond them, her face pinched with worry.

"You will answer my questions," Frederic repeated, his gaze pinning me back like a bug on a board.

The hairs on my arms stood on end as I fought the compulsion that washed over me like waves of pounding intention.

"Yes," I said against my will.

"The man you were with last night, he was a Dark One, was he not?"

"Yes," I heard myself answer, as if from some great distance. I wanted desperately to get away, to run from the suddenly scary man, but he held me prisoner with just the force of his will.

Magda gasped.

"You knew he was a Dark One and you provided him access to the Zorya Anniki,"

Frederic said, more a statement than a question.

"No." I shook my head. "I didn't know until this morning about him being a vampire."

"Why did Anniki come to your room?" Frederic asked.

"I don't know. I really don't know. Maybe because I was the only one she'd talked to last night?"

Frederic was silent for a moment. I was aware of the others, but couldn't seem to drag my eyes from his to look at them. "Where is the Dark One now?"

"I don't know. He left just like I told you — sometime in the night."

His gaze bored into me with a sensation of stripping away all my thoughts and revealing my innermost self. I wanted to squirm away, to stop the examination, but was powerless against his will.

Suddenly he turned away, evidently satisfied with what he'd seen. I slumped against the wall, sliding to the floor in a boneless heap as he returned to the desk, absently picking up one of the sheets upon which Kristjana had been writing. "I believe that will be enough. We will hold the marriage ceremony immediately, so as not to delay your initiation."

Magda rushed to my side and squatted next to me, her face filled with concern. "Are you all right?"

I nodded, my arms and legs feeling shaky in the aftermath of Frederic's display of power.

"You will allow this to go forward?" Kristjana asked, storming over to the desk and slamming her hands down on it. "She is tainted by a Dark One!"

"Tainted? No. Used, yes, but perhaps that can be to our advantage. She has a knowledge of the one who killed the Zorya. We will use that to find him."

"I will not allow this!" Kristjana declared, anger crackling off her. "I will not allow her to pollute the office of Zorya."

"You have no right to refuse her," Frederic said calmly. "She was chosen by the Zorya. A blood pact was created between them. That must take precedence over the fact that she was soiled by a Dark One."

"Gee, thanks," I said wryly, getting to my feet with Magda's assistance. "You really know how to make a girl feel special."

No one paid any attention to me until my stomach growled so loud it was audible to all.

"My word is final," Frederic said, leveling a stern look at Kristjana. "Unless you wish to challenge it?"

I thought for a moment that she might do just that, but after a few moments of her jaw working tightly, she fisted her hands and jerkily shook her head. "It shall be as you order."

Frederic smiled, and I was amazed at how ordinary he appeared. A few minutes before, he'd held me prisoner against a wall, using nothing but his own personality, and now he looked like a perfectly normal middle-aged accountant. "I would suggest you feed your bride before the ceremony, Mattias. We wouldn't want her fainting away before the vows were complete, would we?"

CHAPTER 10

"Are you sure this is a good idea?" Magda asked an hour later as I hoisted myself onto the windowsill of a large house that sat directly behind the church used by the Brotherhood. "I don't think your husband is going to like you missing your wedding night. Your second husband, that is, not your first."

I grimaced and let myself drop to the ground, *oof*ing as quietly as I could. Magda's feet appeared next to my head. Hurriedly, I moved out of the way so she could climb out. "My husband has nothing to say about it. Either one of them. And as far as the latter one goes, I told him I was too tired to play house tonight, and wanted to sleep."

"He bought that?" she asked in disbelief.

"He had no choice." I gave her a quick smile. "One of the perks of being Zorya is that he pretty much has to do what I say."

"Hrmph."

"I will say that I'm glad the Brotherhood folk were content with their version of a marriage ceremony rather than a civil ceremony, because I really would have hated to explain to them why they couldn't take out a marriage license in my name. You *really* want to do this? Audrey and Ray must be worried about where you've been all night."

Magda brushed off my concerns and led the way out of the tiny yard to the street, being careful to stick to the shadows. "I called them while you were chatting with your hubby, and told them I'd see them in the morning."

"Can we drop references to Mattias as my husband? It makes me feel . . . I don't know, uncomfortable somehow. As if I'm doing something underhanded. Which I realize is silly because that's exactly what I am do-ing."

"Except you're doing it for a good reason," she said, completing my thought. We paused at an intersection, carefully eyeing the streets for signs of police, tour members, Brotherhood people, or incredibly hand-some vampires. "So it really doesn't count as a sin, if that's what's worrying you."

We hurried across the street, heading toward the section of town where our hotel was located. Luckily, at that time of night, there wasn't much traffic, either pedestrian or vehicular. "I'm not overly concerned about sinning — I just don't want them to find out the truth and hack off my head or burn me at the stake, or whatever it is they do to people they think have signed on with the enemy. Which is just one more reason why I wanted to get away tonight — if something happens to me, I don't want them coming down on you."

"Pfft," she said dismissively, giving me a friendly little shove. "What's a friend for if not to face almost certain death with, eh?"

"A worthy attitude, but you don't know to what lengths these guys will go," I answered, rubbing my arms. "That little chat I had with Mattias after the ceremony wasn't just to discuss the sleeping arrangements. Did you know that even though Anniki picked me to be her successor, and I have ghostly charges and such, I'm still not officially recognized as Zorya? Evidently they have to conduct some sort of recognition ritual where the Brotherhood people assemble to acknowledge me. Only after that is over will I be able to take the ghosts to their destination."

"A ritual?" she asked. "Like an initiation at fraternities and such?"

225

"Assumedly without the wild orgies and drunkenness."

She grinned at me. "But that's the best part! Did Mattias say what the initiation is?"

I rubbed my arms again, not sure if the goose bumps were from the cold air or nerves. "He didn't really go into it much, other than to say that just as the Zorya requires the stone to channel power, so does she require the acceptance of the community to be recognized as Zorya. The ceremony is supposed to do the latter bit, and I gather after that I'll be put through my paces in front of everyone. It sounds kind of creepy, to be honest."

"Very Masonic," Magda agreed as we kept to the shadows at the next intersection. I recognized a couple of buildings, guessing we were a few blocks away from the hotel. "So that's going to take place tomorrow night?"

"That's the plan. In the ruins we were supposed to go to the other night."

"Oh, good. I really wanted to see that place. I hope no one minds if I come along tomorrow? Ack. It's almost ten. You'd better get some sleep or you're going to be exhausted."

"Yeah, I'm a bit pooped. Whoops. Come

back. I think that's a cop car."

We pulled back as we were rounding a corner, both of us watching suspiciously as a man strolled out of the front of the hotel, pausing to talk to someone sitting in an unmarked car.

"Cop?" I asked Magda.

"Definitely. They must be watching for you. Let's go around the back. Maybe there's a way we can get in there without them seeing."

We slipped around the block, coming up against the kitchen entrance, but there was a policeman there, too, talking with easy amiability with a woman wearing a traditional white chef's hat.

"Damn. OK, how's this? I go in and distract the cop in the lobby, and you sneak through to the side stairs and go up to your room."

"I don't have my key," I whispered, my hopes sinking. Although the Brotherhood people had said they would give me money, I wanted my own clothing and things, which Magda thought were still in my room. "It was in my room when I left, but I'm sure the manager or police picked it up."

Magda pulled out her hotel key — really a plastic card with a magnetic strip — and looked thoughtful. "There's the bathroom.

That's a way in for you."

I ran my mind back to the morning, shuddering at the memory. "I left the door unlocked when I went to bed, in case you needed to use the room, but this morning when I found Anniki, it was locked."

She gave a little grimace, then said thoughtfully, tapping the key card on her lips, "That's as may be, but the police unlocked it at one point. I caught them peeking in while I was getting dressed. If they didn't lock it, I bet you could get into your room from mine via the bathroom. Or in a worst-case scenario, use the balcony our rooms share."

"There's still the matter of getting up into your room."

She smiled and fluffed her substantial cleavage. "Oh, I don't think that's going to be too difficult to overcome. The girls and I can keep the lobby cop's attention long enough for you to slip in and go up the side stairs. I would avoid the elevator, though."

"And if we're caught? I don't want you to get into trouble with the police for helping me."

"If you're seen, I'll simply point at you and scream bloody murder," she said confidently, giving me her key card. "There's nothing they can do to me since I haven't done anything wrong. Just a little aiding and abetting, but what's that? Nothing, really."

Whereas I'd honored Anniki's last request, which left me running from the scene of a murder, I thought with a twinge of guilt.

"Come on, let's go in via the verandah, and I'll go dazzle the cop inside with my fabulous breasts."

Her plan — or breasts — worked like a charm. She had no difficulty engaging the cop's attention long enough for me to slip inside and along the far wall to the hallway that led to a set of lesser-used stairs. The reception clerk was too busy watching Magda to notice me, and my luck held all the way to Magda's room. With a quick, fearful glance up and down the hallway, I opened her room door and let myself in.

I was about to turn on the light when a muffled snore emerged from her bed. Evidently Raymond had decided to wait for her here. I knew where the door to the bathroom had to be, and edged my way carefully through the room, but it was dark and impossible to navigate without running painfully into things. The third time I smashed my toe against a piece of furniture and uttered a smothered yelp, Raymond snorted, and groggily asked, "Honeycakes?"

I murmured something that I hoped

sounded Magdaish, and almost sighed with relief when the door to the bathroom opened easily. I closed the door behind me before turning on the light, hesitating for a moment as I considered locking it in case Raymond decided to follow me, but decided against such an action. It wouldn't be fair to keep Magda from using the room for a second night.

The bathroom had been cleaned up, so presumably the police were done with their forensics work. I eyed the spot where Anniki had lain, begging me for justice, and renewed my intention to fulfill her dying wish.

"If it was Kristoff that killed you, he won't go unpunished," I told the empty room.

And if it was Alec? my inner critic asked. I moved toward the door, mentally shaking my head. It couldn't be Alec. I would know.

The bathroom door that led into my room wasn't locked. I sagged with relief for a moment before peeking inside. The room was dark. "Thank heavens for police who don't stay at a crime scene."

I was halfway into the room before the voice spoke. "Not to mention women who just can't live without their things."

I gasped and whirled as the lights came on. Kristoff stood next to the bed, dressed entirely in black, the golden glow from the lamp casting sinister shadows across his face.

"What are you doing here?" I asked in a high, wavering voice. I started to back away from him but realized I had nowhere to go. There was no safety for a fugitive.

"Waiting for you. Alec had an idea you'd be back. I packed up your things."

I looked where he gestured. My large leather bag was sitting on a chair.

"Why are you following me?" I asked without thinking.

"Why did you run from me?" he countered.

"You killed a man! Right in front of me," I said.

"I killed a reaper," he corrected. "One who was about to kill you."

"He was not. He was just using me as a shield so you wouldn't bite him and turn him into the evil undead."

Kristoff adopted a martyred expression that for some reason, I found endearing. "Dark Ones are very much alive, and we do not turn people without a profound reason."

My eyes widened at his words. Until that moment, I wasn't sure what part of the vampire myth was true. "You mean you *can* turn people into vampires?"

"We can. It strips the soul from the person, so it is not done frequently. Certainly we are not building some sort of Dark One army to take over the world, if that's what you were about to ask."

I closed my mouth. I was, in fact, about to ask that very thing.

"Now, if there are no more ridiculously misinformed ideas you'd like debunked, I'd like to get going. The night is young, and I have much to do." He started toward me as he spoke.

"Don't you come near me," I said with rising panic, backing up and reaching around blindly for an object to use as protection.

He stopped, a mildly amused look on his face. "Why? What will you do? Call the police?"

My heart sank as I realized the veracity of his words. There was no one I could call to help me. Magda must be in her room by now, but I didn't really want to get her involved. Not with a vampire.

"I thought you wanted to see Alec. Or was your night with him so unmemorable?"

My spine stiffened at his mocking tone. "I do want to see him, not that the night I spent with him is any of your business. I have several things I'd like to ask him, not the least of which is why he felt it necessary to give you my passport."

"Come along, then," he said, opening the door to the hallway a smidgen. He closed it quickly. "We have to leave. Now."

"Is someone coming?" I asked, torn between a desire to seek help and a knowledge that I was better off without becoming involved with the police.

"Yes. Police. Evidently you aroused suspicion getting in here." He turned off the light, grabbed my suitcase, and flung open the French doors on the balcony.

"But no one saw me . . . unless the desk clerk caught a glimpse. Oy."

Kristoff didn't say anything, just leaped off the balcony. I followed, closing the French doors behind me, peering hesitantly down to the ground, where he stood waiting impatiently in the indigo shade cast by a nearby hedge. The midnight sun was still up, but at its lowest point, which left everything bathed in a lovely twilight glow.

Everything but the vampire glaring up at me. "Hurry. My car is parked a block away."

"It's a long jump down," I said softly, trying to gauge the distance between the ground and the balcony.

"I thought you said you jumped down this way earlier." Exasperation was beginning to make itself heard in his deep voice.

"Yes, but that was in the heat of the moment. I was scared and panicky. I'm not panicking now."

Setting down the bag and holding his arms up, he muttered something that I suspected wasn't at all a good reflection on me. "Jump down and I'll catch you."

"You have got to be kidding."

His teal eyes glittered wickedly in the moonlight.

"I'm too big! I'll squash you flat," I pointed out.

"For god's sake, woman, jump now, or I'll leave you to the police."

I swung my legs over the railing, sitting on it for a moment as I tried to make up my mind.

Light filtered out from the curtains on the French door. Someone was in my room.

"I'll squash —" I started to say again.

"Jump!" he commanded, and I threw all caution to the wind and did just that.

"You see? I told you I was too heavy!" I looked down at Kristoff's face. As I suspected, I had toppled him like a bowling pin. He lay beneath me with a dazed look in his eyes that quickly faded to familiar irritation.

"All women think they're too fat. I am

perfectly capable of catching you, regardless."

His fingers were splayed on my hips, his breath brushing my lips. We were fitted together in an intimate way that seemed to make thinking difficult. His gaze dropped to my mouth, and I started to tingle all over at the thought of kissing him.

A voice shouting from the balcony roused us both.

"Get moving," he growled as I rolled off him, quickly getting to my feet.

He grabbed my suitcase in one hand and me with the other, dragging me after him as he raced out of the garden.

The sound of someone hitting the ground hard behind us kept me from protesting the cavalier treatment. I concentrated on keeping my feet beneath me as we raced down the block, around a corner, and back behind a small brick building. Kristoff tossed my bag into the back of the red car, shoving me inside before getting in himself.

A uniformed policeman appeared just as Kristoff slammed his foot onto the accelerator, sending us rocketing out of the small parking lot. He swore and jerked on the wheel, narrowly avoiding the cop.

"Holy crap!" I yelled as he took the corner on what felt like only two wheels. "Are you trying to kill us?"

"The thought had crossed my mind," he ground out, his eyes glittering in the darkness as he sped out of town.

"Where are we going? Are you and Alec staying at a hotel in town?" I asked, looking behind us to see if we were being followed.

"Yes, but that's not where we're going."

"I think we're clear. I don't see any cars racing up the hill after us," I said, looking back down at the town as Kristoff shifted gears and sent us flying out of town on the road that led to the main highway. I sat back down in my seat, relieved to have escaped at least one form of trouble. I eyed the other one. "Why not?"

"Because you stalled so long getting off that damned balcony that the police saw my license plate. It won't take them long to trace it back to Alec, which means they'll know where we're staying."

"I'm sorry, I just wanted to keep from flattening you," I said, wrapping the tattered remains of pride around myself.

He snorted. "Women."

"Yeah, well, you have to admit, I was right. I did knock you down."

"I was off balance," he said, his gaze fixed on the road. "And you'll notice that you didn't flatten me."

"That's just a matter of semantics," I said righteously, looking out the window. "If we can't go to Alec's hotel room, where are we going?"

"Somewhere safe."

"Where's that?"

But he wouldn't answer. He didn't say another word for the next twenty minutes as we drove through the twilight. I ignored him ignoring me and admired instead the lovely soft colors of the sky.

"Why are we stopping here?" I finally broke the silence when Kristoff pulled off a winding road and stopped in front of a long metal gate.

"Welcome to our accommodations for the night."

My gaze moved from him as he climbed out of the car and opened the metal gate, to beyond where the outline of a rickety pink barn lurched drunkenly against the glowing sky.

Kristoff got back into the car and drove us around to the far side of the broken-down barn, tucking the car neatly away between the barn and a large, corroded metal cylinder, obviously some sort of farming equipment.

"We're staying here?"

"Yes." He got out, grabbing my bag and

hauling it around to the front of the building.

I stayed staring at the back of the barn for a moment or two, noting with mild interest that a rat was observing me from the top of the metal cylinder.

"We're staying here," I told the rat.

It didn't look impressed.

"I'm not, either," I told it, then gathering my wits, marched my way through thick, smelly mud to the front of the barn. Kristoff and my suitcase were nowhere to be seen, but a faint light glowed from inside the barn. I entered through one of the double doors that had been left slightly ajar.

Kristoff had a cell phone to his ear, then closed it with a quick, jerky motion. "Alec isn't answering."

"Do you think something is wrong?" I asked, watching him closely.

His lips thinned a smidgen. "No. The police probably arrived, and he got out quickly. He might have left his phone behind. I'll try again in the morning."

"Ah. Um. Why are we *here?*" I asked Kristoff as he jerked a couple of mildewy bales of hay off a platform. He had set a flashlight on an overturned bucket, since the interior of the barn was almost completely dark. "That is to say, why are we not at a hotel or something like that? I know we can't go to yours if they saw your license plate, but that doesn't mean we can't go to somewhere civilized."

He yanked an empty moth-eaten grain bag onto the upper half of his bale platform. "Unfortunately, I did not think to bring a false passport with me, so once the police have my name — which they will get from the hotel where Alec and I were staying — they will simply track that no matter what hotel I register at."

"Oh." I thought about that for a moment, distastefully eyeing the refuge he'd found us. There was a suspicious rustling behind the bales. "You couldn't . . . you know . . . *make* someone give us a room without registering under your real name?"

He stared at me. "And how am I supposed to do that?"

"Well, I don't know!" I slapped my hands on my legs in exasperation. "You're a vampire, aren't you? Doesn't that mean you can mind meld with people? Or brain wave them into doing what you want?"

"With my mesmerizing powers, you mean?"

"Yes! Those!"

He sighed a martyred sigh. "I am a Dark One, Zorya."

"My name is Pia."

"I do not have magical powers that affect mortals. So no, I cannot stare deep into someone's eyes and convince them to give me a room without first providing my passport and credit card." He went back behind a half wall and brought out a really filthy-looking blanket.

"Well, what's the use in being a vampire if you don't get any special powers?"

"I didn't say I don't have any powers — I simply said that I do not have any over mortals. And the only one I can *mind meld* with, as you put it, is someone close to me, like a Beloved, and I sincerely doubt such a woman exists." He plopped himself down on a couple of the bales of hay, and pulled the blanket over him.

"What are you doing?" I asked, feeling somewhat lost and alone. I rubbed my arms against the cold — it was cold and dank in the barn, the night air teasing its way in through a dozen or more missing slats in the walls.

"Going to sleep." The words emerged with a surly edge to them.

I considered the black lump that he made in the near darkness of the barn.

"Where am I supposed to sleep?" I asked, hating the pitiful tinge to my voice, but feel-

240

ing particularly vulnerable at the moment. Being helpless in the company of a murderous vampire will do that to a girl.

"I made you a bed over there."

The black lump bulged in the direction of the clumped bales of hay with the dirty feed bag. I looked at the so-called bed, moving hesitantly toward it. The rustling had stopped. Maybe it was the wind, not rodents.

"Turn off the flashlight."

"Not on your life," I said, edging my way over to the bed. One squeak, one sign that there were rats or mice near my bed, and I'd go sleep in the car, small as it was.

"Fine. If you want the police to come investigating who is hiding out in a barn that's supposed to be unoccupied, leave it on."

"Are you deliberately being as obnoxious as possible?" I asked, hefting the flashlight. It had a nice solid feel in my hand. It would make a reasonable weapon in case anything with four legs decided to attack.

Why did I have a feeling it was the two-legged predators I had to worry about more?

"I thought I was being pleasant."

"Pleasant." I snorted. "You wouldn't know the meaning of the word. Don't I get a blanket?"

"No."

I sat gingerly on the edge of my makeshift bed. "You have one. I'm cold. Why can't I have one?"

Kristoff sighed heavily and rolled over to glare at me, his eyes glowing with a teal light in the dimness of the barn. "Because I don't have a bloody bag full of clothing, and you do. Now, will you turn off that light and go to sleep?"

He rolled back over, leaving me staring balefully at his back.

CHAPTER 11

I had to admit that Kristoff, no matter how brusque, had a point — I had all my clothing, while he had nothing but what he wore. I opened my suitcase and pulled out a sweater and scarf that were intended for use during a visit to a glacier . . . a visit I wouldn't get to make.

Bundled up as much as I could manage without actually crawling inside the bag, I sat huddled on my appointed bed and shivered, flicking the light around the barn to make sure there weren't bats or anything that could come swooping down on me while I slept, occasionally sending the light over to the lump Kristoff made.

He didn't move.

I told myself to stop worrying and just go to sleep, but tired though I was, the cold and discomfort kept me from relaxing. At every little rustle, every cold draft, every breeze wafting the smell of mildewed straw and ages-old manure, I hunkered down, more and more miserable, until I couldn't stand it any longer.

"I'm still cold, Kristoff."

He was silent so long, I thought he might be asleep. Finally he sat up and tossed me his blanket. It stank of mildew and horse and sweat, but it held delicious warmth from his body.

"I'm not going to take your blanket!" I said, reluctantly throwing it back to him. "Isn't there another one?"

"No." He didn't insist I take the blanket, just wrapped it back around himself and laid down. "Put on some more clothes."

"I've put on everything I have that's warm, and I'm still too cold to sleep."

The silence was even longer this time, and I could have sworn I heard another martyred sigh, but at last he yanked the blanket out from where it was tucked underneath him. "Get under the blanket, then."

I didn't wait to be told twice. I also didn't examine the wisdom of cuddling up next to a murderous vampire — I clutched my flashlight and scooted over to his bed, crawling in behind him, shivering as I carefully tucked the blanket over me. It didn't quite reach all of me.

He suffered through a good ten minutes

of my teeth chattering and shivering before he swore in Italian, sat up, jerked off his leather coat, and slapped it over the top of me, on the outside of the blanket. He laid back down on his side, giving me his back.

"Oh, thank you," I said gratefully, and scooched in until I was pressed against his back, blissfully soaking in the warmth he radiated. It took a few minutes before I realized that he wore nothing but a thin black T-shirt. The blanket itself wasn't very warm, and with his leather jacket draped over me, and my cold body pressed against him, he couldn't be staying very warm in the cool summer night air. I sat up and peeled off the couple of extra layers I'd donned, draping them over our bodies on top of the blanket before curling up behind him again.

"You are a strange woman," he said after a few minutes.

Pressed against him as I was, I could hear his voice rumble around in his chest. It was an oddly pleasing sound.

"So I've been told. If you didn't kill Anniki, and Alec didn't, who did?" I asked, drowsy enough that my mouth operated without its regular inhibitions.

He was silent for a few minutes. "I don't know."

I opened my eyes and looked at the back

245

of his head. There wasn't much I could see but a black outline, but I looked at it and wondered why he was lying, then wondered why I knew he was lying.

"Are you an Ilargi? One of the soul-sucking ones, that is?"

He stiffened for a moment, then spun around inside the cocoon of blankets and clothing, those beautiful eyes of his narrowed as they examined me. "Who exactly are you?"

I blinked in surprise at the question. "You know who I am — I'm a tourist from Seattle."

"No tourist knows about the soul reapers without having some experience with them."

"I spent some time with the Brotherhood people, so I'm not entirely clueless. I found out about the difference between their folk and the Ilargi."

"They're *all* reapers." He snorted derisively and rolled back over.

I listened to the sound of his breathing, slow and even and rather soothing.

"Was that man who attacked us really going to kill me?"

It took a few minutes for him to answer. "Yes. He was a reaper."

"But that can't be right. They knew I was the Zorya. Why would they want to kill me?"

"You were with me. Go to sleep and turn off that light."

"You didn't answer my question. Are you an Ilargi?"

His sigh was truly admirable, filled with martyrdom. "No."

I bit my lip. Did I believe him? I had believed it when he said he didn't kill Anniki, but everything was pointing to him doing just that. Only . . . I shook my head at my crazy ideas. He didn't feel to me like he had killed Anniki. Yes, he took down the reaper who attacked us, but that was a self-defense situation. Going on my gut instinct, I judged he was telling the truth.

"Go to sleep," he grumbled again.

I took one last wary glance around the barn, worried that a gang of rats might be stealing up behind me, but there was no sound but the wind. Even the rustling seemed to have died down. I turned off the light and snuggled tighter into Kristoff's back, not even bothering to try to figure out why I felt safe with him.

A soft, breathy groan slowly pulled me out of an erotic dream. I opened my eyes to find myself pressed against Kristoff. No, not just pressed — plastered. Our legs were tangled together, my arm wrapped around his torso, my mouth pressed against a bare patch of shoulder. Somehow during our few hours of sleep, he'd turned toward me, and I had draped myself over him like we were lovers. It was warm in our little cocoon, a lovely warmth that was filled with his scent. I breathed deeply, sleepily trying to analyze it, recognizing somewhere deep in my brain that what I was smelling was a man, sexy, dangerous, and at that moment, incredibly arousing.

His lips moved over my neck, soft little caresses that left me feeling boneless. I tipped my head back a smidgen and bit his earlobe, swirling my tongue around it, noting in an absent way that he tasted just as he smelled — masculine, enticing, and oh, so warm.

A dull wave of red hunger rose between us. My mind, oddly analytical, sensed that the hunger was coming from him, and I was just feeling it.

"You're hungry," I murmured into his ear, pressing a few kisses along it.

"Yes," he said on another breathy groan, his lips burning down my neck. A scrape of teeth had me arching my back, my breasts thrusting themselves wantonly against his chest.

A distant part of my brain recognized that what I was about to do was wrong, very wrong, not just because I felt guilty over betraying a possible relationship with Alec, but because Kristoff was a vampire, an enemy, a man who stood for everything I was about to work against. There could be no rational reason why I suddenly was filled with the need to satisfy his hunger.

"You can have me," I murmured, pulling him toward me as I rolled onto my back. I bit gently on his lower lip as he rolled halfway on top of me, one hand stroking my breast.

"It isn't right," he murmured, kissing his way down to my collarbone, his tongue sweeping a path that made me arch up into him again.

"Go ahead," I said, breathing heavily as he slid down a smidgen, his hands busily unbuttoning my shirt to expose my bra. "I want you to."

And I did. I felt oddly detached from the world, as if everything had narrowed down to this one moment with Kristoff, in our safe, warm little nest. All my concerns, all my worries, had focused to one shining point: I must satisfy his hunger.

His mouth was hot on my breasts, so hot it left me gasping. He licked the exposed skin first on one breast, then the other, his hands sliding beneath me. I clutched his head, my fingers stroking the soft curls as he unhooked my bra, gasping again when his mouth closed around an aching nipple.

"So warm," he groaned. "So soft. Like silk over satin."

I writhed beneath him, my mind so filled with sensations, I couldn't begin to separate them. The scent of him ignited a base desire in me; the taste of him on my tongue left me wanting more. The feeling of his body lying half on top of mine made me want to squirm to feel more, all of him, on me and around me and inside me.

His teeth scraped gently over my nipple, tugging in a way that ignited blind passion. I dug my fingers into his shoulders, my breath sounding loud and ragged in the soft morning air.

He murmured something into the underside of my breast, words that made no sense, but which felt like a caress. "You're sure?" he asked, the stubble on his cheeks rubbing against the now sensitized flesh of my breast. Before I could answer, I saw a glint of white and felt a momentary sting that seemed made up of more pleasure than pain.

I let my head loll back at the incredible sensation of him drinking from me, a mixture of arousal and satisfaction that left me teetering on the edge of an orgasm all the while feeling a deep, intense gratification that seemed to originate in Kristoff. It was as if we were sharing emotions, and I knew with absolute certainty that he was as aroused as I was.

His tongue swept across my breast as he pulled his head up, his eyes almost glowing with a mix of desire, passion, and arousal.

I let my hands slide down his shoulders, my fingers tracing out the shape of his muscles through the cloth of his shirt. He started to move up my body, froze for a moment, then reared back and pulled his shirt off.

I cooed with happiness when he returned to my arms, kissing the valley between my breasts. My hands danced over the smooth, hard stretches of muscles in his shoulders, swept down his back, and up along his ribs. He was moving upward, slowly kissing a trail until his mouth was poised above mine.

"This is wrong," he said, his voice deep and lyrical with the Italian accent. "It is not right."

"No, it isn't," I agreed, and arching up to him, kissed him with all the desire that he'd stirred within me.

He groaned into my mouth as I let my tongue do some wandering, my toes curling with the taste of him, hot and sweet and slightly smoky, so good it made me want to yell. He tolerated my exploration for a few minutes, tugging me upward to remove my shirt while never breaking the kiss.

My hands slid down his chest as I sank back down, enjoying the sensation of slick, silky chest hair.

He groaned again, and took control of the kiss, his tongue dancing around mine as he tasted me.

A sharp, short cry of a rodent caused me to jerk suddenly, my fear that we were about to be assaulted driving all other thoughts from my mind.

"Rats!" I said, simultaneously clutching him and trying to find the flashlight so I could pinpoint where the attack was going to come from.

"That was outside," he answered, his hand going to his mouth. He stared in surprise at his fingers.

"Are you sure?"

"Yes."

I looked at his finger. There was smear of red on it. "What happened?"

"You made me bite my tongue."

"Oh. I'm so sorry."

We stayed frozen where we were for the

count of eight; then I said, "We should stop."

"We should," he agreed, his eyes searing a blue light deep within my soul.

"I don't want to," I said, moving my hands up his arms, braced on either side of my head.

"Neither do I," he answered just before claiming my mouth in another one of those breath-stripping, mind-numbingly fabulous kisses. I welcomed his invasion into my mouth, rubbing my breasts against his bare chest as I slid my hands down to his pants. He tasted just as good as he had a moment before, but this time, there was a slightly spicy note added that I put down to the dab of blood on his tongue. I didn't stop to wonder about the fact that his blood actually tasted good rather than coppery, like my own, and just gave in to the sensations he was driving to the point where I thought I might spontaneously combust.

He tore his mouth from mine, glaring down at me almost angrily as he reared back and pulled his jeans off. "I don't want this."

"I know you don't. I don't, either," I answered, struggling to get out of my own linen pants. He was quicker with his clothing than I was with mine, and helped yank my pants and shoes off before he was kissing me again, but this time, his entire body moved into the kiss. I pulled my knees up around him, feeling the proof of his arousal against my pubic bone, relishing the weight of his body on mine. The feeling of him filled my mind, but there was more I wanted from him.

I suckled his tongue, causing him to groan again deep in his throat. His hands were touching me all over, stroking my breasts, my neck, my arms. I mimicked his moves, somehow feeling his pleasure as I pushed it even higher. He rolled over onto his back, pulling me with him, never breaking the kiss that left me hungrier for more.

"Condoms," I said, a sudden thought trying to catch my attention in the ecstasy-fest that was my brain.

"We don't need them," he answered, his head dipping to take the tip of one of my breasts in his mouth.

We didn't need them because he was a vampire and had no diseases, said a distant thought. I squirmed against him, knowing what I was about to do was wrong on every level, but not giving a damn. At that moment in time, the world had shrunk down to one man, and he was all that mattered.

He threw back his head and moaned when I sank down on him, his penis a welcomed invader in my hidden depths, muscles I wasn't aware still functioned tightening around him as I rocked my hips, sending him deeper and deeper into me. His hips lunged suddenly upward, making my eyes cross with pleasure.

"I don't think . . . don't think . . ." I stammered, trying to tell him that I wasn't going to last long, so aroused was I, but my brain seemed to have shut down with the overwhelming sensation of him lodged so firmly inside me.

"Don't think," he agreed, pulling me forward, his mouth hot on my shoulder. Pain flared for a second as he bit, his fingers hard on my hips as they forced me into a rhythm that pleased us both.

He drank deeply of my blood, his own passion mingling with mine until I simply ceased to exist. Wave after wave of ecstasy rolled through me as I climaxed, waves that were amplified by his own moment of exquisite pleasure. The combination of my emotions coupled with his were too much for me, sending me whirling into a chaos of rapture that was accompanied by his shout of completion.

I woke up probably an hour later to find I was alone. I sat up, pushing my hair out of my face, looking around the now visible interior of the barn. Kristoff was nowhere to be seen. My mind was a hazy muddle of half-remembered sensations; my body felt somewhat bruised and fragile. I looked down at myself, surprised to see that I looked the same as ever. I felt as if I had fingerprints visible all over me, marks that would allow anyone who looked at me to know I'd slept with a vampire.

No, not one vampire . . . two. What sort of a horrible woman was I that I so callously threw away my relationship with Alec in order to give in to lust for another man?

Shame washed over me, leaving me hotly uncomfortable and perilously close to tears. What was I going to say to Alec when I finally saw him again? How was I going to face him when I'd slept with his friend?

And how on earth was I going to look Kristoff in the eye? I'd all but thrown myself at the man. He said time and time again that he didn't want me, didn't like me, and yet I took advantage of the fact that he was a man and I was a woman, and we were thrown together for a night of such erotic sex that I seriously expected to see scorch marks on the blanket.

"Bull," I said aloud, quickly getting to my feet and gathering up my clothing. "He wanted it as bad as I did. If I'm to blame, so is he, and if he tries any of that crap on me, I'll let him have it."

I put on a fresh pair of pants and shirt, stuffing yesterday's clothing into my bag before emerging from the barn. I could see more of the area around us, some sort of farm that had clearly known better days. Fields lay in unkempt wilderness, while a good mile away sat a low, squat farmhouse and a couple of outbuildings. There was no one there but me.

"At least he left the car this time," I muttered sourly, shoving my bag into the backseat. "But I'm beginning to be a little distressed about this recent trend of men disappearing rather than sticking around to face the morning after."

There was a movement at the end of the barn. Kristoff stood in the shade cast by the building, frowning at me. "Who are you talking to?"

I had a momentary pang of embarrassment. How do you face a man who you know doesn't like you, but who a few hours ago was moaning his pleasure into your mouth as you writhed around together?

I eyed him. He stared stonily at me, no emotion visible whatsoever on his face. Well, if that's the way he wanted it, that was fine with me. Two could pretend nothing had happened between us.

Besides, I wasn't entirely sure anything had. Oh, we'd engaged in some pretty intense sex — my still-shaky legs reminded me of that fact. But emotionally, had anything changed?

I shook my head at that question, not wanting to try to evaluate the tangled mess that was my emotions. I lifted my chin and gave him an equally cool look. "Oh, there you are. I was talking to myself. Is there an outhouse or something around here?"

He shrugged and remained where he was.

"What, you don't have to ever pee?" I asked, marching toward him, looking for a spot I could use to relieve my bladder.

"Not unless I eat food."

I paused as I was about to pass by, glancing at him in surprise. "You're kidding. You don't really ever have to . . . go?"

"We can, if that's what you're asking," he said with an unreadable look. "But it usually isn't necessary unless we've ingested food."

"Oh." I thought about that for a moment, then continued behind the barn. "That must be awfully darned handy. I'll be back in a few minutes."

He was in the car when I returned, the driver's overhead flap pulled down and to the side, so it blocked the sunlight filtering in.

"I never thought about it, but you must really hate the midnight sun," I said, getting in the car while avoiding looking at him. Try as I might to ignore him, I was very aware of his nearness in the close confines of the vehicle, aware of the way his leg moved as he started up the car and backed out onto the road, aware of the unique scent he seemed to possess that still lingered in my nose just as the almost indescribable taste of him lingered on my tongue. A little zing of electricity shimmered up my arm when his hand brushed it while shifting. Oh, yes, I was aware of him . . . but he seemed just as remote and threatening as he had the day before.

Nothing had changed, not really. We might have sought comfort from each other for a bit, but that was all it was. I could stop beating myself up for betraying Alec's memory, since clearly our little interlude meant nothing to Kristoff.

Alec was who I should be thinking of. But as we drove back to town, I realized with a sick feeling that whatever I might have had with Alec was now over. I wasn't the sort of woman who hopped from bed to bed without a care, despite my actions of the last few days.

"Did you get ahold of Alec?" My voice seemed somewhat hoarse. I cleared my throat and tried again. "Did he get away from the police?"

"Yes to both questions. We're going to meet him in Reykjavík."

"Why Reykjavík?" I asked as he got onto the highway that would take us into the capital.

"That is where the airport is."

"Alec is leaving?" I asked, my heart dropping despite the fact that I'd only just decided we had no future together. Still, it left me feeling oddly deflated to know I was being abandoned so thoroughly.

"We all are."

I glanced over at him, ignoring the little flutter in my stomach. "By 'we all' you mean you and him, not me, correct?"

"You're coming with us. The council will want to talk to you."

I stared at him in blank incomprehension. "You do realize that the police are after me, don't you? They are bound to be watching the airport. There's no way I can get out of Iceland, even if I wanted to, and quite frankly, I don't intend to go anywhere else with you. In fact, I'd appreciate it if you could drop me at the north end of Dalkafjordhur. I'll take it from there."

"Alec told me to take you to the airport," he answered without bothering to even glance toward me.

"And you always do what Alec says?" I asked waspishly, feeling some horrible need to be snarky to him. I beat it down as being a symptom of hurt feelings.

What did I care that a night spent (literally) rolling in the hay meant nothing to him? So he drank my blood and gave me the most incredible orgasm of my entire life, and then proceeded to act as if I was a complete stranger — no, not a stranger, a slight acquaintance who was barely tolerated. So what? It didn't mean I had to feel rejected. Again.

Damn Kristoff. Damn Alec. Damn, damn, damn.

"Hardly. But about this, we agree — the council wants to see you. He can't take you all the way to them, so I've been elected babysitter."

"Babysitter!" I gasped, outraged.

To my utmost surprise, a quick smile flickered on his lips. "I thought you might appreciate that term."

I was too incensed to be charmed by the smile, even though I had a feeling there were few enough of them. "So you intend to haul me in front of this vampire court? To charge me for crimes against other vampires? You know, as tempting as that thought is, I think I'll pass. A few days ago, I didn't even know you guys existed. I'm sorry that your girlfriend died at the hands of the Brotherhood, but I'm not going to make myself a martyr over it."

At the mention of his girlfriend, Kristoff's fingers tightened on the steering wheel. He said nothing, however, just kept driving.

I had no intention of being dragged out of the country, either. "Do you have any knockout drugs with you?" I asked in as calm and sweet a voice as I could muster.

He shot me a startled glance. "No."

"I see. Perhaps you have a gun?"

He frowned. "I prefer bladed weapons to guns."

"Ah. And do you have any knives, daggers, swords, axes, or other weaponry that might possess a blade upon you at this very moment?"

Another quick glance showed I had his interest. "At this moment? No. I left them behind since it's hard to get them through airport security."

"I imagine it is."

"In case you had any ideas, I'll point out

that I don't need a weapon to defend myself."

"Indeed." I was silent for a moment. "How about a Taser?"

His frown deepened. "What, exactly, are you getting at? That I'm unarmed? I admit to that, but if you think you can overpower me, you're sadly mistaken."

I smiled at him. "You yourself admitted you have no hypnotic powers, so how, exactly, do you propose to get me onto a plane?"

The light of understanding dawned in his eyes, his jaw and fingers tightening. "You wouldn't."

"On the contrary, I most definitely would. I will make the biggest scene that has ever been made in an airport. I will attract the attention of anyone with ears in a five-mile radius. I will bring down the full force of security, airport officials, and airplane employees. In short, I will throw the hissy fit to end all hissy fits. You'll have to drug me or knock me out to get me onto a plane, and I'm willing to bet that much as you talk tough, you're not going to hurt me."

He pulled the car over to the side of the road, and before I could even take a breath, he was leaning over me, one hand on my throat, squeezing out almost all the air. "I

263

have killed reapers before, and will kill them again. What makes you think you're any different?"

"You didn't marry any of them," I croaked, realizing with some surprise that something had changed since I'd spent the night with Kristoff — I no longer feared him.

His lips pulled back. "That was a sacrifice on my part to keep you from gaining your full powers."

"A sacrifice that ruined my life as well as yours," I said, swallowing as his fingers released their grip slightly. A little song of triumph sang in my head. I was right — he wasn't going to hurt me. He might be a revenge-motivated vampire, a man who thought nothing about killing those who tortured his own people, but there was something in him, something honorable that I must have sensed during the night.

His eyes narrowed in question.

"Not that I believe for one minute that the marriage ceremony you forced me into was legal, but let's just say it was. Did you ever stop to wonder what happens if you find a woman you really *do* want to marry? Or me? What if I run into the man of my dreams tomorrow? I won't be able to marry him."

"Marriage is a mortal legality." He snorted, releasing my throat to sit back in his seat. "It means nothing to Dark Ones."

"Well, it means something to me," I said, rubbing my throat. "And you ruined any chance I had of having happiness with a man."

His fingers twitched. "You do realize if you create a scene at the airport the police will be down upon you instantly?"

"Oh, I realize that. And thank you, I think I'd rather take my chances with the Icelandic police than a kangaroo court filled with vengeful vampires."

He sat staring out of the front window for a few minutes, clearly realizing that he wasn't going to be able to bully me into submitting to his wishes. "I should just dump you on Alec's lap and let him deal with you."

"I really do need to talk to him," I said, indulging in a little frown of my own. There was a lot I wanted to ask him, but more importantly, I needed to see how he felt about me. If he wanted to continue a relationship, I'd have to tell him about the night spent with Kristoff. And I could just imagine what his reaction would be to that.

Kristoff hesitated for another couple of seconds, then slammed his hands on the wheel and jerked the car into a very illegal, and highly dangerous, U-turn. "I will take you to Alec. I am through with this."

What was "this"? I wondered. Me? The whole situation? Seeking revenge for his girlfriend's death? I pondered that, and what I was going to say to Alec, while he drove us back to town.

CHAPTER 12

I blinked a few times to adjust my vision to the relatively dim light of the library as compared to the bright sunshine outside, smiling at a librarian who glanced up at me as I made my way to the very back of the library where I remembered that a small clutch of study carrels were arranged against the wall. As I thought, the area was empty. I plopped down on one of the carrels and waited.

"There you are!" Marta appeared out of nothing and wafted over toward me. "We were worried when you didn't come back! Is everything all right?"

"As all right as we can expect. I'm sorry I couldn't call you like I did the Brotherhood folk and let you know I was OK, but obviously, that wasn't possible with you all. Where are the others? Oh. Good morning, everyone. Can you gather around, please? I'm going to have to talk kind of quiet so no

one overhears. Er . . . please remain transparent, too. We don't need to wig out some
innocent library patron."

The ghosts appeared one by one, forming
a small circle around me, each of them with
an expectant look that I hated to dash,
however briefly. "First of all, I'm very sorry
for disappearing last night and not coming
back. I ran into a . . . well, you can call it a
situation with Kristoff, and I couldn't get
back here until now."

Ingveldur exchanged a knowing glance
with Old Agda, who cackled rustily and
said, "Had your wedding night, did you? I
told you that man of yours looked like a
lively one."

My cheeks flared in response. "It wasn't a
wedding night."

"Eh? Then why're you blushing like my
arse after a soak in the hot spring?" Agda
asked.

"It wasn't like that," I said quickly, intending to move on to important points.

"Maybe he wasn't any good," one of the
other women said. "Maybe he didn't have
stamina. I said it was important. A man
needs to be able to last more than a few
pokes."

"He lasted just fine —" I stopped myself,
closing my eyes for a moment to avoid look-

ing at the amusement in Agda's eyes. "My evening activities notwithstanding, I do have some news."

"You're with child?" Ingveldur said, her eyebrows raised. "That was quick work, although if he was particularly skillful, not surprising."

"I am not pregnant!" I said loudly, running my hands through my hair in agitation.

A woman with a handful of books paused at the nearest aisle and leaned out to look at me. I gave her a feeble smile. "Sorry."

She sniffed and moved away.

"Listen," I said, trying to will the blush to fade. My cheeks felt so hot I could probably fry an egg on them. "Last night I talked with the Brotherhood people. They explained to me how the whole Zorya thing works. I had to get married to one of their people, a man who represents the sun, to start the process of gaining powers. The next step is a ceremony tonight."

"You've gone and been married again?" Hallur asked.

"Is that legal?" asked Ulfur at the same time.

"It's perfectly legal because (A) it's not a real marriage — it's just some ceremony they conduct within their group — and (B) the marriage to Kristoff wasn't legal. I don't think. No, I'm sure it's not, so therefore, I'm still technically unmarried."

"But you've been bedded by your husband," Ingveldur said, frowning.

"Which one?" Hallur asked. "I'm confused."

"The first husband, the Dark One," Agda said. "My gold is on him. He looks to have the wind for a long race."

"What about the other husband?" Hallur asked, still puzzled. "Did he bed you, too? Just how many men have you bedded since you've arrived here?"

"She gets two husbands? I want to be a Zorya!" announced the teenage Dagrun. Her mother shushed her.

"That's not the sort of question you ask a woman," Ingveldur went on to tell Hollur. "And by my count, it's three."

"I didn't sleep with Mattias. And it's only two!" I took a deep breath, trying to calm my frazzled nerves.

"Two in two days. That's a pretty good start, if you ask me," Agda said. "But don't let that stop you bedding your other husband. Try his paces and then make a decision about which stallion you'll keep in your stable."

"I am not keeping a stable of lovers or

270

husbands!" I said, desperately trying to get off the subject.

"You just took another husband," Ulfur pointed out. "I believe more than one would qualify as a stable."

"Will you people just forget Mattias? He's not really important!" I said, wanting to scream and tear my hair out at the same time.

"Well, I think that Dark One of yours'll think he's important," Agda said, nodding.

I opened my mouth to dispute that, allowed my mind to dwell on what Kristoff's reaction would be to the fact that I had taken another step toward gaining Zorya powers, and closed it again.

"Do you think so?" Ingveldur looked thoughtful for a moment before nodding. "Aye, I reckon you're right."

I took a deep, deep breath, involving approximately half of the available oxygen in the room. "Do you people want to go to Ostri?"

They all nodded, including Ragnar.

"Then you need to listen closely. I cannot take you there until I have undergone a ritual."

"One involving your husband?" Ingveldur asked, a faint wrinkle on her forehead.

"Which husband? The Dark One or the

271

one named Mattias?" Hallur asked, scratching his head. "Who is the third man? Is he a husband, too?"

"Will you forget about my husband!"

"Which —" Hallur started to say.

"All of them!" I squawked. "Just forget all of them! Forget they ever existed! This has *nothing* to do with *any* man in my life, whether or not I've slept with them!"

"Seems to me that you've slept with all the ones you *have* met," Agda's voice said from behind the others.

"Argh!" I wanted to scream, and spent a moment looking for something to throw.

"She hasn't slept with me," Ulfur said with a rakish grin.

"I'd rather sleep with Ragnar than you!" I growled, pushed beyond my endurance.

"Would you, now," the stamina woman drawled, looking at the horse with speculation.

I swear to god that Ragnar winked at me.

I dropped down into the chair next to the carrel, my head in my hands as I tried to keep myself from screaming. Or sobbing. It was a toss-up which I'd go with.

"You're saying we have to wait here until you complete this ritual tonight before we can go to Ostri?" Marta's soft voice cut through the mental hysterical screaming that filled my mind.

"Yes. Thank you. A voice of sanity at last." I took a couple more deep breaths, then rose and faced the maddening group of ghosts. "You should know that there's a possibility that I won't be able to take you to Ostri. If that's so, I will find someone who can take you — you don't have to worry about that."

"You won't be taking us?" Karl asked, his brow wrinkled. "But why?"

"It's a bit complicated. It hinges really on whether or not my marriage to Kristoff is legal. If it is, then the one to Mattias isn't, and that means I'm still a Zorya-in-waiting. If it isn't, then I'll be a true Zorya, and I should be able to find Ostri for you. Either way, I want you all to know that I will make sure you're taken care of. I'm not going to abandon you until you've made it there."

The ghosts looked as confused as I felt.

"Regardless of all that, you seem to be safe at the library, so I want you to stay here until I can finish the official Zorya recognition process, at which point we'll know the answer to the question about which marriage is valid. OK?"

"Oooh, look, it's the husband," Dagrun called from where she was perched on another carrel.

"Which one?" Hallur asked, craning his neck. "Oh. That one."

Kristoff emerged from between two stacks, pausing for a moment with an odd expression on his face as he glanced around. "Who are all these spirits?"

My eyebrows rose as I checked that none of them had slipped into solid form. "You can see them?"

"Yes." He frowned at them. "How many have you collected?"

"Sixteen, counting Ragnar."

Ragnar snuffled the back of Kristoff's head. The latter swatted him away. "I've reached Alec. He will be here in a few minutes. He is not happy."

"Welcome to my world," I said, eyeing Kristoff. "How come you can see my ghosts? You couldn't see them the other night, could you?"

"No," he answered, doing a double take at Dagrun, who was openly leering at him. He looked back at me with one of his regulation frowns. "Why are you keeping them here?"

"It's the safest spot we could find."

"Safe from what?"

Ragnar snuffled Kristoff again. Kristoff turned around, glared at the horse, then made an elaborate gesture that had the horse opening its eyes wide for a moment before it disappeared.

"Holy . . . what did you just do?" I asked, taking a couple of steps forward to make sure Ragnar really was gone.

"The horse was annoying me." Kristoff looked at Hallur, who was standing next to him, examining his clothing closely. The second Hallur realized he had gained Kristoff's attention, he gave an embarrassed smile and backed off quickly.

"I didn't think you had any powers. You said you didn't!"

"I said I didn't have any powers against mortals." His lips tightened as he gazed at all the ghosts. "I do have some against spirits."

The group backed off as one body.

"But where did Ragnar go?" I asked, since I knew Ulfur was fond of the horse.

"Nowhere. I just dispersed his energy. As soon as he gathers it back up, he'll be back. But not, I trust, before we leave. Are you ready?"

"Yeah, I guess so. Does anyone have any questions?"

"I do," Dagrun said, smiling with wicked intent at Kristoff. "Does this husband know about your *other* husband?"

The floor dropped out from under my

feet. Oh, not literally, but it sure felt that way. I stared with wide, blank, deer-caught-in-the-headlights-of-a-really-big-truck-driven-by-a-deer-hating-maniac eyes at Kristoff, who turned his head slowly to me.

"Other husband?" he asked. "Were you married before?"

"Hush, child." Ingveldur bustled over to Dagrun. "That'll be enough from you."

"Before? I'm talking about the husband she wed yesterday." Dagrun snorted, evading her mother. "You know, the reaper husband."

"You married a reaper," Kristoff said after a moment's pregnant silence during which my mind had come to a screeching halt. His voice was flat and emotionless.

"Who married a reaper? Ah, love, there you are. How I've missed seeing you. You are looking particularly lovely this morning, but that shouldn't surprise me in the least since you are the epitome of loveliness. Miss me?" Alec strolled out of the stacks looking just as handsome as ever, his long hair pulled back in a ponytail, his leather jacket slung casually over one shoulder. His eyes twinkled merrily at me as he took one of my hands and kissed my knuckles in a lingering manner that probably would have melted me at any other time.

As it was, I was feeling somewhat as if I'd been turned to stone. "Um . . . yes," I said, my gaze flickering between him and Kristoff, who, oddly enough, also seemed to be sporting a stony appearance.

"That's the other Dark One she bedded?" Dagrun asked, moving around to get a better look at Alec before turning amazed eyes on me. "This is so unfair! Why can't I be a Zorya?"

"Love? Is something the matter?" Alec asked, his smile slipping a smidgen.

"I have just been informed that the Zorya has wed the sacristan." Kristoff finally spoke. His voice was flinty and remote.

"She has?" Alec frowned at me, then glanced around. "Who informed you?"

"One of the spirits," Kristoff said, waving toward Dagrun.

The little wretch had the nerve to grin at him.

"One who may just not find herself going to Ostri after all," I said in an undertone with a particularly potent look her way.

She stuck out her tongue at me.

"Child!" Ingveldur smacked Dagrun on the shoulder. "You do not behave such to the Zorya."

"Spirits? What spirits?" Alec asked. His frown deepened as he eyed me.

"You don't see them?" Kristoff asked.

"No."

Both men frowned at me now. The ghosts all stood around watching expectantly, obviously enjoying the strange soap opera my life had become.

"Why don't we go somewhere a little less public to discuss things," I suggested wearily. I couldn't look Alec in the eye — it was too unnerving with Kristoff standing right there pretending nothing had happened the night before, particularly when both men stood discussing my marriage to a third. I shook my head at my own thoughts and waved a hand at the ghosts. "I saw a restaurant a couple of blocks from here where we can have some breakfast and talk."

"All of us?" asked Ulfur, giving Kristoff a doubtful look.

"No, you guys stay here, where you're safe. I'll be back as soon as I can."

"Take care of yourself, child," Agda said, her eyes alight with mischief. "And get some food into your belly. By the look your man is giving you, you're going to be needing it."

I know Kristoff heard her because his expression grew blacker as I passed. I tried not to burst into hysterics as I left.

"Ragnar!" Ulfur cried as Alec, Kristoff,

and I left the library. "You've come back!"

"Which one is her man?" Hallur's voice asked, drifting out after us. "And are any of them her husbands?"

Alec found us a quiet, nearly empty pub that served food, with a dark interior where the two vampires could sit without being in direct sunlight.

"I've missed you, love," Alec said as he escorted me back to a semicircular booth in the back. He pulled me close, as if he was going to kiss me.

I squirmed out of his hold, casting a quick glance at the still stony-faced Kristoff.

Alec laughed, gently tucking a strand of hair behind my ear. "Don't tell me you're shy all of a sudden?"

"No, it's . . ." I glanced toward Kristoff. "There's something I need to tell you."

"Tell away," Alec said cheerfully, pulling out the table so I could scoot around into the seat.

He sat close to me on my right, his leg pressed against mine in a casually intimate gesture. It was both thrilling and disconcerting. Mostly the latter.

Kristoff took a seat just about as far from me as he could on the left. I gave my order to the waitress, absently noticing that while

Kristoff waved away the idea of a meal, Alec duplicated my order.

"I thought you guys didn't eat food very often," I said in a low voice to Alec as the waitress toddled off.

He looked surprised for a moment, then sent Kristoff a rueful smile. "You told her who we are?"

"It seemed best," was the curt reply.

Kristoff avoided my eye just as much as I tried to avoid his. I felt incredibly uncomfortable. There I was, fat, frumpy, and almost forty, a woman so desperate to find a man, she had to take a singles' tour, sitting between two of the most gorgeous men I'd ever in my life seen, men I'd engaged in sex with, and I was so uncomfortable, I seriously thought about just walking away from it all.

Only I couldn't. It wasn't just about me now. There were others involved, others I had to consider.

Alec took my hand. "I see. I'm sorry, Pia. I would have told you, but most women don't take well to the idea of Dark Ones, and I didn't want you to slip away from me."

My level of discomfort rose significantly. I squirmed.

"You're all right with it?" he asked, kissing my fingers again, gazing at me over them with pleading eyes.

I defy any woman not to melt in that situation.

"Well . . . I was a little taken aback, but I knew you couldn't be evil," I told him, guilt interfering with my pleasure.

"I should have known you'd understand." He kissed my knuckles again. "So what is it you wanted to tell me?"

I gently pulled my hand back, trying to find a sophisticated way to tell him. In the end, my mouth took over and just blurted it out. "Kristoff and I slept together."

Alec froze, his smile fading. "You what?"

"We slept together." I took a deep breath. Kristoff slid me a surprised glance. Clearly he hadn't been expecting me to reveal the truth about what had happened. For some odd reason, that hurt. "It wasn't intentional. That is, we didn't plan it. It just sort of happened. I was cold, and he shared his blanket with me, and one thing led to another, and . . . well, you can fill in the rest."

Alec turned his gaze to his friend. "You slept with my woman?"

"Yes," Kristoff said, an interesting parade of emotions passing quickly through his eyes. Surprise, speculation, and acceptance all passed by. "Yes, I did. As the Zorya said, it meant nothing."

"My *name* is Pia," I said through clenched teeth, hurt by his words. I hadn't said it meant nothing. Was that what he really thought? I wanted to curl up into a ball and sob for an hour or two.

"You *slept* with her?" Alec asked again, obviously having difficulty with that point.

"I'm very sorry if you're hurt," I said, trying to focus on him and not the hateful monster sitting on my other side. "I didn't intend to betray you in that way. Obviously things can't be the same between us now, but I do want you to know —"

"You knew she was my woman, and you just . . . what? Thought you'd screw her while I wasn't around?" Alec interrupted me to ask Kristoff.

The two men glared at each other.

"It wasn't like that —" I started to say, but this time Kristoff cut me off.

"I just told you it meant nothing. We've had each other's women before — what's the problem now?"

"The problem," Alec growled, jabbing a finger toward me, "is that she is mine. You knew that and you didn't care."

Kristoff said something in what I was sure was Italian. Alec answered in German. The two of them started arguing in their respective languages, both clearly understanding each other, and I reflected for a moment on just how annoying it was that the only language other than English of which I had a reasonable comprehension was Spanish.

"*Habla español,* anyone?" I asked, feeling hurt, abused, and left out, not to mention extremely guilty about trampling all over Alec's finer feelings.

You made your bed with another man in it, my inner critic said. *Now you have to sleep in it alone.*

"You want her? You can have her," Kristoff suddenly said in English, his lovely deep voice sounding very frayed about the edges. He snatched up his leather jacket and, without a single look my way, stormed out of the pub.

CHAPTER 13

I stared in amazement at the retreating figure of Kristoff, guilt rising with every second.

"Alec, I'm so sorry," I said miserably, slumping down and wishing I could just melt into the floor.

He frowned. "Sorry about what?"

"About everything." I waved a hand toward the door through which Kristoff had just made his stormy exit. "Coming between you two. Sleeping with him. Ruining our relationship."

To my complete and utter stupefaction, he laughed, taking my hand again. "Sweet, adorable Pia — do you think I hold you responsible for Kristoff forcing himself on you?"

I goggled. I truly goggled at him, and I don't believe I've outright goggled at anyone before.

"I've known Kristoff for at least three

hundred years. We've worked together for the council, you see, so I know well what sort of mesmerizing power he holds over women." He glanced at his watch and pulled out a cell phone. "Stay here. I'll be back in a minute."

I continued to be stupefied, and goggled a bit more as he strode off, and ducked outside the door.

"I've lost my mind," I told myself, going back over the last couple of minutes, and looking up to ask, "Did he just say he didn't blame me?"

The waitress gave me a bit of an odd look as she deposited our plates. "I don't know. Are you to blame?"

I thought for a moment. "Yes. I wasn't forced, no matter what Alec says."

"Well, then." She nodded as if that settled the matter, and toddled off to deal with other customers.

"My life has become one long confusing situation after another," I told my breakfast.

The door at the front of the pub opened. I glanced up, expecting to see Kristoff, but the two people who entered had me half rising to my feet.

"I'm so hungry I could eat one of those adorable Viking ponies we saw the other day," Magda said, laughing up at Ray. He murmured something and was about to hold out a chair for her when she glanced at the back of the room, freezing momentarily when she saw me. "Oh, dammit, Ray, I left my camera back in my room. I'm so famished I'm going to faint if I don't get some juice or something. Would you mind horribly going back to get it for me?"

Ray must have objected slightly, because Magda stood on her tiptoes and flicked her tongue on the tip of his nose. "It's not the same. I want *my* camera. You wouldn't want me worrying about it all day, would you?"

I wondered absently what it would be like to flick my tongue over the tip of Kristoff's nose . . . Alec's nose! I meant Alec's nose!

My inner critic shook her head at the slip.

Ray, putty in Magda's adept hands, hurried off to do her bidding. She waited until the door was fully closed behind him before making a beeline to me.

"There you are! I wondered what happened to you last night. I tried checking on you this morning, but you were gone, which really wasn't a surprise, because there's no way I'd stay in that room if the police could come barging in at any moment. Which evidently they did, since there were a couple of them in there when I looked for you. They were a bit rude about it, actually, and locked my door to the bathroom, so we had to use the one at the end of the hall again. Are you all right? Did you get your things? How did your wedding night go?"

"I'm fine, just a bit confused, but you know, it's becoming a familiar emotion. And yes, I got my things. The rest of the tour isn't going to show up at any moment, are they? If they are, I'd better leave now."

"No, no, eat your breakfast. That waffle looks delicious. I think I'll get one once Ray comes back, which should be in about ten minutes or so. You skipped answering the question about the wedding night," she pointed out helpfully.

I blushed.

"That good, was it? I have to admit, I don't go for the Viking type, myself, but Mattias seemed nice enough."

My blush deepened. I tried to hide it by eating some of the delicious-looking breakfast that sat before me, but I was so filled with guilt, I couldn't swallow a single bite.

"Either you're having two breakfasts, or the new hub is here with you," Magda said, pushing Alec's food slightly to the side so she could lean her elbows on the table. "In the men's room, is he? Don't worry, I won't intrude when he comes back. I know how it is with honeymooners."

287

"For heaven's sake, Magda!" I finally snapped. "You know it's not like that!"

She laughed, whomping me on the arm. "Finally got a reaction out of you that wasn't an embarrassed blush. Of course I know it's not like that, but I couldn't resist teasing you. Although . . ." She eyed me a bit more closely. "You do have that air about you of a woman well satisfied."

My mind drifted to the activities of the last evening and my face reddened even more.

"Ooh, I think I struck a nerve. So it wasn't all sacrifice for a good cause with the manly Viking, eh?"

"I didn't spend the night with Mattias," I muttered, shoving my whipped-cream-drenched waffle around the plate.

"No?" Her eyebrows rose. "Oh, with what's his name . . . Alec?"

"No. Kristoff."

Her eyebrows rose even higher. "Really, now. And you . . . ?"

"I didn't mean to," I said hurriedly, desperately wanting a shoulder to cry on, someone who would understand what had happened. Someone who could make sense of it all for me, because clearly I was beyond that. "It just kind of happened."

"Wow," she said softly, watching me with

sympathy in her eyes. "And now you feel guilty about it?"

I nodded. "Horribly so. At the time, it just seemed so . . . right. Kristoff was there, and he . . . he . . . oh, it sounds hokey, but I felt like he needed me. Me — not just a woman, but me. And despite everything, I gave in, and now Alec is back and he and Kristoff had a fight about it, and I just don't know what to do. Or think. I'm so confused about everything, Magda. I keep hoping that things will straighten out so I can make sense of them, but they just get more and more complicated."

"Men will do that to you," she said, patting my arm. "They mess with your head."

"No, that's not what I mean. They're not playing mind games with me . . . at least I don't think they are. . . . It's just . . . Oh, it's so hard to explain. The reapers tell me the vampires are bad. I know they are — Kristoff killed a man right in front of me, and neither he nor Alec makes any bones about working for some murderous council that sanctions the killing of reapers."

"So that pretty much cinches who killed the other Zorya," she said quietly, still watching me intently.

I rubbed my forehead. I felt a headache coming on. "Not necessarily. They said they

289

didn't. Or at least Kristoff said he didn't, and the damned thing is, I believe him. I believe — oh, hello."

Alec appeared as if by magic, smiling benignly at Magda before turning his attention to me. "I hope I don't interrupt?"

"Not at all. This is my friend Magda. She's on the tour with me."

"Alec Darwin," he said, scooting in on the other side of me.

"I'm sitting in your seat," Magda murmured, about to leave.

"Don't mind me; I'm just here to gaze with admiration upon the fair Pia," he said, shooting me a positively steamy look.

Magda's gaze flickered back and forth between Alec and myself.

There was a moment of uncomfortable silence. I took a deep breath. "Alec, there's something I think you should know."

"Another confession?" he asked, giving me a quizzical look before glancing toward Magda. "Are you going to tell me that she is your lover, too?"

"No."

Magda stifled a giggle.

I didn't think it was possible for me to blush any harder, but I'll be damned if my cheeks didn't light up even more. Wearily, I held a glass of water to one side of my face in an attempt to cool it down. "She knows about you and Kristoff. About what you are."

"Ah," he said, eyeing her with a little less happiness. "Does she indeed."

"I do," she answered gravely. "I was with Pia for much of last night, you see. Well, not the part she spent with the other . . . that is, I was with her while she met with the . . ." Magda floundered a couple of times, stuck in a verbal dead end in her attempt to not broach the touchy subjects of my time spent with Kristoff or the Brotherhood folk. She gave a feeble smile. "Let's just say I was with her. I helped her get her things out of the hotel room. And I know about Anniki."

"Ah," Alec repeated, leaning back. "The Zorya, I presume you mean."

"How did you know she was a Zorya?" I asked slowly, my head starting to pound. It seemed to me as if the room darkened a smidgen. I glanced at the window, but it appeared to be sunny outside, not clouding over as I surmised. "I didn't know who she was when we . . . when we went back to my hotel room."

"Didn't you?" He frowned, toying with a glass of water. "I thought you said she was."

"I think what Pia's trying to ask and is too nice to do so is whether or not you killed her," Magda said bluntly.

Alec glanced at her in surprise before turning his lovely green eyes on me. "Is that what you think? That I killed the Zorya?"

"You did leave without saying anything to me," I pointed out. "I didn't know what to think when I woke up to find you gone and a dead woman in my bathroom."

"But I left you a note," he said, frowning, his eyes sincere. "I told you I had to leave unexpectedly to handle some business, but that I'd be in contact later in the day. You didn't get that?"

"No," I answered, shaking my head. "A note?"

"Yes. I left it in the bathroom so you'd be sure to see . . . Ah. I begin to see it. Whoever murdered that Zorya must have taken my note. My sweet, sweet love. What you must have thought of me!" he said, wrapping an arm around me and pulling me up close to him, his lips whispering along my jaw. "I'm surprised you didn't run screaming from me."

"Or at least stick a stake through your heart," Magda said, watching us with interest.

Alec broke off nibbling on my face to grin at her. "Beheading is the preferred method of execution for Dark Ones. Staking is difficult unless you know exactly where the heart is." His gaze returned to me, rueful and contrite. "Not that I would blame Pia for thinking the worst of me. Forgive me, my love?"

"I . . . I . . ." I stammered a little, not knowing what to say. I was relieved at the thought that he hadn't just up and left me without a word, but at the same time, I was incredibly bothered by the idea that either Kristoff had lied to me, or someone else, a stranger, had marched through my room while I was sleeping. "I didn't think the worst, Alec, so there's nothing to forgive. But it does leave the question of who killed Anniki. And why she was killed in my room."

"I was thinking about that," Magda said, absently pulling a strawberry from my plate and eating it. "You said that you'd run into Anniki earlier in the evening, right? She got the stone from you and told you all about Zorya-ing."

"More or less, yes. But the Brotherhood people were here. She knew that. So there's no reason why she should try to seek me out over them."

Alec's gaze narrowed sightlessly on the glass of water. "Not unless she was afraid of seeking help from them."

I stared at him in surprise. "Why would she be afraid of them?"

He shrugged. "Perhaps she had a change of heart about the reapers. Perhaps she learned something about them that made her hesitate committing herself to them. I think, my love, you've had a very narrow escape, and although I am not pleased with Kristoff's high-handed actions in marrying you himself rather than allowing me to do so, it relieves my mind to know that you are safe from the reapers."

Magda and I exchanged glances.

She was about to speak when the door opened and Ray entered. "And there's my cue to make a graceful exit." She pressed my hand quickly. "Call me later, OK?"

"I'll try," I said, giving her a grateful smile. "You're supposed to go to the glacier today, aren't you? Have fun."

"Will do. It was nice meeting you, Alec," she said, standing up.

Alec rose and took her hand, bowing over it. "It is a pleasure to meet a friend of Pia's. We will be moving on to Vienna shortly, but I hope to see you again soon."

Magda sent me a curious glance, but murmured only a polite good-bye before hurrying to intercept Ray before he saw me. She hustled him out of the restaurant without a look back.

"Vienna?" I asked, trying to postpone the discussion that I knew had to be had. "Why are you going to Vienna?"

His eyes were as warm as his smile as he scooted back in, pulling me over so I was smooshed up against him, and brushing a strand of hair back off my forehead. "That's where the council is based. Kristoff told me of your reticence to meet with them, but I fear it will be required. You truly are a most remarkable woman, Pia. You thought I had left you without a word, and not once did you chastise me, as any other woman might. I can't believe my fortune in finding you."

His lips were warm on mine, coaxing me, teasing me into opening up for him. I allowed him to kiss me, my mind divided between acknowledgment of his expertise and the awareness of just how different an experience it was compared to the overwhelming, forceful invasion that was Kristoff's method of kissing. Where the latter was constantly dominating and aggressive, Alec's kisses were sweet little sips. He nibbled my lower lip for a moment before moving a line of kisses along my jaw. "My adorable one. I am so hungry for you. Can you feel it?"

I glanced down at his lap, somewhat

startled that he was feeling aroused in such a public place.

His chuckle sounded warm and breathy on my ear, making little shivers of delight ripple down my back. "Actually, I meant literally hungry for you, although I desire you in that way, as well. Will you yield to me, my love? Will you give me what only you can?"

"People can see us," I protested, reluctant to do what he wanted. Why, I had no idea . . . it just seemed wrong.

"No one will notice," he murmured, pressing a hot kiss to the sensitive spot behind my ear. "Give to me, my love. Let me taste again the nectar that only you can provide."

Why not? my inner critic said with a mental shrug. He knows what happened last night and doesn't blame you. Why not let him go for broke?

Because it's wrong, a tiny little voice answered.

There was that word again — "wrong." It felt wrong, but for the life of me, I couldn't decide why.

"What happens if you're somewhere without people?" I asked, stalling just a little bit. "Somewhere isolated?"

He made a face. "We can survive on the blood of animals if we have to. It is not preferred, although sometimes necessary, such as when we are separated from loved ones. But that will not happen with us."

Absently, I fingered my fork, trying to analyze my reluctance.

"Pia, my love, you hesitate. You wound me. Can it be that you prefer Kristoff?" Alec asked, pulling back.

His jade eyes were filled with pain.

"No, of course not." I felt lower than a snake's belly — here was a perfectly nice man, a man who cared about me, one who I knew was trying his best to help me, and I was spurning him for what? Kristoff? Mentally, I shook my head at that. I didn't want Kristoff. I might not be deathly afraid that he would kill me, but there was a darkness in him that boded ill for everyone. It wasn't for Mattias's sake, either, that I was hesitating. So then why was I not at this moment allowing Alec what he wanted?

"It is me, then," Alec said, withdrawing both physically and emotionally. "I have failed to capture your heart as you have mine."

"The situation with Kristoff," I said, using a feeble excuse. "It's —"

"Unimportant. You worry unduly that I blame you, love. I do not. I have known Kristoff for a long time. He has taken many women from me." Alec's lips curled in a wry smile. "And I have repaid the compliment, but you he shall not steal. You are mine . . . if you wish to be."

"I think that's the sweetest thing anyone has ever said to me. I'm flattered beyond belief, but after last night . . . well, I think I need to take things a little slower. I like you, Alec. I like you a lot. And if you really want to" — I waved my hands around vaguely — "for lack of a better word, feed off me, then go ahead."

His smile was tinged with regret. "I have rushed you, have I not? For that, I am sorry, and we will, naturally, proceed slower if that is your desire. You must forgive me for being impatient, my love, but when you have lived as long as I have, you have little tolerance for being made to wait."

I opened my mouth to protest, but he silenced me with a swift kiss. "No, you are right. You must have time. And I will be happy to give it to you, but I am very hungry for you, and since you said I may . . ."

He waited until the waitress, who had been within sight, moved off before returning to the spot behind my ear. "You do not know how much I anticipate this moment."

I clutched the edge of the table, bracing

myself as if for an injection, torn between a desire to run away and a guilty sense of obligation.

The pain, when it came, was almost instantly over. Alec jerked back with an astonished look on his face, a smear of blood on his lip, which he quickly wiped off.

"Is something wrong?" I started to ask, but at that exact moment, several things happened in a whirlwind of action.

Two people who had been strolling toward us stopped, one of them pointing and calling out, "Dark One!"

The waitress, hearing that, dropped her tray and snatched up a steak knife, vaulting a table as she lunged toward us.

Alec leaped to his feet and jerked me after him, literally dragging me out from behind the table. A slight shimmer to one side resolved itself into the form of Marta, who clutched at me with intangible hands.

"Pia! You must come! The Ilargi has found us! He's taken Jack the sailor, and now he's trying to get Karl!"

CHAPTER 14

"Stay back!" I ordered Marta, which was utterly foolish because no one but me could see her, let alone harm her.

"The light must purge him!" the man who had screamed out the warning about Alec shouted as he, his companion, and the waitress closed in on us. "We must take him back for cleansing!"

"Run!" Alec said, pulling a gun from his jacket. He shoved his cell phone into my hands. "If I am captured, Kristoff will help."

"But —"

"Run, my love!" He pushed me to the side as he waved the weapon at the three on-comers. The other people in the restaurant, alerted by the scene, leaped to their respective feet at the sight of the gun, stampeding to the door with various startled cries and warnings.

"I'm not going to leave you," I said softly, assessing the three people who were now warily eying Alec's gun. I didn't recognize them, which meant they likely didn't know who I was. "If I can explain to them who I am —"

"Don't be stupid — they'll kill you before you could get the words out of your mouth. Get out of here now, while you can."

"You don't understand," I said, reluctant to explain that in the Brotherhood's eyes, I was the new Zorya. "If you let me have a word with them —"

"Go!" he bellowed, and threw himself forward, knocking down two of the three Brotherhood people. The waitress rushed me with a frenzied look in her eyes, one that, coupled with the sharp knife in her hand, triggered my flight instinct. I leaped over the ball of writhing men on the floor, and bolted for the door. Pain burned deep as the waitress lunged at me, the knife slashing into the flesh of my arm.

She yelled something at me, but Alec, in a supreme effort, kicked out with one of his legs and sent her flying.

"Pia!" Marta cried, running alongside me as I hared down the sidewalk, ignoring the startled glances of passersby. I spun around a corner and headed for the busy center square, panic spurring my flight.

"Pia, what was all that about?" Marta

asked as I dashed into a covered alley that featured arts and crafts booths.

"It's a long story," I panted.

"You must come," she wailed, and I pulled up, dropping to my knees to hide behind a tarp-covered stack of soft-drink boxes that was located next to a food booth. "Jack, the sailor who was always looking for rum, he is gone. The Ilargi has taken him. And now he's back for Karl."

"I can't come right now," I gasped, trying both to get air into my lungs, and to keep my breathing down to a dull roar so any pursuers wouldn't hear it. "I'm a little busy."

"But you must!" Tears were evident in her voice. I looked up to see her standing before me, transparent as ever, but her face torn with anguish. "The Ilargi will claim Karl's soul just as he did Jack's if you do not stop him."

"They'll kill Alec if I don't find help," I told her, my heart torn in two.

Her lip trembled as fresh tears spilled down her face. "I love him, Pia. I love him so much. Please save him."

"But Karl is already dead, and Alec is . . . technically undead, I think, but still . . ."

The look of betrayal in her eyes wrung my heart.

"Marta," I said, hoping she'd understand,

but she stopped me with one word.

"Please."

I couldn't turn my back on her. I had sworn to the dying Anniki that I would take on her responsibilities, and I couldn't ignore that oath now just because Alec was in trouble.

"Let's go," I said, getting back on my feet and peering cautiously out down the line of vendors. No one seemed to be paying me any attention.

"Thank you," she said with a throb of gratitude. "We must hurry. The Ilargi will not be held off for long."

"Alec has lived several hundreds of years without being caught," I muttered to myself as we dashed off toward the library, winding our way around strolling sightseers and shoppers. "He won't let them catch him now. I hope."

"Hurry," Marta urged as I paused for a traffic light. "There is no time."

I don't know what the librarians thought as I flung myself through the doors. I only had a glimpse of startled expressions as I waved a friendly hand at them before heading to the back study area.

"The Zorya has come!" one of the women ghosts yelled out from her spot at the end of one of the stacks, evidently acting as sentry. "She has come!"

"About time, too," Dagrun sneered.

"Karl!" Marta screamed, rushing past me in a flurry of ghostly nothingness. "Is he . . . Karl!"

Just as I emerged from the stacks there was a loud crashing noise, followed immediately by the tinkle of glass.

"There! He's there!" Ulfur cried, rising from the ground and pointing at a shattered window.

"Karl?" I asked.

"I'm here," came the shaky, somewhat muffled reply. I ran to the window and looked out, voices calling behind me indicating that other library patrons had heard the crash.

"Did he take anyone else?" I asked softly.

"No. We wouldn't let him," Hallur said with grim victory in his voice as he faded to a translucent state. He limped slightly and appeared to be bleeding, but grinned. "He'll know better than to attack the lot of us again, he will."

A woman behind me, assumedly a librarian, stopped next to me and started pelting me with questions.

"I'm sorry. I'm American. I only speak English," I told her, clutching my side where a stitch pulled painfully.

"What has happened here?" the librarian asked, switching into flawless English. She waved a hand toward the window as others arrived, all of them viewing the display with confusion and ire.

"It looks to me like someone went through the window," I said, peering out of the shattered window to a tiny patch of greenery. A few people who evidently had been strolling through the area were clustered together, pointing at a direction opposite the library.

"I will call the police," the librarian said with thinned lips. She gave me a piercing glance. "You will not leave."

"No, of course not," I lied, giving her a bright smile.

She evidently issued orders to the other librarians, herding the patrons out of the bits of shattered glass. I waited until they had gone about fulfilling her commands before turning back to my ghosts.

"Come on, folks. We've got to find you all a new hiding spot."

I smiled at the patrons who stood in the stacks, chatting about what happened. They stopped talking when I flung myself out of the window, managing to tear the leg of my pants on a shard of glass I'd been taking pains to avoid.

"Do not hurt yourself, Pia," Ingveldur

called as they drifted out the window after me. "Oh! You are bleeding. Hallur, the reaper is bleeding."

"So am I. That Ilargi was a tough one. But we were stronger." His face sobered. "But it wasn't enough to save Jack."

"I know you tried," I said as we hurried away. "It's my fault, really. If I was any sort of a proper Zorya, I'd have had you to Ostri by now."

"Do not blame yourself," consoled Marta, clutching Karl's arm and sending him a look of love so profound it brought tears to my eyes. "If it was not for you, the Ilargi would have taken Karl, too."

"No, you all saved him," I said, feeling the full extent of my guilt.

"We were near the end of our strength," Ulfur confessed. "We could not have opposed him much longer. He ran because he heard you."

I felt moderately better, but strengthened my determination to see that my friends received their reward. If I couldn't take them, then I would move heaven and earth to find someone who could.

We managed to get away from the area just as the police sirens were heard, although I kept looking over my shoulder as we headed for the open spaces and busy area that was the waterfront park.

"Where are we going?" Ulfur asked as we pulled up en masse at the edge of the park.

"That is a very good question. I wish I had an answer to it." I scanned the area, looking for somewhere safe to hide for a bit while I made some plans. My arm burned with an increasing pain that I put down to the fading of adrenaline. I garnered some odd stares as people noticed the blood flowing down my arm, driving me to take up a position under the trees on the far side of the park.

"Pia, you are hurt. You should see a doctor," Marta's soft voice chided me.

I knelt in a slightly damp bed of discarded fir needles cast down by the tall tree that shielded me from the sight of the rest of the park, rocking for a moment as I tried to get a grip on the pain now radiating with increasing intensity from my arm.

"We should get to safety," Agda said, her voice even reedier than normal. "That Ilargi may come back."

"We can take care of him," Ulfur said, flexing his muscles in that time-honored male attitude of bravado.

"Aye, and just how are you expecting to do that?" Agda asked, squatting a few feet away from me. "I'm all done in. I don't think I could so much as move that pebble if my life depended on it."

There were murmurs of assent from the others.

My head swam suddenly.

"Pia?" Marta's face came into view. "She's fainting!"

"I'm all right, just a bit woozy from the loss of blood," I said, wrapping my tattered sleeve around the bleeding gash. The pain from that act almost left me retching. "I've got to find somewhere safe for you guys. Only I don't know of anywhere safe, and Alec might be captured, and Kristoff is gone off who knows where, and I don't even know where Magda is, and if the Brotherhood people find out I've been seen letting a vampire drink my blood, they may not listen to me. . . ."

"Weeping never served anyone," Agda said, peering at me as tears of self-pity welled in my eyes. "You've got a brain, child; use it."

I sniffled back the unshed tears and remembered the cell phone Alec had shoved into my hands. I'd stuffed it into my pocket absentmindedly as I made my escape from the restaurant. I pulled it out now with a minute sense of hope. I might not be high on Kristoff's list of people he was willing to aid, but he wouldn't turn his back on Alec, would he?

I brought up the phone's address book, quickly finding the number for Kristoff.

"What is she doing now?" Hallur asked, studying the cell phone with interest.

"She's calling someone. That's a mobile phone. I've told you about them. All the fishermen in the village have them," Dagrun said with the voice of a teen who can't believe how stupid adults are.

"I've told you not to hang around those docks." Ingveldur rounded on her. "They're too rowdy for a young lady."

Dagrun rolled her eyes. "I'm *dead!* They can't do anything to me! Besides, how do you expect me to keep up on things if I stay along the shore with the rest of you?"

"You might be dead, but I'll not have a daughter of mine making sheep's eyes at the local fishermen," the ghost I assumed was her father said gruffly.

Kristoff's short, "Yes?" in my ear interrupted the scene.

"Kristoff? This is Pia. I know you're pissed at both Alec and me, but I could really use your help." I described in succinct sentences the happenings of the last half hour.

The ghosts, prompted by Dagrun's description of a cell phone, crowded around with their heads pressed closely to mine so they could hear.

"Where are you now?" Kristoff asked in a weary voice.

"At the north end of the park, near the cliff. Behind a tree."

The silence that followed was rife with annoyance. "Stay there. I'll fetch you as soon as I can."

"You'd best be hurrying," Old Agda yelled. "The reaper is bleeding something fierce."

"I'm fine," I interrupted. "Just get here as soon as you can. I have a feeling the police are going to be crawling over this area any minute."

I slumped back against the hard face of the cliff that edged the park, closing my eyes in an attempt to keep a handle on my emotions, the sounds of the seagulls and ghosts as they chatted seeming to blend and blur in my mind until they lulled me into a state of unawareness.

Fingers on my wounded arm roused me from my stupor. Sharp eyes of the purest teal considered me when I jerked upright.

"You came," I said without thinking, a little spike of hope starting anew within me.

"You asked me to," he answered. His brows pulled together as he gently removed the wad of cloth I'd tried to bind around my arm. "This is deep. It is still bleeding."

"It hurts like the dickens, too." I tried to keep my voice light, but judging by the assessing glance he shot at me, I suspected I failed.

He hesitated for a moment. "You should see a doctor."

"I don't think that would be a very good idea, not unless you know of someone who can patch me up without involving the police."

"Can't you help her?" Ulfur asked Kristoff.

"I am not a healer." He gently probed the area around the deep cut, his fingertips coming away red with my blood.

Instantly, a deep, consuming hunger rose within me. I shook my head at the fantastic thought. The hunger was within him, not me . . . but how did I know that?

"But you're a Dark One," Ulfur insisted. "You can close a wound, can't you?"

"I must be going into shock," I said aloud in a distant, somewhat abstracted voice.

Kristoff stared at his fingertips, swallowing hard as he struggled to control the hunger.

"Oh, you might as well," I said, leaning back as I closed my eyes. At that moment, I didn't care what happened to me. I was tired and in pain, and I just wanted to go to sleep forever. Let someone else take my burdens for a bit. "The blood's there, why let it go to waste?"

"You must help her," Marta insisted.

"I'm going to take a little nap," I announced, my voice sounding distant even to me. "Do whatever you want."

I let myself drift, too tired to care anymore. Heat built up in my arm, a persistent sensation that wouldn't allow me to float away entirely. It was an annoying feeling, nagging at the edges of my awareness, pulling me back to a body that suddenly seemed too burdensome to bear.

I opened my eyes and found myself staring at the top of Kristoff's head, the rich brown curls a few inches from my nose. "What are you doing?"

He looked up, bumping his head on my chin. The warmth I felt had been his mouth on the gash, now partially closed in a raw-looking welt. "You've lost too much blood."

"You're healing me?" I asked, amazed and even more confused at the dichotomy of his actions. "I kind of got the impression you never wanted to see me again."

Irritation flashed across his face. "You summoned me, if you recall."

"Yes, but that was because I knew you'd want to help Alec. I didn't think you'd give a snap about me."

He was silent for a moment, his expression stony and unreadable. "Alec would have my head if I let you bleed to death while I rescued him."

"Yes," I said, insight coming with a rare burst of clarity. "Did you drink enough? You seemed awful hungry."

A look of indignation flickered in his eyes. "I am not so desperate that I must prey on wounded women. I closed your wound, nothing more. If I have your permission, I will finish so we can ascertain what trouble Alec has managed to find now."

I nodded, watching with interest as his mouth moved over the remainder of my wound. Something like that would have grossed me out a few days before, but the touch of his mouth on my skin was sensual, erotic, and anything but repulsive. It sent little shivers of pleasure up and down my arms, and it was only with a great effort that I managed to keep my face placid.

"That's so weird," Dagrun said sulkily from the pack of ghosts, who were clustered around, watching intently. "I thought you said you couldn't heal."

"I can't, not in the true sense of the word.

But I can stop the bleeding. It is a necessity for Dark Ones to know how to do so," Kristoff said as he examined his handiwork. The entire wound was closed now, still somewhat red and raw, but not open or bleeding. Dried blood pulled at my skin, however, making it feel itchy. "It would not do to have one's source of blood hemorrhaging to death. Are you able to stand?"

The last bit was addressed to me. I nodded and got to my feet, staggering a moment when the blood seemed to rush from my head. Kristoff's hands were warm on my arms as he steadied me. "I'm OK. We'd better go see what's happening to Alec. If he'd only let me explain to the Brotherhood guys who I was, I'm sure I could have avoided the whole scene."

"Don't count on it," he said grimly, adjusting the collar of his coat and picking up a hat he must have taken off earlier. Without another word, he turned and strode off.

I looked at my collection of ghosts. They looked back at me, oddly silent. I realized that they were waiting to see whether I was going to abandon them or not.

"Right. I'm not quite sure how we're all going to fit into the car. Especially Ragnar."

"Don't worry about that," Ingveldur said

with a smile. "We'll all dematerialize."

"You can do that? Excellent."

"I'm too old for that sort of foolishness," Agda said with dignity. "I will ride in the vehicle. I've always wanted to, ever since they started coming to the new village."

"You rode on the bus with the rest of us," Hallur pointed out as we started toward the now distant figure of Kristoff.

"It's not the same. I will ride in this mortal car."

"I want to ride, too," Dagrun said quickly. "I want to watch *him*."

There was no doubt whom she was referring to.

Ingveldur rolled her eyes. "You'll be behaving yourself, in that case. I won't have you giving the reaper any difficulties."

Ulfur patted his horse's nose. "Don't worry about us — I'll ride after you."

I thought Kristoff was going to kick up a fuss when the ghosts started piling into the car, but as one by one they disappeared — except Agda, Dagrun, and Hallur (who claimed he was there to keep an eye on the two women) — he said nothing, just asked where I thought Alec would be taken.

"The only place I know of that the Brotherhood uses is the church and house behind it. Do you think they'd harm him?"

315

"Without you? Probably not seriously. They'll wait for their so-called ritual before they kill him," Kristoff said matter-of-factly.

I opened my mouth to tell him there was no way I'd participate in a ceremony that would bring harm to anyone, let alone the man who had more or less professed his love for me, but Kristoff continued with a curious look cast my way.

"Why did you proceed with the marriage to the sacristan when you knew it was invalid?"

"For one, I don't know that the marriage you forced me into is legal."

"It is," he said flatly.

"And for another," I continued, "I decided that you had a point about them not being happy to see me if they knew I was married to you. Which meant I had no reason *not* to marry Mattias when they pushed the ceremony. Normally I wouldn't do something so underhanded, but . . ." I bit my lip, absently rubbing the welt on my arm where the knife had cut.

"But you realized the end justified the means?" Kristoff gave a sharp nod. "I understand now."

"No, you don't, because that isn't why I did it. It's confusing. I just thought that I'd like to see a little more about them. I mean,

I've heard what you've had to say about the Brotherhood. I've heard what they've said about your people, too, and while both sides seem reasonable, neither one meshes completely. One of you has to be bad, and the other good. I'm just trying to figure out who is who. Unfortunately — oh, crap!"

Kristoff slammed on the brakes as we came upon a traffic backup. While there weren't many cars in line, it was the police cars with flashing lights that sent my heart into my throat.

"What is it? Some sort of a checkpoint?" I asked as Kristoff opened his window and leaned out to see what was happening.

His expression was grim as he sat back down. "Cordon. It's likely they're checking ID for everyone leaving the town."

"But we're not leaving," I pointed out.

Kristoff grunted and took a left turn into a bank parking lot. "No, but this road leads out of town. Get out. We'll walk the rest of the way."

"But I was enjoying the ride," Agda protested as she crawled out of the backseat.

"Are you sure that's wise?" I asked Kristoff as I got out, noting that the police were also stopping people on the street.

"We don't have much of a choice. This way." He flipped up the collar of his coat and angled his hat, moving immediately to the side of the street that was in the shade.

The ghosts came back from absolute invisibility to their normal nearly translucent state, trailing behind in an odd sort of train as I followed Kristoff through winding streets. I was worried about an intersection right outside of the church. Five roads met there in a cobblestone square, and the police, if they were searching people, would be sure to have someone there.

Kristoff didn't even pause as we reached the five-cornered intersection. He wrapped one arm around me, pulling me up close to his body, his head angled toward mine as if he was murmuring sweet nothings. The brim of his hat was most effective in blocking the view of our faces. "Do not say anything if they stop us. Just act giddy."

"That's not going to be any problem," I answered, the nearness of him suddenly causing memories of the night before to come flooding back with vibrant intensity. My legs felt more than a little wobbly as I breathed in the faintly smoky scent that always seemed to be around him. It reminded me of a fall afternoon, with burning leaves tinting the crisp air.

Two police officers were on our side of the street as we strolled up to the church, the trail of ghosts behind me thankfully not visible to their eyes. Kristoff's mouth touched my ear. I giggled in a loud, high voice, and said very quietly, "I'm going to kiss you. Don't freak out," before wrapping both arms around him, stopping right in front of a policewoman.

The moment my mouth parted under his I knew I'd made a mistake. What I had intended for the benefit of the cops immediately turned serious as his tongue started bossing mine around in the way that left me mindlessly craving more.

The policewoman said something, amusement rich in her voice.

Kristoff groaned into my mouth when I sucked on his tongue, his hands sliding down to grab my butt.

The policewoman spoke a little louder, muffled laughter coming from her companion.

Hunger and need rose in him again, accompanied by a sexual drive that washed over me like lava. I burned for him, ached for something undefined, something that only he could give me . . . something I could give him . . . it was all so muddled in my head, I couldn't organize my thoughts.

Someone tapped on my shoulder. I broke off the kiss, burying my face in Kristoff's chest as he spoke over my head, a forced lightness in his voice when he answered the policewoman.

I kept my head lowered and angled toward Kristoff, leaning heavily on him as he urged me forward, my cheeks burning with very real consternation. What on earth was I doing? What sort of person was I that I could act that way with him when Alec, the man who a short time ago had professed all sorts of affection for me, had sacrificed himself to ensure I got away safe?

I stumbled as we passed a couple more police officers, but they paid us no attention as Kristoff led me toward the church.

"That's it. I'm going to be a Zorya if it kills me," Dagrun announced behind me.

"Too late," Ulfur said cheerfully.

"Are we going to the house or church first?" I asked Kristoff, trying to drag my mind from the horrible well of guilt that filled me to concentrate on the situation with Alec.

Kristoff hesitated outside the front of the church, holding me in an embrace that would have given me pleasure if his eyes hadn't been wandering with calculation over the front of the church. "The house, I think. The church is too public. They'll put him in some sort of cell to hold him for a ritual later."

"Your ritual?" Dagrun asked me.

I wanted to throttle the little snot.

Kristoff's gaze shifted to me, his eyes narrowing. "What ritual?"

I cleared my throat, shot Dagrun an evil look (she smirked in return), and met Kristoff's flinty gaze. "I'm being sworn in tonight as Zorya. Or whatever the ritual is, exactly."

"You can't do that," he said, the familiar frown he usually wore starting to form. "I married you first. The marriage to the sacristan isn't valid."

"So you say, but since they don't know that, there wasn't any reason I could give them to not have the ceremony tonight."

Kristoff looked heavenward for a moment, his hands tightening on my shoulders. "Do you have any idea what they will do when they find out what you've done?"

"How are they going to find out? They'll do their ritual tonight, and proclaim me Zorya. I admit I don't like misleading them, especially Mattias, who seems like a nice, if rather misguided, guy, but what harm is it going to do? You yourself just said it's not going to be a valid ceremony, so how can it hurt anyone?"

He started walking to the side of the church, leading me down a narrow street to the house behind, his hand biting into my uninjured arm as he said tersely, "There will come a point where they will expect you to act as Zorya, and when you exhibit no particular powers, they will begin to wonder why. Do not doubt for a moment that their form of ascertaining the answer will be extremely unpleasant for you."

"I figured I'd just tell them I need some practice, or use some excuse like that. That should buy me a little time, which I'll use to find another Zorya, a real Zorya, who can take the ghosts to Ostri for me."

"Procrastination is not a solution," he said stubbornly. "The day will come when the reapers here find out you are a Zorya in name only."

"Yes, and I plan on being a long way away from here on that day." I pointed to the house. "The most important thing is to get Alec out. Since they will pretty much attack you on sight, I'll go in and see how things are."

I started to go to the front door of the house as I spoke, but Kristoff pulled me back.

"That would be foolish in the extreme. You stay here while I get a reaper and find out what they've done with Alec."

"Oh, no," I said, grabbing his arm as he started to leave. "I know how that'll end up."

"Um . . . Pia?" Ulfur said.

"What do you mean?" Kristoff asked, frowning at me.

"You'll torture the truth out of whoever you nab. Go ahead, admit it."

"Of course I will," Kristoff said, almost snorting in disgust as he turned back toward the house.

"Pia, I think you really will want to — oh, too late."

"What?" I asked, turning to see what it was that had Ulfur in such a swivet.

Visible through the ghosts were two men: Frederic and Mattias.

"I believe we can save you the trouble of torturing one of our people," Frederic said with a misleadingly bland smile.

Kristoff whirled around at the sound of his voice.

"I wish the same could be said of you, but you see, it's not often we have two Dark Ones in our grasp." Frederic's dark eyes moved to me with an assessing glance. "Not to mention a Beloved."

CHAPTER 15

"This is absolutely uncalled for. I am, if you recall, the Zorya. I do not expect to be treated like this!"

My exaggerated outrage fell upon deaf ears. Well, almost deaf ears.

"That's telling them," Ulfur said, giving me a nod of approval.

"Aye, our reaper has spirit. But what is this place?" Hallur asked as the ghosts trooped after me.

"I told you this would happen," Kristjana almost spat as I was shoved toward a flight of stairs.

"This is the house that the Brotherhood uses," I said softly to my ghosts.

"Ah. Rather chill here, isn't it?" Hallur rubbed his ghostly arms.

"That's a root cellar down there," Ingveldur said from the stairs. "Are we going down? I don't particularly like closed-in spaces."

"You can stay up here," I told Ulfur sotto voce, so the others wouldn't hear me. "You should be safe in the Brotherhood house. I can't imagine an Ilargi would come here."

He nodded and went to explain to the rest of the ghosts.

"We'll be right up here if you need us," Ingveldur called as I was led down into the basement. Frederic was behind us; Mattias manhandled a handcuffed Kristoff before me. I glanced at Kristoff, who was being unusually silent. He hadn't gone easily, his face still showing the effects of the battle with Mattias that had been ended abruptly when Frederic pulled out a wicked-looking gun and held it to my chest.

Kristjana gave me a shove between my shoulders that almost sent me tumbling down the stairs. Trussed up like a turkey, I would have preferred to have a hand free to hold on to the railing lest she act on the idea of getting a new Zorya.

"I told you that she was tainted," the woman in question said to the man behind her, giving me another shove. "She's a Beloved!"

"Hey, watch it! I almost fell! You could have broken my neck!"

Behind me, Kristjana snorted. "A Beloved is immortal."

I flared my nostrils at her. "Look, I don't know what sort of relationship you think that Kristoff and I have, but we're not dating, much less in love," I told her as I stumbled on the last step. "And I'm certainly not immortal."

"Not him, the other one," she answered.

"Alec? Is he here? Is he all right?" I stopped, refusing to go any farther. "If you've hurt him —"

"Stop treating us as if we are fools," Kristjana interrupted. "Yes, your Dark One is here." A slow smile crept across her face. It wasn't particularly nice. "He has not been cleansed . . . yet. But I very much look forward to watching him embrace the light."

"If you strike us down, you will simply bring more of the council upon your heads," Kristoff said, breaking his silence. "We do not act alone. Nor will we tolerate your persecution."

Kristjana spat at him, literally spat at him, moving around him but being careful, I was interested to note, to stay just out of his reach. "We will purge the earth of your kind just as the light was purged of darkness."

"Rhetorical gibberish," Kristoff said, and probably would have continued if Mattias hadn't slammed his head into the wall.

"Stop that!" I yelled, starting toward

them, but Kristjana jerked me back.

A moment of sadness gripped me as her face lit with a pleasure bordering on the fanatical. I wondered if she was mentally stable, or if her belief in the Brotherhood had consumed her past the point of reason. "You will watch when the light cleanses your Dark One. You will see as I have seen how the darkness can be stripped from them."

That pretty much answered the question. I kept my voice calm and soothing as I said, "I understand why you think they are evil, but I assure you, Alec and Kristoff are not. You might have good intentions, but where they concern these two men, you're way off base. If you would untie us, I'd be happy to sit down and explain everything to you."

"The time for talk is past," Kristjana said with dismissive self-righteousness. "Now is the time for action. We will be conducting three cleansings tonight?"

The question was asked of Frederic.

"Who do you expect will conduct the ceremony?" Frederic asked in his soft, French-accented voice. "You just declared the Zorya tainted."

"And you cannot deny that!" Kristjana cried. "You can't deny that she was unsuitable for the job from the very beginning.

Look at how she's deceived us! By the light, Frederic, she's a Beloved!"

Frederic said nothing as he strolled down the last of the stairs, merely nodding toward a door. Mattias shoved Kristoff up against the wall, whipping out a set of keys to unlock the door.

"I told you that I'm not dating anyone —" I started to correct Kristjana.

She spun around. "Oh, shut up, you ignorant fool. A Beloved is not a girlfriend, it is a so-called savior of Dark Ones, not that they can be saved by anything but the purity of the light."

I decided the best defense was a good offense, and whirled away from her, taking an assertive stance in the middle of the room. "You will not talk to me that way! I am the Zorya, not you, and you will treat me with the respect and honor due someone in my position!"

Kristjana slapped me. She just reached right out and smacked me smartly across the left cheek. "How dare you! You pollute the very air we breathe, and you expect us to treat you with respect? You, who have betrayed everything we stand for. You, who have aided the Dark One we hold by promising him salvation. Well, we shall see that he has it — but it will be true salvation, not the farce you call redemption."

Kristoff made a low, growling noise. "Hypocritical diatribe. You murder my people, then claim to save them, hiding your true intentions behind a cloak of righteousness, but not even your precious light can hide the truth about your actions. You deal in death, not divinity; torture, not salvation."

"I will enjoy watching you cleansed, too," Kristjana said, her face as rigid as a mask. "But I think you should be given the chance to see the truth when your friend receives the light first."

I stared at her in horror, the zeal in her voice raising goose bumps on my back as I had a mental image of the sort of light Alec would be forced to endure. "Please, listen to me. I swore to Anniki that I would right the injustices done her, and I am trying to do that. But she was wrong — you're wrong — about Alec and Kristoff. If they were what you say they are, I'd do everything in my power to help you, but you're damning them without reason."

She straightened up, clearly about to launch another physical attack, but Frederic's soft voice stopped her. "That will be enough, sister. You will not strike Zorya Pia again."

"She is not worthy of the name Zorya," Kristjana spat.

"That has yet to be determined," Frederic said, eyeing me. "We will leave that to the Zenith to decide."

I turned to him as a bastion of sanity. "May I see Alec, please? I'd like to make sure he's all right, then I would like to explain to you what's been going on."

Frederic looked thoughtful for a moment, then nodded toward Mattias.

Mattias shoved Kristoff through the door he'd unlocked and slammed it shut, locking it before he marched over to the door on the opposite side of the room, quickly opening it.

A maw of darkness gaped open before me as he flung open the door.

"Alec?" I said, taking a hesitant step toward it.

"Pia?" From the obsidian depths a shadow appeared, stumbling out. "Love, is that you?"

"Love," Kristjana said, her voice dripping with scorn.

"Are you hurt?" I hurried over to him, but Mattias leaped in front of me, his normally placid face hard and unyielding. "Mattias, please."

His eyes narrowed on me. "You marry me,

330

but you are *his* Beloved? I did not believe that of you, Pia."

"I'm sorry about that, but there were . . . reasons . . ."

"I'm all right, just a bit bruised," Alec said as I stopped. He peered over Mattias's shoulder at me. Like Kristoff, he'd been handcuffed, although his hands were bound in front of him. "I'm sorry I didn't give you enough time to get away, however."

"I did. We came to rescue you," I said with a wry smile.

"We?"

"Kristoff is here, too."

"He always did have more brawn than brain," Alec said, his gaze warm on me despite the circumstances. He turned to consider Frederic. "I take it you have plans to use Pia to destroy Kristoff and me?"

Kristjana started to answer, but Frederic held up a hand to stop her. "You are Dark Ones. We are obliged to purify you. However, the Zorya has asked for a chance to speak, assumedly in your behalf."

"Yes, I would like to do that." A tiny little flicker of hope rose despite the situation. "I think if you could get to know them as I do, you will see that they are not the murderous, vengeful monsters you paint them."

"Just yesterday two of our brothers were

injured, and a third killed. By all accounts, the murderer was the Dark One you name as friend."

"There were extenuating circumstances," I said, licking my dried lips. "Your people attacked Kristoff and me without provocation. The man who was killed held a knife to me and threatened to kill —"

Frederic raised his hand again. "We will save this discussion for the Zenith to hear."

"You're not going to let her go?" Kristjana asked in outrage.

He looked thoughtful for a moment. "I believe that would not be wise. However, we will allow you to have your say, Zorya Pia. As you know, the liturgy of light is to be held tonight, to endow you with the powers of Midnight Zorya. We will hold a convocation then to bear witness to all you wish to say. Following that . . ." His gaze went to Alec, who glared back at him. "We shall see."

"I'm glad someone is willing to listen," I said, holding up my hands, which, unlike those of the two men, had been bound together with duct tape. "I'd appreciate it if you could take this off me. It's beginning to chafe."

Kristjana looked like she wanted to chafe the rest of me, most likely with a chainsaw or large tub of explosives, but Frederic simply gestured toward Mattias.

"Love, don't let them —" Alec's voice was cut off as he was shoved back into his hellhole, the door slammed after him.

"Is that really necessary?" I asked Frederic as Mattias flicked open a penknife and cut through the tape on my wrists. I peeled off the grey wad and absently rubbed my tender flesh. "Couldn't you at least give him a light and something to read?"

He ignored my comment, still watching me with an impassive gaze. "You will understand that we cannot allow you to roam freely until the convocation and the liturgy have been conducted."

"I don't understand, but I have resolved myself to confinement," I said loftily.

"We only have two secure cells," Kristjana said, her expression doubtful as she looked at Frederic. "You do not intend to leave her with her Dark One. The two of them together . . . they could be dangerous."

"I am not so convinced of that as you are," Frederic answered slowly. "But I agree that it would be unwise to leave them together."

"I'm perfectly happy staying in a hotel room," I said with only a little nudge of my conscience about leaving Kristoff and Alec behind. "Or I could —"

"Place her with the other one," Frederic pronounced before turning and starting up the stairs.

"What? No, wait —"

Before I could rally a protest, Mattias grabbed my arm, unlocked Kristoff's door, shoved me inside, and slammed the door closed behind me.

"Hey! I'm the Zorya, remember?" I threw myself back into the door and pounded on it. "Mattias, let me out! I promise I won't run away or marry anyone else, OK? Mattias? Hello?"

"Perhaps you shouldn't make such hasty promises," Kristoff's deep, rich voice rolled around in the darkness of the room. "You never know when you might wish to take a third husband."

"Oh, be quiet, you. Mattias? Damn." I turned to face the room but saw nothing. There was no light in the room, not one tiny little smidgen peeking in from outside, which meant either there weren't any windows, or they were boarded up tightly. There was a smell, however, an earthy, slightly musty scent that must have been what Ingveldur had picked up on when she looked down into the basement. It smelled like a bag of potatoes left sitting in a pantry too long. "Where are you?"

A painful-sounding thud came from a few feet away, followed by a muttered oath and slight scuffling noise that finished with a wooden creak. "On a chair."

I held out my hands, taking baby steps to avoid running into anything. "Where on a chair? Lovely, now I sound like Dr. Seuss. I don't suppose you can see in the dark, can you?"

Kristoff snorted. "No. Nor can I turn into a bat and escape this prison, or change into a wolf and attack your second husband the moment he opens the door, or even dissolve into a wisp of smoke and slip through the crack under the door. I'm a Dark One, Zorya, not a djinn."

"I'm having just as bad a day as you are, so you needn't be quite so snarky. I don't know where you are," I said, taking a few more shuffled steps forward, my hands still reaching into the darkness.

"Why do you care where I am?" he asked sullenly.

"My hands are free. I might be able to get yours free, as well, and then we can do something about this business. Could you talk some more so I can find you?" I shuffled a couple more steps, and suddenly my fingers met something soft and squishy. I jumped back, startled. "Ack! Something else is here!"

"Yes. My eyeball."

"Oh. Sorry." I reached out carefully, baby stepping forward until my questing fingers landed on a nose with a little break in the middle. "Did I hurt you?"

"No, but if you don't let go of my nose you'll make me sneeze."

"Sorry." I took the last couple of steps forward, feeling my way down to his shoulders, then around to his back where his hands were bound. "I suppose you've tried wiggling your hands out of the handcuffs?"

"Yes. I am not a magician, either."

I knelt and felt the bindings. They seemed pretty secure, snapped tight around Kristoff's wrists. I sat back on my heels, sighing. "And I do not know how to pick a lock, unfortunately. Well, no use in crying over spilled milk. What else is in here? Nothing we can use as a weapon?"

"I didn't find anything."

It didn't take me long to examine the room. There were a couple of wooden bins that had evidently been used at one time to hold root vegetables, but all that was left now was a fine dirt at the bottom of the bins, and a couple of shriveled lumps that could only be desiccated potatoes. I searched the last bin, finding nothing but an especially odd-shaped potato. It had sharp little pointy eyes, and a soft coating, as if it had sprouted a growth of fungus.

"Other than what smells like a mummified rat, that is."

I screamed and dropped the horrible thing my fingers were still examining, and leaped to the side, bashing into Kristoff and knocking him over. As we fell, our heads clunked together painfully.

"Oh my god. Are you hurt?" I hurriedly scrambled to my feet and leaped backward when I stepped on something soft and gooshy. "Eeek! Rats! *Rats!*"

"That was my hand," Kristoff said in a rather pained voice.

"I'm so sorry! Let me help you up —"

"No!" he said quickly, his breath coming sharply. There was a ruffling noise, a muffled groan, and then the chair creaked again.

I huddled against the door, my arms wrapped around myself, my forehead throbbing where it had smacked against Kristoff. "Are you hurt?" I asked again with what I thought was noble, if miserable, concern.

"Not really. Why, were you planning on attacking me again?"

"I didn't attack you. I was trying to help you."

"By poking me in the eye, twisting my

nose, knocking me down, beating me about the head and shoulders, and attempting to break the bones in my hand?" His voice was as deep and rich as ever, but there was a distinct note of dissatisfaction in it that riled me.

"Well, I'm doing the best I can, but you didn't tell me that bin had a dead rat in it!"

"I couldn't see what you were doing to tell you to avoid it," he said with maddening reason.

"You know how much I hate rats. You could have warned me."

The sound of a tiny sigh reached my ears. "Zorya, there is a dead rat in the far bin."

"Very funny. What are we going to do?" I was almost glad it was dark in the room, so Kristoff wouldn't see the tears of frustration and self-pity welling in my eyes.

"Christ, you're not going to cry, are you?"

"No, of course not. I'm not the crying sort," I said with a betraying wet sniffle, defiantly wiping my eyes. "It's just that it's been kind of a long last couple of days, and I'm a bit tired and stressy."

He didn't say anything to that, but he didn't need to.

I rocked myself, feeling absolutely pathetic at that moment. I'd failed miserably in trying to do what Anniki had begged of me before she died, failed in getting the ghosts to their final reward, failed trying to make the Brotherhood people see reason. And now Alec and Kristoff were likely going to be subjected to the clearly insane Kristjana's most demented tortures, and there was only myself to blame. I'd botched the whole thing horribly, and I wanted nothing more at that moment than to go home and cry for a week or two.

Kristoff sighed again, this time loudly and aggressively. "Come here."

I swallowed the painful lump in my throat. "Why?"

"Because you're miserable and I can't stand the sound of you sniffling over there." His voice was gruff and abrupt, but there was an underlying note that had me carefully moving forward without questioning why I sought comfort from him.

"Sit down," he commanded.

"I'm not touching those bins again —"

He swore in Italian. "Sit on me, woman."

My fingers brushed against his chest. "I'll squash you —"

"Sit!"

I swiveled around to sit across his legs, swearing that if he made one little intake of breath that indicated I was smashing his legs into a pulp, I'd leap off.

All he said, however, was, "I can't pat you in a suitably calming manner, but you can consider yourself patted. Now stop crying."

"Why are you being nice to me?" I asked, blinking like crazy to keep the tears from spilling over my lashes.

"Would you rather I yelled at you?"

"No. I'd rather you answered a question."

"What?"

"Why did Kristjana keep referring to me as Alec's Beloved? I told her we weren't dating, so even if she knew that Alec and I had spent the night together, that doesn't constitute a relationship."

Kristoff was silent for a few moments, reluctant to speak. I relaxed on him a smidgen, refusing to allow myself to admit just how much I enjoyed breathing in his smoky scent.

I didn't want Kristoff, I reminded myself. It was Alec who indicated he loved me, Alec who clearly felt I was something more than a pest to be endured.

"My people have a long history," Kristoff finally said. "Males can be either Dark Ones or what are generally referred to as just Moravians — men born with a soul, but still needing blood to survive."

"You really don't have a soul?" I asked, amazed at such a thing.

"No. I was born with one, but lost it. The only redemption is to find a Beloved, a woman who will take the seven steps of Joining and, in doing so, will return a soul to the Dark One."

"You lost your soul? How can you lose a soul? I mean, it's not something you can misplace easily, is it?"

"It is if another Dark One strips it from you."

I gawked at him despite the fact that I couldn't see anything. "Another vampire turned you? I thought you said that doesn't happen often."

"It doesn't. My circumstances were . . . unique."

I waited for him to continue, but he didn't. "You're not going to tell me about it, are you?"

"No."

I sighed. "All right. Where are these women you mentioned? The Beloveds?"

I felt him shrug. "They can be anywhere, at any time. There is only one Beloved for a Dark One, and if their paths do not cross, there is no other. At least . . . One of the members of the council claims his Beloved was not the woman born to that role, but I am not privy to all the details, so I can't say if that's just a rumor or not."

"Good lord. So if you're in the wrong place at the wrong time, and this soul-redeeming woman gets married to someone else, and spends her life without knowing you . . ." Profound sadness leeched into the air. "Oh, Kristoff, I'm so sorry. The Brotherhood killed your girlfriend, the one who was going to do that for you. I didn't blame you before for being so determined to have justice done, but now I feel even more horrible about it."

"Angelica was not my Beloved."

I could feel his grief, feel the anger that filled him when he thought about her. Without thinking, I put my arms around him and pressed his head to me, wanting to comfort him as he'd given me comfort. "She wasn't? How do you know?"

"I'd know," he said, somewhat muffled since his face was pressed into my cleavage.

"How? Is there some sign? Because if I'm supposed to redeem Alec's soul for him, I'm going to need some help. I don't have the slightest idea how to do that."

Kristoff froze for a moment, then relaxed, his face moving slightly against me.

"What are you doing? Are you sniffing me?" I asked, pushing myself back.

"Yes. Beloveds smell."

"They what?"

I stared down at where his face was, even though I couldn't see so much as a glint from those lovely blue eyes.

"Beloveds, when claimed, have a different scent. It's . . . Some have described it as unpleasant. I've never found it particularly so, but they do definitely smell different than other females."

"You're saying I stink?" I said, jumping off his lap.

"No, you don't, you smell . . . It doesn't matter. You don't smell like the other Beloveds I've met."

"I honestly don't know whether to be offended or grateful," I said, stumbling back until I felt the rough stone wall behind me. I sank down onto the floor, feeling it was better to put some distance between Kristoff and me. Sitting on his lap had brought up far too many memories, memories that for Alec's sake I should squelch.

"You should be grateful. Once a couple has Joined, they are bound for life."

"Joining requiring some steps, you said?" I was curious as to what, exactly, made one a Beloved.

"Yes."

"I'm probably going to regret this, but what, exactly, are they? Maybe I'm like partway to being Alec's Beloved, and that's what Kristjana picked up on?"

"Or she could just be jumping to conclusions."

"True. What are the steps?"

"Nothing very profound. The first is a marking. That can mean anything from the ability to share thoughts without verbal communication, to being able to sense things that were hidden before."

"You can share thoughts? You mean like mental telepathy?"

"Yes. It is not unknown for Dark Ones who are very close to do so, and it is always the way with a Beloved."

"Wow. Interesting. Still, that first step sounds pretty vague," I said, thinking about how I knew Alec was hungry and needed blood. Or had that been Kristoff?

"Second step is protection from some sort of a danger."

"Alec sacrificed himself for me earlier, in the restaurant," I said, but the image that flashed into my mind was of Kristoff turning to face me after he'd killed the man who'd held a knife to my throat.

"Third is an exchange of the body."

I raised my eyebrows.

Kristoff's voice held a slight note of amusement. "More like a kiss than what you're thinking."

I blushed despite the darkness.

"Fourth is an issue of trust — will the Beloved betray the Dark One or keep his faith?"

I moved uncomfortably on the cold dirt floor. I wouldn't perform on Alec and Kristoff whatever horrible ceremony the Brotherhood folk wanted. I just wouldn't.

"Fifth is another exchange of the body. Yes, your night with Alec would qualify." His voice ceased to be amused, and was back to being hard and flinty.

"Sixth is a need that the Beloved can fulfill to overcome the Dark One's true self."

I frowned. "A need? What kind of need?"

"It's personal to each couple. Something the Dark One needs that the woman provides."

"Blood, you mean?"

"Possibly. I don't know; I don't have a Beloved to ask."

"Hmm." I thought about that for a few minutes. Both Alec and Kristoff had needed blood from me, but it was Alec who said he needed me, wanted me in his life. "And the last step?"

"Exchange of blood. After which the Beloved makes some sacrifice, and the Joining is complete."

"Well, I certainly haven't drank Alec's

blood," I said, my nose wrinkled at the thought of such a thing. "That sounds extremely unhygienic, not to mention dangerous if one person was diseased."

"Dark Ones don't get mortal diseases."

"Still, it doesn't sound very good. You know, I think that may be what's going on — I fit all the rest of the steps but that one. I just don't know if I can drink blood, even to save him. It's just so icky."

Kristoff was silent, but a sudden wave of hostility from him had me wondering if he would be jealous if I found his friend's soul.

I didn't want to break up their friendship, but he couldn't expect me to turn my back on his friend if he needed me, could he? More importantly, how were we to get out of this horrible fix so I would even have the chance to find out if I *was* a potential Beloved?

I sighed. It was shaping up to be a long, unpleasant day, and I didn't have any expectation of it getting better soon.

CHAPTER 16

"What time do you think it is?"

The silence that met my question was almost as thick as the blackness wrapped around us in the miniscule basement storeroom.

A tiny little snuffling sound finally broke the silence.

"Kristoff!" I said loudly.

A muted snort answered, followed almost immediately by Kristoff saying, in a voice thick with sleep, "What?"

I stood in the middle of the room, or what I assumed was the middle, and put my hands on my hips. "You were sleeping, weren't you?"

"No. Possibly." He cleared his throat. The chair creaked as if he had been leaning back and suddenly sat upright. "What was the question?"

"How can you sleep at a time like this!"

"I'm male. I fall asleep after sex, and when

I'm trapped in a small room with my arms handcuffed behind me, and nothing else to do but think about how hungry I am."

"Well, I like that. Here I am talking to you about various escape plans, and you're using the fact that I can't see you to doze off! *And* you snore!"

"I do not snore. Dark Ones do not snore," he said sternly, and I imagined that he was, at that moment, frowning at me. I swam my way through the darkness toward him, my hand sweeping in front of me in case I was going in the wrong direction. "What are you doing?"

My fingers struck his chin. I followed the line of his jaw up to his forehead. As I suspected, there was a wrinkle between his brows. "Just seeing if you were frowning at me. I figured you were."

Silence filled the room for the count of seven. "Do you care that I'm frowning?"

"Oddly enough, I do," I said slowly, after some consideration. My fingers idly twined through his hair, playing with his curls until I realized what I was doing and stepped away a foot or so. "I've always maintained that a jolly vampire is better than a pissed-off one. When do you think they'll let us out? We've been down here for hours and hours."

"Are you so anxious to see me murdered?" he countered.

"Don't be silly." I recommenced pacing the length of the room. I was getting good at estimating just where the walls were. "I'm not going to let them murder you."

"And just how do you expect to stop them from trying?"

I paced toward him, absently counting the steps. "They can't do anything ritualistic without a real Zorya, can they? If you're my husband, then I'm not real. At least, not by their standards. And if I am real, then all I have to do is refuse to participate in the cleansing ceremony."

He gave a disbelieving grunt.

"It's not like they can make me kill you," I pointed out.

"On the contrary, assuming you were a Zorya, I can think of any number of ways they could force you to do just that, but if you wish to persist with the belief that ignorance will protect you, so be it. Now, what are you doing?"

"It just occurred to me what you said." While he had been speaking, I felt my way along the wall over to him, kneeling beside him. "You said you were hungry. When's the last time you ate?"

His voice had a slightly surly tinge to it.

"You should know; you were there."

"Last night, you mean? No wonder you're hungry. Here, have an arm."

I thrust my arm roughly in the direction of his face.

He head butted my offering. "Whatever else you may think of me, I am not a cannibal."

"Don't be obstinate. You know full well I was intending for you to have a sip of Vino Pia, not eat my arm."

"I don't need your blood," he said in a voice that continued to bristle with surliness.

Hunger hung in the air like a thick, red mist.

"Yes, you do. Look at it this way — you'll be weaker if you don't, and frankly, I'd rather have you brimming with health when we have to deal with Kristjana, especially if the ritual fizzles. That woman is just not right in the head."

He grunted an assent.

"So stop being stubborn, and eat. I had breakfast, you didn't. Eat." I shoved my wrist in the direction of his face.

"I don't like to drink from wrists," he muttered. "It's so cliché."

"Oh, for god's sake . . . fine." I hauled myself onto his lap and half turned to face him, letting him have the inside of my upper arm. "Better?"

His breath was hot on my arm, sending little pinpricks of pleasure along my back and belly.

"I don't think that would be wise," he said, his voice sounding oddly choked.

I couldn't help myself. I leaned into him, his curls brushing against my mouth. That faintly smoky scent that seemed to be uniquely his seeped into my pores, making my stomach tighten with anticipation. "It's all right, Kristoff. I don't mind feeding you, I really don't."

"You know what happened last time," he warned, his voice getting rougher and rougher. I heard him swallow. "I told you before that to a Dark One, the act of feeding can be arousing."

"You said there had to be a shared attraction." My heart was beating madly. I knew I should stop, knew I should back off to the farthest corner of the tiny cell and let him go hungry. I knew that what he was saying was absolutely true — not only was the proof growing beneath my right hip, but I was tingling just from the nearness of him. The scent and feel of him filled my mind, and more than anything, I wanted to taste him, wanted him to taste me.

"Yes." His voice made me shiver.

"It's all right," I repeated, too overwhelmed by emotions to listen to my common sense.

"Alec —" he said, choking to a stop.

"I don't think Alec and I are meant to be," I said, realizing with surprise that it was true. It was a dream, a pleasantly enticing dream, but a dream nonetheless.

"If you're his Beloved, your blood will be poison to me," Kristoff murmured against my arm, his lips caressing the suddenly sensitive flesh.

"We won't know until you try," I whispered into his hair, unable to keep from pressing little kisses along the top of his ear. I shifted on his lap so that I was straddling his legs, undoing the top couple of buttons on my blouse so it sagged open. "If it is, we'll have the answer, and we'll stop. If I'm Alec's Beloved . . . well, I'll deal with that."

"He'll kill me for this," Kristoff said hoarsely as I arched my back. His head dipped down, kissing a hot line along the upper slopes of my chest. He stopped for a moment, his breath coming fast as I pulled off my shirt and reached behind to unhook my bra, his groan of pleasure echoing mine when his mouth descended again. "To hell with it. You taste too good. . . ."

"Too much talking, not enough biting," I said, moving restlessly against him. I wanted more, wanted him inside me, wanted him drinking from me, wanted that amazing sensation of sharing that we had the previous time he fed off me.

He kissed a path over to my shoulder, moving a bit down my upper arm, his tongue painting a hot brand along my flesh.

"You're sure?" he asked, his voice sounding as rough as his breathing in the confined space.

I thought of Alec, locked in an identical room just a few yards away, thought about what he meant to me, and what I apparently meant to him. I thought about how he made me feel wanted, cherished, even loved. Kristoff didn't want me, didn't want anything from me but satisfaction for the sexual itch that we seemed to share, and he certainly didn't need me. He was bound to his grief, and I suspected that I simply filled the role of physical relief, and yet I felt closer to him than I did to the man with whom I might very likely spend the rest of my life as his Beloved.

I thought about all of that in the space between heartbeats, and wrapped my arms around his head. "I'm sure."

The pain was fleeting, a momentary burning sensation that was quickly lost in sweeping pleasure. Kristoff moaned as he drank deeply, the sensation of that winding me up tighter than I had ever been. I moved against him, wanting his touch, mindless to everything but the sensations that were rippling through me like waves.

"Pia . . ." His tongue lathed a spot on my arm.

I felt the need in him, a need not just for my blood, but one that was instantly answered by my body. I was wound tighter than a clockwork, and felt like I might explode at any second.

"Well ahead of you," I said, sliding back on his legs to find his buckle and zipper. He lifted his hips slightly as I made frantic little noises while struggling with the former. At last I got the zipper down, not at all surprised to find him hot and hard and clearly as aroused as I was. I held him in my hands, enjoying the unabashed groans of ecstasy my touch drew from him.

Another need burned through me, one I couldn't help but give in to. He made a distressed noise as I rose off his lap, but that quickly changed to an unintelligible gurgle as I knelt and tentatively took him in my mouth, the sensation flooding my mind with rapturous images that drove out all other thoughts.

All of them but one — I'd used him for my own satisfaction the night before, self-ishly used him even though I knew he was still mourning his lost love. I wouldn't do that again.

"Pia, I don't think I'm going to last if you keep doing that," he warned, the huskiness of his voice sliding along me like velvet on bare skin.

"I want to give you pleasure, Kristoff," I murmured against the base of his penis, set-ting a rhythm that had his hips moving with quickening pace. "To thank you for what you gave me the other night."

He sucked in a huge amount of air as I let my tongue curl around the sensitive under-side of his penis, the muscles of his thighs as hard as cement beneath my hands.

"Stop," he cried, his legs tightening. "Dammit, I wish my hands were free. You don't owe me any thanks. We gave each other pleasure, and we will do so again."

There was a command in his voice, an order that had me smiling against the velvety tip of him. He understood what I was offering. "I think it's my turn to ask you if you're sure," I said, giving him a swipe of my tongue.

His muscles trembled with strain. "Quite sure."

"Will you be grossed out if I kiss you?" I asked as I rose, quickly removing my jeans and underwear before straddling his legs again. At least I wouldn't have to worry about him seeing all my pudgy parts.

"Try me," he growled.

His mouth was as hot on mine as it had been on my arm, his tongue the same bossy tongue that immediately charged into my mouth and set about pushing me over the edge of tolerance.

I positioned him and sank down slowly, the movement making us both moan.

"Do you have any idea," I gasped as he slid in another inch, my body gripping him tightly as he invaded delicate, sensitive parts, "any idea how good that feels?"

"Hrng," he answered, his head lolled back as I flexed my hips. I leaned forward and kissed his neck, smiling as I nibbled my way up to nip his earlobe. "Christ, woman! Do that swivel again."

I swiveled. He made a noise from somewhere deep in his chest, a primitive sort of noise, a mating noise, one that seemed to thrum through me as I moved against him. That was all it took — that noise, and the feel of him so deep inside me, and the wave after wave of exhilaration that wound me even tighter until I teetered at the edge of a climax.

His teeth pierced the skin behind my ear, the burn racing through my body, setting me alight and pushing me over the edge. I clutched at his shoulders, shaking with the strength of the climax even as he cried against my neck, his sensations pushing me beyond awareness into a new place, something made up of the two of us.

I collapsed against him, almost sobbing with the euphoria of the moment, confused about what I'd just experienced. This was beyond normal sex, beyond even incredibly fabulous sex. What we'd just done was earth-shattering, profoundly momentous in a way I couldn't begin to understand, but disturbed as I was, I knew one thing for certain — I would die before I let the Brotherhood people sacrifice the man in my arms.

I had to get him out, get Alec and him both out, and away from Kristjana. Frederic and Mattias might be reasoned with, but I knew with chilling conviction that Kristjana wouldn't be happy until both vampires were dead.

I just wouldn't let that happen.

■ ■ ■ ■

"Heea."

A voice, muffled and indistinct, reached my ears. I drifted on a cloud of post-orgasmic insensibility, finally realizing that the word spoken was my name.

"What?" I asked, too boneless to move. I had collapsed onto Kristoff, and was draped across him now, his face smashed into my breasts, my knees still gripping his hips.

"Mrrphm reef."

"What?" I asked, pulling back in order to hear him better.

"I couldn't breathe," he said, a slight edge of amusement in his voice.

"Oh, I'm sorry, I didn't think about you breathing." I scooted off him, groping around on the ground to find my clothing. "That is, I didn't think about the fact that my boobs were smothering you. Are you all right?"

"Yes."

"Full? Or do you need another go-round?" I pulled on my clothing, my face flaming for no good reason. Yes, I'd just had the best sex of my entire life, but it was with a man who saw me as nothing more than an annoyance who could occasionally scratch an itch — or fulfill a hunger. There was no cause for me to be blushing like a virgin.

"That was quite sufficient, thank you," he said politely, but the humor was gone from his voice, replaced by a flinty note that made me, for some reason, want to throw something large at his head. Or cry. Possibly both.

Sufficient, my shiny white ass! Once again I was left swearing that if that was the way he wanted to deal with the fact that we had quite possibly the best sex in the entire history of the world, then I would certainly not disillusion him.

Sufficient. The bastard.

I was formulating an extremely cutting comeback when there was a noise at the door.

"Zorya Pia? Are you there?"

A crack of light appeared along the edges of the doorway.

"Mattias?" I asked, astonished.

The door was pulled open a few inches. Mattias's eyeball was applied to the open space. "Has the Dark One turned you?"

"Turned me? You mean made me a vampire?" I rushed to the door, pausing when Kristoff hissed at me.

"My trousers," he said softly.

A little shaft of light fell across the room, striking him on the leg, allowing me to see that he was still exposed to view.

"Yes. Kristjana said that he would do so in order to keep you from becoming Zorya tonight." Mattias's eye examined me with calculation.

I moved to block his view of Kristoff, backing up until I reached him. "Don't be silly. Kristoff wouldn't vamp me. Would you?"

"At this moment, I'm considering the very attractive idea of throttling you," was the answer.

"See?" I told Mattias. "He wants to strangle me, not make me a vampire. Are you going to let us out?"

"I should not," Mattias said, his eye considering me with unblinking interest. "Kristjana said I was not to come down here. But you are the Zorya, and my wife."

"Actually, she's mine, but don't let that stop you from freeing us," Kristoff said.

"Hush, you," I said, giving a little trill of horribly false-sounding laughter as I squatted awkwardly next to Kristoff, reaching behind me to tuck him away and do up his pants. "He's such a joker. But you know, Mattias, I don't feel that we've really had the time to get to know each other, and as I have a few hours free now, why don't we have a nice, long talk about things? Out of the basement."

"Kristjana would not be happy," he pointed out.

"Well," I finished fighting with Kristoff's zipper and moved toward the door, smiling my most winsome smile. "She doesn't have to know, does she?"

He hesitated, clearly not sold on the idea of letting us out, but I was not going to let this chance slip by me.

"Mattias," I said gently, batting my lashes ever so slightly at him. "I'm the Zorya. Anniki picked me to be her successor, and I'm wholly committed to doing what's right. There are a dozen ghosts upstairs right now just waiting for me to make good on my promise to take them to Ostri. I'm not a bad person — you know that, don't you? Please let us out. I promise I'll be responsible for both Alec and Kristoff."

"No, I could not let the Dark Ones out," Mattias said, shaking his head. "That would be wrong. They are to be cleansed."

"You are completely misjudging the situation —" I started to say, but Mattias suddenly pushed the door open a little wider, enough for his entire face to glare in at me.

Or rather over my shoulder. Kristoff had come up behind me, as silent as a panther. I turned to see what it was that had Mattias so angry.

Kristoff's shirt hung open, part of it poking out of his fly.

"No wonder I had such a hard time with that zipper," I muttered, frowning at it.

"What?" Mattias asked suspiciously.

I turned to face him with a bright, innocent smile. "Sorry?"

His face darkened. I looked down and saw to my horror that I had buttoned my blouse incorrectly — half the buttons were in the wrong buttonholes, while the other half weren't buttoned at all.

"You have slept with the Dark One!" Mattias accused, and I had to admit, the evidence of obviously hastily donned clothing was pretty damning. "You had sex with the other one, and now this one, too? You have sex with everyone but me!"

"I don't have sex with everyone!" My fingers danced along the front of my blouse, fixing the button issue.

Kristoff snorted.

I elbowed him in the gut.

"Right here, in the very house I was in, practically in front of me!" Mattias continued, his face turning red.

"Would I do that?" I asked, trying very hard to assemble my facial features into those depicting innocence, but I couldn't seem to remember what that looked like.

The door slamming closed and the key scraping in the lock were the answer to *that* idiotic question.

"Well, hell," I said, leaning my head against the door.

CHAPTER 17

"Would I do that to you?"

"Oh, be quiet, Mr. Actually-she's-*my*-wife. That didn't help matters one little bit. You just had to mention that, didn't you?"

"Are you attempting to blame me for our current predicament?"

I took a deep breath to answer him, and realized that I was, in fact, trying to blame him for just that. I slumped against the door in defeat. "No, I realize full well that it's my fault we're here."

Kristoff was silent for a few moments. "I believe Alec shares some of that blame. He should have known better than to take you to a public place where he had no easy means of escape."

"Probably."

"I suppose I should have made you stay back while I checked the perimeter of the house, as well."

"Hindsight and all that. Besides, shifting

blame won't do any good." I sighed, my spirits drooping. "If there was just some way to reason with the Brotherhood people. I know if I could talk to them, they would see that you and Alec don't deserve their wrath."

"It won't do any good. We've tried for centuries to show them the truth about us, but they refuse to accept it."

"Maybe if —" I stopped, hearing something that had me taking a step away from the door, watching in surprise as once again it was opened a crack.

"Pia?"

I grabbed the door and hauled it open, relief swamping me as I beheld the welcome sight of Ulfur and Ragnar. Ulfur was in solid mode, his smile filled with warmth as we emerged from the cell. "Ulfur, I could kiss you, but given the fact that lately I seem to end up married or in some other way bound to any man I kiss, I'll settle for a heartfelt thank-you. How did you get the keys?"

Ulfur's smile widened to a cheeky grin. He flexed his fingers. "I saw that one who had the keys come upstairs a few minutes ago. I figured he must have confined you down here somehow, and . . . er . . . persuaded him to give me the keys."

"Is there a handcuff key on there?" Kristoff asked, nodding toward the key chain.

There was. He was still rubbing his freed wrists and shaking the blood back into his arms when we released Alec.

"My love, I knew you would find a way to free us," Alec said with a wet and hurried kiss.

I slipped out of his hold, not wanting to mislead him, but hesitant to say anything. Now was not the time to discuss personal relationship issues. I shot Kristoff a glance, but he was frowning down at his wrist as he rubbed away deep red marks. "You can thank Ulfur, not me."

"Ulfur?" Alec looking around the basement area.

"He's one of my ghosts. Is it safe to go upstairs, Ulfur?"

He flitted up the stairs, once again translucent. "Yes."

"Then let's get the hell out of here," I said, starting for the stairs, but was shoved back by first Kristoff, then Alec.

Just as my foot hit the bottom stair, a sudden explosion of noise filtered down to us. Kristoff and Alec froze for a moment, then both shouted something and bolted up the stairs, right through Ulfur and Ragnar.

"What the — what is it?" I asked Ulfur as I ran up after them.

He stood in the doorway, his brows raised in surprise. "It's Dark Ones."

"More? Good lord, how many are there on this island?"

Behind me, a door slammed. I whirled around to see who had just left the kitchen area, but the sight of Kristjana, a knife raised high in her hand as she ran toward me, screaming what sounded like a Viking battle cry, instantly absorbed all my attention.

"Ack!" I yelled, and, turning on my heel, raced out of the kitchen toward the front of the house, from which all the noise was originating. "Help! Mad Brotherhood woman!"

I dashed into the main room, skidding to a stop at the sight of the room's occupants. Mattias was on the floor, his arms twisted up behind him as Kristoff slapped on the handcuffs that he'd just shed. There was a distinct look of pleasure on his face as he did so. Around him stood four men, all dark haired but for one blond. Alec spun around as I flung myself toward him, Kristjana in hot pursuit.

She was screaming something in Icelandic, but the murderous look in her eyes pretty much translated her intent. She'd gone off the deep end.

Alec shoved me behind him and lunged for her, while one of the other men — I recognized him as being Kristoff's brother Andreas — jumped toward her at the same time. Andreas grabbed her neck in some sort of disabling move, causing Kristjana to fall to the ground with a solid thud.

"Is she dead?" I asked, about ready to scream.

"No," Andreas answered, prodding her with his toe. "She's just unconscious. For now."

I shivered at his last words.

"Do we kill them now?" the blond man asked, a wicked light in his eyes as he stalked forward to help Andreas haul Kristjana onto a couch.

Andreas looked to one of the other men. Alec and Kristoff did the same. I examined the two men who were strangers to me — both were tall and well built, although the blond was a bit stockier.

The dark-haired man pulled off his fedora and gave me a long, considering look, his eyes so dark they were almost black. "Not yet. This, I presume, is the reaper you mentioned?"

"This is Pia, yes. My love, this is Christian Dante, one of the members of the

368

council," Alec said. "The other is Sebastian."

"You're all vampires?" I asked, gazing at them with a kind of awed wonder. Each and every man could have graced the cover of a men's magazine. I couldn't help but wonder if being drop-dead gorgeous was one of the requirements to be a vampire.

"We are all Dark Ones, yes," the one named Christian answered. He made a little bow to me, although I noted he shot Alec a questioning glance.

Alec answered by putting his arm around me and hauling me up to his side. "Pia is not Zorya by choice. She is not responsible for what is happening here."

"You know, I really can speak for myself," I said, a tiny bit irritated with Alec's protective gesture. I twisted my way out of his hold and gave Christian, who clearly held some sort of a position of authority with the others, a level look. "I did not choose to become Zorya, that's true, but I have accepted the job now, and I am, in fact, responsible for my own actions. But . . ." I stopped, puzzled. "I thought you were in Vienna. Isn't that where you were trying to take me?"

Kristoff, to whom I had addressed the last question, quirked his lips. "Yes."

"We took a portal," Christian answered as the blond vampire walked around me, obviously examining me.

"A what, now?" I asked.

"A portal allows one to move from one area to another quickly, via a tear in the fabric of time and space," Christian answered.

My mouth hung open for a minute before I turned to Kristoff. "You guys can teleport like in *Star Trek*?"

"Not quite," Alec answered for him. Kristoff shot his friend an unreadable look. "But it's a similar principle. We don't use them often, since they can be tricky at best, but they are sometimes used in a time of emergency."

"Which this clearly is." Sebastian finished his examination of me and resumed his spot next to Christian. "An unmade Zorya, a sacristan, and a reaper elder — not a bad day's work."

Kristoff hauled Mattias to his feet and shoved him into the chair. At the sight of the latter's angry face, it struck me that Frederic wasn't anywhere in the room. "Did you hurt Frederic?"

"Unfortunately, no. He escaped," Kristoff's cousin Rowan said as he entered the room from the kitchen. He had a nasty burn on the side of his face, which, to my amazement, started fading even as I watched. "He had a car. The last I saw of him, he was headed out of town."

"You won't catch him," Mattias said sulkily. "Not before the Zenith gets here."

Christian spun around and stared at him in surprise. "Your leader is coming here?"

"To welcome Pia as a daughter of the moon." Mattias shot me an angry glance. "I am beginning to believe Kristjana when she says that you do not deserve to be Zorya."

"I think it's safe to say that Kristjana is not the most mentally stable person in town," I said dryly. "And I only know four of the six vampires here, and out of those four, three of them hate me, so you really needn't be so quick to judge."

"The Zenith is coming," Christian said softly, sharing a look with his friends. "How very interesting."

The one named Sebastian smiled. It made me shiver.

"Why do I have a horrible idea that I'm going to be used as bait to capture yet another member of the Brotherhood?" I asked Alec.

He brushed a strand of hair from my face. "It must be, Pia. The Zenith is the leader of the reapers — to have him is to deal a great blow to them."

"And if I say I won't cooperate?"

"You will not have a choice," Christian answered. He strolled over to gaze down into my eyes, holding my gaze with one that seemed to strip away everything and leave me bare and exposed. "You are a Zorya, a potential means of horrible death to my people. We cannot allow you to gain the power to do that. Do you understand?"

"Oh, I understand."

"Good." Christian nodded and released me from his hold.

"I understand that you're just as blind as the Brotherhood people are."

All six vampires froze, and I realized just how stupid a thing it was to challenge them when they were en masse. But I have never been known for having an overabundance of common sense, so I raised my chin and added, "It obviously doesn't occur to you that perhaps I can be a Zorya who doesn't destroy your people. And yet, that is exactly what I intend to do. Assuming I can, that is."

I shot a quick look at Alec and Kristoff. Alec was looking puzzled, while Kristoff avoided my eyes all together.

"And how do you propose to do that?" Christian asked in a velvety soft voice. He had an odd sort of an accent, part English, part something slightly Germanic, but as nice as his voice was, it was nothing like the silky tones that Kristoff could utter when he so chose.

I dragged my mind from that subject to the one at hand. "A lot of that depends on your answer to a question."

Christian's eyebrows rose. "What is the question?"

"Did you kill Anniki?"

He frowned.

"The other Zorya."

His brow cleared. "Ah. The one Kristoff said was discovered in your hotel room." He was silent for a moment. "Her death, while unlamented by my people, was not caused by any of them."

I stared hard at him, trying to read his body language. I had a pretty good sense of when someone was lying to me, and his words rang true. Of course, it could be that one of the vampires had killed her, and just not told his buddies, but that didn't seem very likely. "You may not have mourned her death, but I did. She was innocent of any wrongdoing. She hadn't been formally recognized as a Zorya, so she couldn't have hurt any of you."

"The point is moot," Sebastian said with

a note of finality. "Sooner or later, she would have destroyed us, just as you would have done if Kristoff had not taken steps to stop you."

"You mean the marriage?" I asked him.

He nodded.

"Marriage?" Mattias's face turned red. "You *married* a Dark One?"

"Yes, but not legally," I said, trying to calm him down before he burst.

"It was a legal marriage," Kristoff said stubbornly.

I raised an eyebrow at him, crossing my arms. "Possibly, but you know, I've been thinking about this, and everything I've seen and heard the last few days has left me with the idea that a group like the Brotherhood is more likely to accept as valid a marriage ceremony that I agreed to and participated in willingly over one where the groom had to bribe people to make it happen, forge the bride's signature, and bring in false witnesses."

Silence filled the room.

"That is a good point," Christian said thoughtfully, his gaze on Mattias.

The latter's face suddenly broke into a grin. "Then you are *my* wife."

"Don't get too excited — that's only a supposition," I said, suddenly worried that

Mattias might demand marital rights. "I don't know for sure which marriage is real."

"It is a reasonable point, nonetheless," Alec said, glancing at Kristoff.

"And one which means that the reaper here could still pose a danger if Kristoff's marriage won't stand," Sebastian added, nodding at me.

I sent him a quick glare. "Even if it's true, it doesn't mean I'm any such thing. I am not going to hurt *anyone*."

The silence that followed that statement was filled with disbelief.

I turned to Alec as the most reasonable of the men present. "Before Anniki died, she begged me to make things right. *'Let justice roll down like waters,'* she said, and I have done my best to do just that. I will find her murderer, and see that he or she receives justice for that act. But I will not persecute the innocent. I didn't want the job, but now I have it, and assuming that I am given the power to back it up, by god, I'm going to do the best I can with it. I have ghosts I'm responsible for," I said, waving my hand around the room.

My little gang had been oddly absent, but I saw now that they had just been hiding. They stepped forward now, all of them, out of the walls, from behind the furniture, and from the doorways. All of them solidified for a moment, until the room was filled with them.

Mattias's eyes bugged out of his head as he took them all in.

Ulfur strode forward until he stood in the center of the room, addressing Christian. "We will not let harm come to Zorya Pia, Dark One."

The other ghosts nodded their heads. Tears pricked in my eyes, a warm gratitude swelling in my chest.

"I see." Unexpectedly, Christian smiled. "You have quite a formidable group of champions, Pia."

"I do indeed. And it's because of them, and others like them who I might be able to help, that I will remain true to my oath to Anniki. I will be the ever-flowing stream of righteousness, but it will be *my* righteousness. I will not be a Zorya who destroys people without due cause."

"You won't have a choice," Mattias said smugly. He blanched somewhat when he saw that everyone in the room focused on him. The ghosts had gone back to a translucent state and were grouped together at one end of the room.

"What do you mean?" I asked Mattias.

He jerked his shoulders. "What I said. You

will not have a choice about using your powers. You think you will, but you won't. You are *my* wife, so once the ritual is conducted, you will not be able to keep from using your powers."

I stared at him in horror. "That can't be right."

"It is. Zoryas must cleanse. It is their reason for being." Mattias looked away, but a satisfied smile lurked on his lips.

I looked aghast at the others in the room. "I will not be used like that. If that's truly the case, then I will just refuse to undergo the ritual. I'll simply remain as I am, a quasi-Zorya, someone who can't do anyone any harm."

"We're not going to Ostri?" Hallur asked.

"I'm sorry." I turned to them. "I said I'd find someone else to take you if I had to, and that still stands. I promise. Barring that, there must be someone who can show me where the entrance is."

"The entrance to Ostri is a time, not a place," Mattias said, apparently engrossed in examining his fingers. "The opening to it is triggered by the Zorya during the ceremony of light. That is the only time you can lead spirits to it."

"Well, crap," I said, as conflicted as hell. I wanted desperately to get the ghosts to their final reward, but not at the cost of being an unwilling weapon of vengeance. "I'm so sorry. If that's the case, I can't risk it. It will have to be another Zorya who takes you to Ostri."

The ghosts murmured amongst themselves. Ulfur looked sad for a moment as he watched them. "We understand," he said. "We know you would take us if you could."

"You'll still get there," I reassured them. "Don't give up hope."

He said nothing, but their acceptance of the inevitable made my conscience sting. Was this what Anniki wanted from me? I knew she'd want the ghosts sent on their way, but the cost was simply too high.

"You do not understand," Mattias said abruptly, picking at his fingernails. "Your desire to protect the Dark Ones does not matter. The ceremony will be conducted whether or not you are present, and you *will* receive the powers of the Zorya. That is a fact."

"But if I'm not there —"

He looked up quickly. "It matters not. You are the Zorya. Once the ceremony is completed, you will receive the light and become a tool of righteousness and vengeance."

The eyes of all the vampires in the room moved to me. My stomach turned over in helpless fear.

"You will destroy the Dark Ones whether or not you wish to. You simply will not be able to keep from doing so," Mattias ended, his delivery matter-of-fact.

"Not unless she is destroyed first," Sebastian said, his gaze hooded.

"No. She will not be destroyed," Alec said, taking up a protective stance in front of me. Kristoff made an arrested gesture, as if he was going to protest. I'd like to think he did have enough feeling toward me that he didn't want me killed by his buddies, but I had to admit, as things stood, the vamps had a strong case for wanting me out of the picture.

"There has to be a way around the ritual," I said. "Is there?"

Mattias shook his head. "No."

"Then we will simply not allow the ceremony to take place," Alec said. "Pia is right — if she is kept in the state she is now, she poses no threat to anyone."

"But if a ceremony is held on her behalf —" Sebastian started to protest.

I was beginning to not like him.

"If we capture the Zenith, we could use him to ensure the ceremony was not conducted," Alec cut him off. "His life would be the price of Pia's safety."

"That might work," Kristoff said suddenly. He avoided meeting my glance, however. "It would mean that we have to find him before he reaches the others."

Christian raised an eyebrow at Mattias. "Where is the ritual to be held?"

Mattias glared at him and refused to answer.

"I think it's going to be at a ruins about ten miles from town," I said slowly, wondering if Alec's plan would work. I didn't want to die, but I also hated to fail Anniki. There had to be a way to accept the power and yet not use it against the vampires. "In some forest that's supposed to be haunted."

"We will search for other reapers," Christian told the others. "And most importantly, the Zenith. If he is arriving for this ritual, he will come here first."

"I'll go search for the trail of the reaper who got away," Rowan said, starting for the back door.

"I'll search around the ruins, in case any of them are already there," Andreas said as he left.

"Sebastian and I will take the town." Christian put his hat back on. He gave me another piercing look. "Alec, you will stay with the Zorya and the prisoners."

"I don't need a babysitter," I protested.

"I will help Rowan with the one who escaped," Kristoff said, not meeting my gaze as he left.

"Do not fret, my love," Alec said, gently pushing me toward the kitchen. "I am here for your protection, not to serve as your jailer. Help me find something to restrain that woman."

Kristjana regained consciousness just as Alec slapped a piece of duct tape across her mouth. Bound and gagged, she may not have been able to say anything, but if the venomous look in her eyes was anything to go by, she was indulging in a detailed fantasy of just how she'd like to see me die.

We laid her on a bed in a room on the ground floor, closing the door and locking it before returning to the main room.

"There you are. I was wondering what was going on."

I blinked in surprise at the sight of Magda standing over Mattias, who was rolling around on the floor, clearly struggling to get free of his bonds. "Oh, hello again, Alec. Pia, can I ask why your husband is handcuffed?"

"The vampire cavalry rode into town," I said, giving her a little hug as Alec, after greeting Magda, hauled Mattias to his feet, escorting him into another bedroom. "What are you still doing here? I thought the tour was leaving at noon."

"We were supposed to leave, but then Denise disappeared." Her smile, which had been filled with sunny warmth, faded.

"Disappeared?"

"Yeah." She gave me an odd look. "I know this is going to sound crazy, but I've come here to warn you. Sometime during the night, Denise disappeared out of her room. The police think it's suspicious because she left everything behind — passport, money, clothes, everything."

I sat down on the couch recently vacated by Mattias. Magda sat next to me. "Well, that's weird, but I don't see why you need to warn *me* about it."

She hesitated. "The police told Audrey that Denise left a note, saying that she had seen you in town, and she was going to follow you to see where you'd gone."

A chill swept over me. "Oh, god."

She nodded. "The policeman told Audrey that they think you did something to Denise. They're combing the area for both of you, and have refused to let us leave the country."

My shoulders slumped. "I haven't seen her. I didn't know she'd seen me, and I certainly wouldn't do anything to her."

"I know you wouldn't." Magda patted my arm. "That's why I wanted to warn you. I don't know what's going on with the Brotherhood people, but I'd suggest you get out of town before the police find you."

"I can't leave just yet," I said absently, wondering what had happened to Denise. She had nothing to do with my situation, so it was likely that if some accident had befallen her, it was entirely unrelated. The police, however, would not entertain that thought.

"You can't? Why?"

I explained to her the happenings since I'd last seen her, leaving out the part about having incredible sex with Kristoff.

"Good lord, you certainly have been busy," she said when I finished up. Alec's footstep was audible as he crossed the kitchen. She leaned close to me and whispered, "So do you think you're Alec's whatchamawhosit? Beloved?"

"No, I don't think so," I answered just as quietly. "Kristoff was hungry, so I let him . . . for lack of a better phrase, dine. He said if I was a Beloved, he wouldn't be able to do that."

"You know, this is really fascinating. And exciting. But what are you going to do about tonight?"

"The ritual, you mean?"

She nodded.

I glanced around the room. Several of the ghosts had drifted off to the kitchen to see what Alec was doing. Dagrun had thrown herself down on the couch opposite, and appeared to go to sleep. Agda demanded to see the inside privy, and the other women had gone with her to see what modern plumbing looked like. Other than Dagrun, we were alone. Quickly, I explained my reasoning regarding the two marriages.

"That makes sense, I guess," she said after mulling it over for a few seconds. "So if Mattias is your real husband, are you going to become Super Zorya?"

"I don't know. I don't want anyone to die, but I made an oath to Anniki."

She was silent for a moment, her fingers absently twisting the material of her linen walking shorts. "You know, I think I'd take what your husband said with a grain of salt."

I cast my mind back to anything that Kristoff might have said that could be in question.

"He said that once you had the power, you wouldn't be able to control it."

"Oh, Mattias? Yes, he did say that. It seems . . . counterintuitive, doesn't it?"

"Yup. You know what I think?" She tipped

her head to the side as she considered me. "I think he was bullshitting you."

"You don't think they can bestow powers on me without me being there?"

"No, actually, I can see that. You've already got this stone that makes you Zorya, so that's the part you're responsible for. You accepted the job. I admit it's a bit odd having the power come through recognition of that by your fellow Brotherhoodians, but eh. People do weird things sometimes. No, it's that whole song and dance about once you have the power, you'll have to use it whether or not you want to. I don't buy that, I don't buy that at all."

Now that I had time to sit and think about it, it didn't seem right to me, either. "I'm very big on the idea of free will," I said, nodding. "No one can make me do something that's morally reprehensible, not even if I had all the power of the moon. Anniki said nothing about being just a tool."

"Exactly. Maybe someone who didn't have a lot of mental gumption couldn't control her powers, but you? Bah. You've got gumption coming out of your pores."

"Thank you," I said, smiling. I felt surprisingly better at that thought.

She eyed me curiously. "So does that mean you're going to go ahead and let them do the ceremony? Or are you going to give in to this Christian fellow and let the vamps bully you into giving up your oath?"

I glanced toward the door. Alec was visible in the kitchen, surrounded by Ulfur and Hallur and a couple other ghosts, all of whom were examining his clothing while Alec spoke to someone on his cell phone.

"I've never enjoyed being pushed around," I said softly. "Not by anyone. And I don't intend to be used, nor will I let anyone die because of me. If I'm in a position of power, I can get the ghosts to Ostri, and keep everyone safe — Brotherhood people and vampires alike."

"Atta girl," Magda said with approval, giving my arm another pat. "That's part of your oath to Anniki done. What about the other part?"

"I don't know," I said slowly. "I honestly don't believe Kristoff or Alec had anything to do with her murder. And Christian said none of his people did."

"You believe him," she said, making it a statement, not a question.

"As a matter of fact, I do."

"So, who *did* kill her? And why was she killed in your bathroom?"

"It's your bathroom just as much as it is mine," I protested weakly.

She gave me a look that made me ashamed. "You said yourself the door was locked on your side. Besides, I didn't know her, and you did. There must be some connection between you and her that led to her being killed in *your* bathroom."

"If there is, I can't figure it out," I said, feeling helpless again. "I *think* it has something to do with the fact that I ran into Anniki earlier, but why would she come to see me in the middle of the night?"

"I still say it's that Ilargi person. You're sure one of the vamps isn't him?"

"I'm not sure, but I really don't think so. None of them feel" — I made a vague gesture — "evil. Dangerous, yes. Mysterious, and unmoving, and not at all the sort of person you want to meet in a dark alley — oh, hell yes! But soul sucking? No. Not that."

"Hrm." Magda looked pensive. "Well, I suppose finding her murderer isn't as pressing as dealing with this situation. I'm sure you'll work it out in the end. Now, what can I do to help?"

I glanced at the clock. Night had set in. "There's about two hours before the ritual is supposed to begin. I don't know how many other Brotherhood people are gathering for the ritual, although I don't think it's a whole lot. There's just not time to bring in people from outside of the area, and Mattias told me a few nights back that there are only like five total members who live in Iceland. So I think the first thing is for me to get out of town. You think you can get a car?"

"Done and doner," she said, saluting. "Then we'll go to the ruins?"

"*I'll* go. I don't think it's going to be safe for you at all," I said, quickly interrupting her protests. "I know you want to help, Magda, but really, the best thing you can do is stay away from the ruins. I don't want to have to worry about protecting you from anyone's ire just because you helped me, especially if that means I can't control whatever is going on at the time."

She opened her mouth to protest, closing it again with a muttered, "Damn. I hate it when you make sense."

"I promise I'll tell you everything that happens," I said, getting to my feet, one eye on Alec. He had his back to me, still talking on the phone. "Assuming I can, that is."

"Don't be such a negative Nelly," Magda said, heading for the front door. "I'll be back in a flash with a car. And I'm going to hold you to that promise, missy. If I have to sacrifice my curiosity, I want a full disclosure on the happenings."

I waved good-bye and sank back down onto the couch. I just hoped I'd be around to fulfill that promise.

CHAPTER 18

"My darling, you know I would move heaven and earth for you," Alec said a bit later. He kissed my hands when he said that, making me more than a little uncomfortable about his unabashed affection for me.

I had to break it to him that things had changed. It was unthinkable to let him believe I returned his feelings when just a few hours before I was engaged in carnal acts with his friend. I blushed just thinking about the manner in which I'd fed Kristoff.

"About that, Alec . . . I think we need to have a talk." I remembered that I was supposed to be coming up with an excuse to slip away from him so I could use the car that Magda was even now bringing to me, and amended my statement. "We need to talk about a couple of things."

"And so we shall, my precious one, but later. Kristoff is on his way back — he and Andreas have located the reaper who got away — and Kristoff ran into a couple more on their way to the ruins. He is bringing them back here. Christian called to say that he believes the Zenith has slipped past them. Sebastian was nearly run over by someone in a rental car."

"Couldn't that have been merely a tourist with bad driving skills?" I asked, distracted by the idea of a homicidal tourist.

Alec's lips quirked. "Not when the driver picks Sebastian out of the crowd and deliberately tries to run him down."

"Ouch. The Brotherhood guys can recognize vampires that easily?"

"Not generally, no, but all the members of the council are well known to the reapers, as are those of us who are tasked with hunting them. That is how I was recognized in the restaurant earlier. But all is well — Sebastian got the number of the car, and they are in pursuit. Kristoff has the three who attacked us earlier. You may rest assured that if the Zenith comes here, I will protect you, but I suspect that he will head straight for the ruins."

"So everyone is going to converge there?" Damn. How was I going to slip away and get to the ruins myself if all the vamps were descending there?

"Not if we can take them elsewhere. Do

not worry, my love, I won't let anyone hurt you." His cell phone rang. He glanced at it. "Ah. That is Andreas checking in. You will excuse me for a moment. . . ."

He wandered off to the hallway. I glanced around the room, saying softly, "Ulfur?"

"He's in the kitchen," Dagrun said from where she reclined on the couch.

I thought hard for a minute. "Do me a favor and round up everyone. I'm going to have to get moving, and I don't feel good about leaving you all behind."

Dagrun sighed heavily, but got up and stomped out of the room. I sidled past the door of the hall and through a small parlor to the kitchen.

A cluster of male ghosts stood marveling at the modern appliances. "What exactly does a Cuisinart do?" Ulfur asked, pointing at the item in question.

"Chops things up. I've sent Dagrun to gather up everyone — we have to get out of here. Now."

Ulfur and the men looked interested. "Where are we going?"

"To Ostri. I'm afraid we can't get your horse in the car, though."

Ulfur blinked for a moment. "We are going to the ruins you mentioned earlier?"

"Yes."

"I will ride there."

"It's almost ten miles," I pointed out. "If the opening to Ostri doesn't last long, I'm not sure if you can get there in time."

"I will not leave Ragnar," Ulfur repeated, a stubborn set to his ghostly jaw.

I gave up, recognizing defeat when I saw it. "Get going now, then. I'll try to delay leaving as long as I can, but I can't let the vampires get to everyone before they complete the ceremony."

Ulfur ran out after getting directions, calling for Ragnar, who appeared out of nothing with his ears twitching excitedly.

I peeked out the door to where Alec stood, still talking on the phone. The ghosts ran down the front stairs, rippling through Alec without him so much as lifting an eyebrow. I wondered again why Kristoff had been able to see them, but Alec didn't.

"The child says we're leaving?" Old Agda asked as she hobbled into the kitchen double time.

"Just as soon as the car gets here. Ulfur went on ahead to meet us. Is that everyone? Where's Karl and Marta?"

"Coming," Marta said, her face alight with happiness as she and her husband hurried into the kitchen. "You've changed your mind? We're really going to Ostri?"

"I'm going to do my best," I said with grim determination. "I'm going to need everyone to get into the car when Magda comes with it. Then we'll drive to the ruins, and we're going to do everything possible to stop the vampires from coming down on the Brotherhood people until they complete the ritual. So save your energy, OK?"

"You want us to help stop Dark Ones?" Hallur asked, looking worried. "We can't do that."

"Of course you can. You stopped the Ilargi."

The ghosts all looked at one another. "That was different," Hallur finally said.

"I don't see how. If anything, the Ilargi was more dangerous because he could suck your soul, and yet you stopped him from taking Karl. Surely if you can all cooperate to stop someone as powerful as that, you can slow down a couple of vampires."

"Dark Ones can disburse us," Ingveldur pointed out. "You saw this yourself when your man was annoyed by Ulfur's horse."

"Which man —" Hallur started to say.

"Ragnar wasn't in solid form then. If you all save your energy for stopping the vamps, and go solid on them, you should be able to slow them down."

"I don't like it," Hallur said, but his

buddy, the one with the two-room house, socked him in the shoulder.

"Don't be such an old woman!"

"Oh!" Agda said, taking a swing at the other ghost.

He ducked. "We stopped an Ilargi! What's a few Dark Ones?"

"That's the spirit," I told him. "Er . . . no pun intended. All right, does everyone know what to do?"

"I suppose so," Hallur said slowly. Marta giggled. Ingveldur ordered her daughter to vanish.

"We'll be here, but unseen, so as to save as much energy as we can," Ingveldur told me before disappearing.

I glanced out of the window. "Excellent. Magda has just arrived, so if you would all go outside and get into the car, I'll be out in a jiffy."

I tiptoed across the kitchen. Alec stood with his back to me. I felt bad about slipping away without him knowing, but there was no way I could take him with me. I did scribble out a quick note, however, and used a magnet on the refrigerator to leave it clearly visible. I didn't want anyone to worry that one of the Brotherhood people had nabbed me.

"I would be happy to come with you —"

Magda said a few minutes later.

I held up a hand to stop her. She sighed and gave me the keys to the compact rental car.

"It's safer this way. Safer for everyone," I said as I got into the car, accepting the map she shoved through the open window.

"Sometimes being safe sucks."

"Yeah, I know. Everyone in?"

Magda looked around in surprise. We were at a tiny garage connected to the house, apparently alone. "Your ghosts?"

"Yes." I glanced in the rearview mirror. There was nothing to be seen, but I could feel the presence of my ghostly friends. They must have been packed in as one solid mass.

"You're standing on my foot!" Dagrun complained. "Mother, Old Agda is on my foot!"

"Hush, child," Ingveldur scolded her daughter.

Agda cackled.

"You can stay behind if you like," I told the unseen teen.

"And miss seeing the vampires kill you? I don't think so."

"No one is going to kill anyone," I said grimly, starting the car.

"So you hope," Magda said, calling after me as I pulled out, "I'll be waiting to hear what happens!"

I waved a hand at her, and drove out of town.

The map that Magda had given me was not very helpful, and I took wrong turns three times before I stopped asking my ghostly friends for directions since it was sadly apparent that they didn't get out of the village much. It seemed like hours had passed before I finally pulled off to the side of the road and considered a sign that bore a ruins symbol, and an arrow pointing to the left.

"I think that's it. Ulfur certainly should have had time to get here. Everyone still all right?"

"No," Dagrun answered.

"We're fine, child," Ingveldur said at the same time. "The ride has been very interesting."

I glanced at my watch. "And a lot longer than I thought. All right, let's hope we made it here in time."

We pulled off the road and bumped our way down a graveled track that had some serious potholes. Ahead of us loomed an inky black expanse of forest, one of the few ancient woods left standing in Iceland. I remembered reading a note in the guidebook that said this spot had long been avoided by locals as being enchanted, thus the trees were preserved when pretty much all the other forests had been decimated.

No sign of the ruins was visible through the trees, but that didn't surprise me. The sun was sinking fast on the horizon now, the sky taking on that strange twilight appearance that was vaguely unsettling.

We arrived at last at a small shaded clearing. "I hope those belong to Frederic and his Brotherhood buddies rather than the vamps," I said, noting the three other cars in the tiny dirt parking area. Two bore Icelandic plates, another had a small rental tag on the bumper.

"Can we get out now?" a distressed voice asked.

"Sure, Hallur. Everyone out, but stay in low-watt mode until we see if the vamps are here."

I shivered as we followed a path that led into the woods. Immediately, we were enveloped in a heavy gloom that seemed more than just visual — it was as if the trees themselves were warning us to turn back, despair dripping heavily from their branches.

"OK, this is creepy," I said, rubbing my arms. "Is anyone else feeling this?"

"Yes," Ingveldur answered. Her voice was

subdued. "This is a haunted place, Pia."

"Haunted with other ghosts, you mean?" I looked around as we picked our way down the path. The trees were pretty solid here, not allowing much light to penetrate their stiff branches. The scent of pine mingled with the slightly acidic odor of damp earth. "I don't see anyone else."

"She means haunted by the spirit of place," Agda said in her dry, somewhat wheezy voice. "There are spirits here, ancient spirits, going back many generations."

I could believe it. I'm not normally someone who gets creeped out easily, but this wood, with its tall, black trees and somber atmosphere, was having an effect on my nerves. Silence hung heavily, like a dark cloud overhead, muffling the noise I made walking on dead pine needles. No other noise reached me, no rustling of small animals in the undergrowth, no night-bird sounds, not even so much as the whine of a gnat. "Maybe we should go back and look for another way to the ruins . . ."

"There," Ingveldur said. I stopped and looked around, finally seeing what she must have seen. A patch of the path ahead of us was lit with an amber glow that was the filtered midnight sun. I hurried forward, relieved to be out of the dark woods. The path turned and wound around a small mound, the top of which was crowned with a few crumbling bits of stone.

"The ruins at last. All right, everyone stay on your toes and watch for vampires. And for heaven's sake, if you see anything that looks like an opening to Ostri, let me know."

I left the path and was just moving to a tree with the intention of using it to shield me until I saw if there were any guards posted, when a hand clamped down on my face, causing me to simultaneously shriek into the hand and jump, twisting as I tried to free myself.

"Hush, love, it's just me," a man's voice spoke in my ear as another arm wrapped around me like steel.

"Alec?" I whispered when the hand had been removed from my mouth.

"It's a Dark One!" one of the ghosts said. "Should we stop him, Pia?"

"No, it's fine," I said quickly, turning in his arms.

Alec frowned down at me in question.

"Sorry. My ghosts are acting as bodyguards tonight. What are you doing here?"

"Finding you," he answered. "Why did you leave me? And what are you doing here?"

Suspicion tinted his words.

"I'm not here to destroy you or any of your friends, if that's what you think," I said quickly, speaking softly so as to avoid further detection. "Are all of you here?"

"No. Kristoff discovered you were gone. He thinks you've gone to join the reapers, and went off to stop you."

"Alec . . ." I hesitated, unsure of what I could say to convince him of my motives. "I have gone to join them, at least in the sense that I want them to complete the ceremony. No, listen to me for a minute — I know you guys don't want me to have power. But I just don't believe that if the ceremony is completed, I'll become some uncontrollable vampire-killing machine. There has to be a certain amount of *me* involved in the whole thing, if you know what I mean. And I don't accept the Brotherhood's story that all vampires are evil and should be destroyed. I am confident that no matter what, I will be able to control myself and not be some brainless tool."

He was silent for a moment, his arms like steel bands around me.

"You've seen other Zoryas," I pointed out, pleading with him to understand. "Were they uncontrollable? Or did they consciously use the power granted them?"

His arms relaxed somewhat. "They seemed very much in control."

"Exactly. Mattias was just trying to convince everyone that they were doomed. I think he's pissed at me because I wouldn't take him seriously as a husband, and he probably wants a wife who doesn't see both sides of the picture."

"The council will not understand, even if I do," he warned, loosening his hold more. I stepped out of it. "They will not hesitate to destroy you should they see that you bear the true power of a Zorya."

"Then we just won't let them see," I said softly. "Where are they?"

"No idea. They were following the Zenith last I heard, then Kristoff and I discovered your note, and he ran off to find you. I had to stay at the house in case the Zenith showed up, but when it was clear he wasn't headed there, I left to find you."

We moved silently from tree to tree, keeping our eyes peeled for any sentries Frederic might have set.

We were just about to emerge from the forest and take up a position behind one of the fallen walls when a noise behind us had me spinning around.

"Dark Ones!" Karl shouted, and my heart dropped at the sight. Emerging from the woods were the other vampires . . . all but Kristoff. They paused at the sight of Alec and me.

"I thought it would be too much for you," Christian told me with obvious disappointment.

The wind lifted and blew our way, bringing with it the reedy sound of voices chanting. Goose bumps rippled along my arms as I realized what was happening — the Brotherhood people were conducting the ceremony to bless me with the power of the moon. I glanced into the sky. The moon wasn't very visible, if at all, during the months when the sun never completely set, but there was a faint, almost invisible sliver showing over the tops of the trees.

"Let justice roll down like waters, and righteousness like an ever-flowing stream," I said, the image of Anniki as she pressed the stone into my hand flashing through my mind with unusual clarity.

She died for her belief in justice, and I had promised her I wouldn't fail in pursuit of the same. And so help me, I wouldn't.

"The ritual!" Sebastian shouted, and started forward.

"Stop them!" I yelled, whirling around to race toward the ruins. The ghosts materialized as a solid group and immediately flung themselves on the four vampires, their cries piercing the night. The vamps were taken totally unawares, and went down in a massive tangle of arms and legs.

Alec stood between me and the ruins. His eyes glittered in the twilight. "Go fulfill your destiny," he said after a moment, stepping aside.

"Oh, thank you." I ran forward.

The ruins loomed before us. It was pretty much like any other relic of centuries long past — large tumbled boulders that had been shaped by the weather into unrecognizable blobs of stone, two walls still standing, most of which had crumbled away, leaving only sharp little fingers of rock pointing to the sky.

The bulk of the building had been pulled back into the earth over time, wildflowers and tall grass claiming the remainder of visible stone. Someone had cut the grass in the very center, however, where part of one of the walls had collapsed, leaving three long blocks laid out like pews.

I stumbled to a halt as I realized that on one of the stones, a figure had been stretched out. Around it, spread out in a triangle, three people stood.

A sudden chill spread over me as I thought for a moment they were some sort of inhuman specters floating above the ground, but I realized with a start that they were simply wearing an odd sort of outfit that reminded me of a Renaissance fair I'd visited sometime back. Their long black robes blended into the shadows in a way that made it seem as if they had no legs or heads, their upper halves swathed with silver tabards, the sort Crusaders used to wear, but where the Crusaders bore a bloodred cross, the Brotherhood sported a crimson crescent moon.

I took a hesitant step forward, but at that moment a strange thing happened. The sun, which was moving slowly ever lower on the horizon, dipped to a point where a shaft of light penetrated the obstacles of trees and ruins, unerringly finding me with an impact that I felt to my toes. I stared down at myself, and my mouth opened in surprise when the light bathing me changed from the rich golden amber of the sun to a silvery blue light that seemed to glow along my skin.

The chanting swelled, ending on a high, triumphant note.

"It is done," Alec said in an odd, choked voice.

I glanced up at him, still stunned by the fact that I now glowed like the moonstone lantern. I raised a hand toward him. He flinched and backed up a step.

"I won't hurt you," I said, gazing with amazement at my glowing hand.

A cry from behind Alec had me gasping in horror. The vamps had worked faster than I thought to disperse the ghosts, running toward me only to stop a few feet away.

"So," Christian said, his voice filled with regret. "It is done."

"Yes," I said, suddenly possessed with a strange calm. I eyed him carefully, wondering if my new power would suddenly reveal to me an evil in him that I had not detected, but there was nothing there but what I had first seen. "And as I said before, you have nothing to fear from me."

"Am I late?" a panting voice called out, and Ulfur emerged from the woods, hauling a reluctant Ragnar with him. "Dark Ones! But . . . Pia, you're glowing."

"The ritual is completed," I told him. "It was as we guessed — the marriage to Kristoff was null. I can take you all to Ostri, assuming the others can gather up their energy."

"We cannot let you proceed," Christian said, and I felt a sense of profound sadness from him. "You are a true Zorya now. You mean death to my people."

He started toward me on the last words, and I threw up my hands, yelling, "No, you don't understand —"

The words trailed off when, to my amazement, a ring of brilliant bluish white light sprang up around the vamps, encircling them.

"Er . . . did I do that?" I asked Alec, staring in disbelief.

Christian started to step through the light, but yelped and jumped back the second it touched him. "What is this you have done?"

"I don't know," I said, wanting at the same time to yell at him and apologize. "I'm sorry, but I have to go stop Frederic. I have a feeling I know who it is they have, and I will not let them hurt him any more than I'll let them hurt you guys. So just . . . stay there."

"Pia," Alec started to say, reaching out a hand to touch the ring of light. He jerked his hand back with an oath. "I am not sure —"

"It's all right. None of you will get hurt if you just stay here," I told all of the vampires. "Ulfur, let's go see about saving husband number one."

"Husband . . . oh, the Dark One? Is he here, too?"

"I will come with you," Alec said as I

turned around and ran toward the ruins.

The vampires confined by the light circle yelled after us, but I didn't listen. I could reason with them later — right now I had a horrible suspicion that Frederic was waiting for me to show up and destroy Kristoff.

"It might be dangerous for you here just now," I said to Alec as we wove our way through the tumbled boulders.

He shot me an odd look. "I trust you."

"Thank you. Ulfur, I think I want you in commando mode."

"Commando?"

"Invisible and quiet until I call for you. Can you do that?"

He smiled and faded into nothing. "I'll be here when you need me."

"I'm counting on it. Holy Mary and all the saints!" I came to a halt as we cleared the last tumbled stone.

The figures in black and silver turned to face us.

Kristoff lay spread-eagle on the nearest stone, his arms and legs tied down to metal hooks that had been driven into the rock. He was covered in blood, and I thought for one horrible moment that they had killed him, but his head turned slowly to me as I stood staring in horror.

"Come to finish me off?" he asked, his

lovely voice broken and hoarse. "May your god damn you for all eternity."

CHAPTER 19

"We're here to save you," I told Kristoff, the strange calmness continuing despite the terrible vision of him covered in his own blood.

"I knew you would come." One of the hooded figures spoke. He pushed back his hood. It was, as I suspected, Frederic. "I knew you would not be able to refuse the light. Seize them."

The two hooded people headed for us, but Alec whipped out a gun. "Touch her, and you die," he warned them.

"It's all right," I started to say, but when I reached out to stop him, a bolt of energy shot down my arm right into him, sending him flying several feet until he smacked into one of the tall fingers of stone.

"Holy Jehoshaphat," I cried, and would have run to him, but one of the hooded people grabbed me. I struggled, knocking the hood off the person, revealing the rather square face of a blond woman. She was built like a wrestler, though, and quickly twisted one of my arms up behind my back, using her other hand to press down on my throat in a manner that could easily disrupt airflow.

The other person, a man, reached Alec.

"If you hurt him, you'll be more than sorry," I swore, making a futile effort to get free.

"There is no sense in struggling, Zorya Pia. Greta is a member of the Norwegian military." Frederic strolled over to where Alec lay prone. He poked him with his foot, rolling Alec over onto his back.

I gasped in horror. The side of Alec's face and neck was a bloody pulp, as if the flesh had been melted away. "Dear god — did I do that?"

"It is the cleansing power of the light," Frederic answered, sauntering over to where I was held by Greta.

"Should I bring him to the altar?" the other Brotherhood guy asked, glancing from Alec to Frederic.

"Not yet. We will attend to this one first, then deal with him. My dear, you do us proud." Frederic stopped in front of me, giving me a benevolent smile. "Only made a Zorya for a few minutes, and you've already begun to wield the light. We are pleased."

I blinked back tears as I dragged my gaze from where Alec lay in a bloody heap to the monster who'd so misled me. Could Mattias have been right after all? Was I going to be nothing but a tool to destroy innocent people?

I closed my eyes for a moment, too sickened by what I had done to be able to face anyone, but I knew I couldn't hide from the truth. "Let justice roll down like waters."

Frederic raised his eyebrows. "How very apt, although I believe we will let it flow as light." He stepped back, indicating Kristoff. "And here is your first opportunity to see that justice done. We will begin the cleansing ceremony."

Kristoff turned his head slightly. His face was in shadow, but his eyes glowed with an intensity that burned. The accusation in them stung, but I couldn't blame him for thinking the worst of me, not when he'd seen me come close to destroying his friend.

I looked from Kristoff to the man who stood waiting in front of me. "No," I said simply, knowing to the very depths of my soul that I would rather die than allow myself to be used to harm anyone. "I won't cleanse anyone. Kristoff doesn't deserve that, nor does Alec."

Kristoff looked stunned for a couple of seconds.

"You really should have more faith in me," I told him.

His jaw worked for a moment, but he said nothing.

"Doesn't deserve it?" For a moment, the mild, pleasant expression on Frederic's face cracked, and rage unlike anything I'd ever seen showed through. I would have taken a step back, but Greta held me immobile.

Frederic leaned his face into mine and hissed, "He killed one of your own people. He killed one of your brothers in the light, apparently before your very eyes. How can you say he doesn't deserve justice for that?"

"He killed in self-defense, and in defense of me," I answered. "I am sorry that one of your people died, but perhaps he shouldn't have been so quick to try to kill us."

"Do you blame him for mistaking you for one sympathetic to this . . . this monster?" Frederic asked, waving at Kristoff.

"I blame you for a lot of things, but most of all for intolerance. I won't do it," I repeated, shaking my head. "I will not kill for you."

Frederic held out his hand. "Mikael?"

The other man gave him Alec's gun.

Frederic pointed it directly at me.

"That won't do any good," I said with a brave little laugh that I didn't feel in the least. "What are you going to do, shoot your own Zorya? I'm willing to bet there are some sort of rules prohibiting that."

"There are, as a matter of fact," Frederic said, a sour look on his face. "There is nothing that says we cannot hurt you, however. So long as we don't actually kill you, we would not be in violation of the laws that govern us."

"What's a little torture between friends, eh?" I said with forced lightness. "Well, try this on for size — there is nothing you can do that will change my mind. I would rather die than harm anyone else."

He must have seen the truth in my eyes, must have heard the absolute conviction in my voice . . . or perhaps it was the cloaked and tabarded figure who emerged from behind him who caused him to lower the gun.

"Difficulties?" the figure asked, the hood muffling the word slightly.

I lifted my head, something chiming a little bell of warning in my head.

"Zenith," Frederic said, bowing. I was momentarily startled — the voice that spoke was definitely feminine.

The warning bell in my head got a whole

414

lot louder.

"We are honored by your presence. Light bless you."

"And you, brother." The woman stood next to one of the spikes of stone that marked where a wall had once stood. "I see the ritual is completed."

"It is. But the Zorya is reluctant to assume her duties," Frederic said, his voice filled with gentle chastisement.

Gentle, my ass. If anyone here was a monster, it was him.

"Oh, I don't think she'll give us any trouble." The woman's hand rose and swept back the hood. A malicious, amused gaze challenged mine. "Not holier-than-thou Pia. Not when her friend's life is at stake."

"Denise," I said, both surprised and, at the same time, oddly *not* surprised to see her. "Somehow, it seems almost fitting that you should be head honcho in a group of self-righteous, intolerant wack jobs."

She smiled and moved out from behind the rock a few feet. I was about to continue when I saw that she, too, held a gun . . . and it was pointed directly at a woman she pulled out with her.

"Hello," Magda said, giving me a weak grin. "Guess who I ran into on the way over here."

I stared at her in dumb horror.

"I'm sorry," she continued, glancing sideways at Denise. "You were right. I should have stayed out of it."

"It's too late for apologies," Denise said, yanking Magda in front of her. "I should have gotten rid of you two thorns in my side at the beginning."

Frederic, who had been frowning, looked from Magda and Denise to me. "You know the Zenith?"

"I thought I did. She's a member of my tour group."

He rounded on Denise. "You have been in Dalkafjordhur and you did not alert us?"

"Be quiet! You forget to whom you speak!" Denise snapped.

Frederic took a step toward her, gesturing with the gun, clearly baffled. "But you are the Zenith. You should have notified us that you were coming early. It would have changed everything had we known you were here —"

"It would have changed nothing," she snarled. "I do not have to explain my plans to you. You are here to see that they are carried out, nothing more. Do you understand, *brother?*"

The emphasis she placed on the word was stark, and left me smiling to myself. Frederic was a self-aggrandized man, and he wouldn't take well to being chewed out in front of others.

"As the Zenith commands," he said stiffly, bowing his head in a jerky concession of submission, but I caught a glimpse of his face — he was furious.

Now, how could I use that to get us out of this horrible situation?

"Just so you understand the situation, Pia — if you do not, in the next thirty seconds, begin the ritual of cleansing on this repulsive specimen, Frederic will begin cutting off parts of your friend. Perhaps after witnessing her torment you'll rethink your foolish stand. If you still refuse after we've hacked her to pieces, I'll kill you."

"You can't kill me; I'm the Zorya," I said, my blood chilling despite my bravado. I truly believed she would torture Magda. She seemed so cold, so heartless . . . and with that thought, a door in my mind opened, flooding me with an absolute knowledge that left me shaking.

"And *I'm* the Zenith. I can do anything I want."

"Including killing the previous Zorya? It was you, wasn't it? You killed Anniki."

Her expression never changed, but surprise flashed in Frederic's eyes.

"You killed our Zorya?" he asked.

She made an abrupt gesture. "She was a fool, an ignorant fool, and impure to boot. She deceived us with a facade of piety, and we were all taken in. But I sensed something was wrong, and it was — she was ready to betray us, betray the entire Brotherhood by helping the Dark Ones. Once I found out the truth, I knew what had to be done."

I was silent, remembering the light of truth that had shown in Anniki's face the night we spoke together in the café. Her absolute conviction was not an act, as Denise would have me believe. Which meant that Denise was lying . . .

"But to kill her without letting us know first?" Frederic's eyes stood out against the pallor of his skin. "We deserved to know."

"Do not even think of telling me how to do my job," Denise snapped at him. "It is my responsibility to ensure the order is protected against those who would drag us down. Your duty — every member's duty — is to protect the order at all costs."

Frederic's jaw tightened. He didn't like what he was hearing, and I didn't blame him.

"I don't believe you," I said, shaking my head, tears burning my eyes as I remembered Anniki's shining face. "She wasn't like that. She believed in what she was doing. She was happy and excited about being a Zorya, about doing what she clearly thought was some way to better the world. She was not a traitor to your cause, however wrong it is."

"You are just like her," Denise pronounced, sending me a look of pure, venomous hatred. "Only you do not hide your taint behind pretended piety. But we know what you are now, and we will take steps to cleanse the darkness out of you as we will your friends."

"Friends into whose arms you pushed me," I said slowly, remembering the stupid bet she'd forced me to accept. "You knew they were vampires then, didn't you?"

"I recognized them." That nasty smile of hers curled her lips again. "I thought of letting them have that little bint Anniki, but it was much easier to just silence her myself . . . especially since it would implicate you in her death."

"You didn't have to kill her —"

"Silence!" Denise raged, jerking Magda forward a few feet. "You exist solely at my whim, Pia, a fact you should not forget. Anniki was nothing, not worth the time it took to get rid of her, but I did it so that the order would be stronger."

"You're absolutely insane," I said, my skin crawling with horror at the woman who stood in front of me, but even as I recognized the madness in her, I realized there was something wrong, something that didn't quite ring true. "You killed a sweet, innocent woman for no reason. You are the one who is tainting your precious group."

Her eyes narrowed on me. "The Brotherhood is all that matters. *In tua luce videmus lucem* — in thy light we see light."

My stomach heaved. Poor, poor Anniki, caught between a madwoman and her delusions of piety.

"Enough of this." Denise nodded toward Frederic. "Start the ritual. I don't have time to waste."

Frederic hesitated a moment, but finally gestured to the other two members. Greta reluctantly released me, taking the gun from Frederic and pulling up her hood to join Mikael as they stood at the head and feet of Kristoff. Their voices started a low, singsong chant that Frederic joined in as soon as he pulled a wicked-looking knife from his boot.

Magda's eyes widened at the sight of the blade as it glinted in the light I cast. "Pia?"

"It's all right. Just stay calm. I won't let anyone hurt you." I glanced at Kristoff. He lay mute, his body stretched taut, as still as if he was already dead. His clothing bore long gashes, testimony to the fact that Frederic was not hesitant to use the knife he held so nonchalantly. I swallowed back a knot in my throat, forcing down the rising nausea at the proof of Frederic's savagery, my gaze locking with Kristoff's for a moment that seemed to stretch to an eternity.

His eyes were filled with neither a plea nor condemnation. He simply watched me with interest, as if I was some sort of specimen he was examining under a high-powered microscope.

"Any last words?" I asked him, keeping my face placid.

His brows rose slightly, and I saw his Adam's apple bob. "None," he finally said.

I nodded and stepped forward, my eyes on the dagger that Frederic held.

As the chanting increased in volume, something whirled off to the side, like a mini cyclone. Grass and leaves spiraled upward into the air, dust from the dirt it raised leaving a cloudy haze that formed itself into an oval about the size of a small car.

"Ostri," Frederic said, glancing at me, a slight smile on his face as I gazed in astonishment at it.

"That's . . . heaven?" I asked.

"It is the gateway to Ostri. It is there that

you will lead the spirits who have looked to you for guidance — once you have completed the cleansing."

The stone that swung gently from my wrist had turned into a lantern, glowing in a light identical to that which shimmered around my body. It grew brighter.

"Is that it?" a breathless voice asked behind me. I turned to see motes of light gathering in the air, reforming themselves into Marta. "Is that Ostri?"

"That's it. Where are the others?"

"Coming. It's so beautiful," she said, her voice filled with awe as she stared at the dusty portal.

"I guess it is." I couldn't help but smile as the other ghosts slowly re-formed themselves, all of them staring with identical expressions of unadulterated delight at their long-sought destination. "Before you go, I just want to thank you all for everything you've done. No matter what else has happened, or will happen, I'm truly pleased that you will be able to move on."

Dagrun clicked her tongue against her teeth and pushed forward, past the other ghosts, past where Frederic stood, past Kristoff and the still-unmoving Alec. "I'm not going to stay for the speeches. Farewell and all that." She stepped into the swirling mist and disappeared.

"Go ahead, all of you," I told the ghosts, turning back from their beatific smiles as they spoke good-byes before drifting into the vortex.

I had a job to do still, a horrible one that lay before me.

"Get to it, already," Denise ordered, jerking Magda forward another couple of steps.

"In tua luce videmus lucem," Frederic said, gesturing toward Kristoff. "Now is the time, Zorya, daughter of the moon. Draw on our strength. Channel the light that flows through you from the moon goddess mother to cleanse the abomination that lies before us. Right the wrongs."

The chanting increased in volume, filling me with a euphoric sense of lightness. The light increased in intensity, surrounding me with a corona of power that threatened to burst free and fill the entire hilltop.

Kristoff's gaze met mine, and for a moment, for a second, I was possessed with the absolute knowledge that I could end his suffering. It would be humane. It would be quick. It would be . . . unjust.

"Ulfur?" I asked, struggling to rein back the light that wanted so desperately to pour forth.

"Here."

The air rippled behind Denise.

"Now," I said, spinning around to face the two women. Ulfur materialized, throwing himself forward onto Denise, knocking the gun from her hand as Magda was sent flying with a startled cry.

I gathered the light and yelled as I flung it at Denise, "This is for Anniki!"

The light hit her with the impact of a sledgehammer, flinging her backward at least a dozen feet.

Frederic froze for a second, then leaped at me, his face twisting in hate. "If you will not use the light, then I will!"

A sharp burning pain bit deep into my side. I stared down in horror to see him pulling the knife from my side. The blade glistened with blood, but glowed with a pure white light that faded from me even as I watched.

Frederic whirled and ran toward Kristoff. Denise, still struggling with Ulfur, screamed an order to kill me. Magda picked up a rock and slammed it on her head, pointing beyond me and yelling.

Alec had risen to his feet, the right side of his body still rather gruesome, but miraculously partly healed. He lunged forward, knocking Mikael aside in a desperate attempt to free Kristoff's hands.

Greta shot him three times in the chest, sending Alec to his knees.

I knew with absolute certainty that Frederic was going to plunge the light-drenched dagger into Kristoff's heart, and I had no power left to stop him.

I acted without thinking. I leaped forward, throwing myself toward Kristoff, screaming, "No!"

Frederic raised the dagger high in both hands, chanting in a high, strange voice, *"In tua luce videmus lucem!"* before jerking his hands down.

The knife bit into my back as I landed on top of Kristoff. Alec hauled himself to his feet, still frantically trying to free Kristoff's hands despite the fact that Greta continued to empty her gun into him.

Pain blossomed slowly as I lifted my head, a hot glow spreading out from the blade in slow waves of heat that quickly picked up intensity.

Shouts rang out through the trees, familiar voices calling to Kristoff and Alec.

"The light must have faded," I told Kristoff, who lay prone beneath me, the waves of heat starting to make thinking difficult. "I told you to have faith in me."

"I do," he said, the lovely teal of his eyes burning bright.

Frederic screamed as the vampires reached him. Magda rushed over to me, gasping at the knife that I knew was protruding from my back. "Dear god in heaven, Pia. Dear god!"

"I'm all right," I said, my voice a croak as hands helped me off Kristoff and the stone. My head was swimming, but I made an effort to clear it. Alec, after having kicked the gun from Greta, sent her flying into Rowan's waiting arms, and staggered toward me, grabbing me in a careful but tight embrace.

"My love, my brave love. It is all over, my Beloved. Do not cry — it is over."

I wasn't crying, but I was shaking with the aftereffects of having been twice stabbed. I didn't complain, however, as Alec cradled me, murmuring words of comfort.

"What are you doing? You can't move her!" Magda ordered, trying to pry Alec's hands off of me. "She's been stabbed! We have to get her to a hospital! Dear god, don't any of you know how to treat someone who's been stabbed? Pia, sweetie, lie down. We'll call an aid unit."

"There is no need for mortal assistance," I heard Christian say. I lifted my head, looking at him. He eyed my back carefully for a moment, then, to my surprise, smiled.

"I realize you don't like me, and you'd

probably like me dead at this very moment, but I would like to point out that I did not harm any of your people, and I *am* wounded."

"That doesn't matter anymore," he said, the odd smile still on his lips.

Alec suddenly stepped back, an indescribable expression on his face.

"There will be repercussions, Pia."

"What?" I dragged my attention from Alec to him.

"I'm sure you still want me dead, but I can assure you —"

"The council will speak to you later, after things have sorted themselves out."

"I must be in shock again," I said, shaking my head. "None of this is making any sense."

"If you are in shock, then so am I. Why are you standing around smiling?" Magda demanded to know.

"She is a Beloved. She is immortal," Christian said, and before I could say anything he plucked the knife from my back.

I yelped and spun around. "Hey!"

"The wound will heal by itself in a few minutes," he told me, glancing beyond to Alec. "I will leave you to Alec. He will no doubt wish to explain to you what it is to be a Beloved."

"But I thought . . ." I blinked a few times, but as usual, that didn't make things any clearer. "A Beloved? How can that be?"

"You sacrificed yourself," Alec said, his expression stunned. "You saved Kristoff. They would have killed me, too, after him, but you . . . I . . . I don't know . . ."

He stumbled off a few feet, looking as if the ground had been pulled out from under his feet.

I looked over to where Kristoff was being assisted to his feet by Rowan and Andreas.

"So I really am a Beloved after all?" I asked, feeling oddly empty inside.

"You are." Christian gave me a long look, then handed me a business card. "We will be in contact."

Then he turned and strode off to where the others were holding Frederic and his buddies.

"What is happening?" I asked no one in particular.

"I'd say your friends are all nutters, but you know, that guy is right — the wound has healed itself up," Magda said, examining my back.

"I'm Alec's Beloved," I said, trying to come to grips with the fact. Saying it aloud didn't seem to help.

Kristoff took a step toward me, hesitated,

then walked past without saying a word.

Pain lanced through me. I saved his life and he couldn't even acknowledge that? More than ever I felt like crying. Kristoff might be upset that I was his friend's Beloved, but it hurt that he couldn't even face me.

"You're welcome," I said, fighting tears.

"He has been gravely wounded," Rowan said before he went over to help the others as they stood guard over the Brotherhood people.

Ulfur stood silently watching us, Ragnar behind him, both of them nearly invisible. They must have exhausted their reserves.

"Thank you," I told Ulfur, and he summoned up enough energy to materialize a physical form long enough for me to hug him. "You saved us all, but the time has come for you to go. Everyone is waiting for you."

He gave me a sad smile and faded back to a translucent state. "It's too late."

I turned to look at the entrance to Ostri, but it was gone. It must have disappeared when the ritual was stopped.

"No," I said, my shoulders drooping. "Oh, Ulfur —"

"It's all right," he said, lifting a hand to me. "I kind of like this world. It is interesting, at least. Be well, Zorya Pia. Go with the blessing of the village."

Pain spun through me, pain and regret so great I wanted to howl to the sky about the injustices of the world that couldn't be made right.

Magda touched my arm. "Is it over?"

"Yes." I couldn't move. My legs were like lead weights, as heavy as my spirits.

"The good guys won?"

"Yes."

She patted me gently, careful to avoid the two puncture points. "You did the right thing, but I never doubted you would. And hey, look at it this way — you not only got a new career and two husbands, now you have a vampire of your very own."

A vampire of my own. I stood numbly thinking about that as she wandered over to offer her help to the remaining vampires. Lucky me, bound for all eternity to a man I didn't know.

But it didn't have to stay that way, did it? We were bound together now — Kristoff had said that Beloveds and their Dark Ones could talk together without words, use some sort of mental telepathy to communicate. It seemed to me that would offer a good way to learn about someone.

Are you out there? I asked, my eyes on the

430

retreating figure of Alec as he caught up to Kristoff, the two of them about to move out of sight into the trees. *Can you hear me? Does this really work?*

Yes, it does. The voice was instantly there in my head, as loud as if it had been spoken in my ear.

My delight was short-lived. The man who turned back to look at me with an expression of stunned surprise wasn't Alec . . . it was Kristoff.

Dear god. It wasn't Alec. My mind whirled around helplessly, trying to understand what had happened.

Kristoff's gaze met mine over the distance, and I realized that the pain and regret I felt originated from him. He didn't want me. He never had. I was merely a warm body to feed him and satisfy a purely physical need. His heart was still bound in grief to the woman who'd been so cruelly killed, a woman who by all accounts should have been the one to redeem him.

Not me. But life is cruel, and we'd been bound together for the rest of our lives.

For eternity.

My heart cried out as he turned away and disappeared into the inky darkness of the forest.

CHAPTER 20

"You are free to go."

"What?" I roused myself out of the stupor that had claimed me several hours before, focusing on the square face of the policeman who sat opposite me. "I'm what?"

"Free to go. Unless there's something else you wish to tell us?" A blond eyebrow rose in question.

"No." I blinked a couple of times, looking around at the police station. It hadn't been busy at all when the vampires arrived with Denise, but that quickly changed.

"You mean you don't want me to tell you about Anniki and Denise anymore?"

The policeman, whose name I vaguely remembered was Jan, shook his head, gesturing toward a stack of paper. "Not unless you have something new to add. The woman you helped to catch has confessed to the murder of the Frenchwoman."

The woman I helped to catch. I rubbed

my head, trying to process everything that had happened in the last few hours.

"Your friend is here, if you wish to leave." He turned to a computer terminal and began to tap on a keyboard.

I gathered together what wits I still had, and staggered out of the room to a reception area, where Magda was chatting with a familiar man.

"I didn't really think you would turn Denise over to the police," I told him.

Christian turned to face me. "I hadn't intended to at first, but then . . . well, let's just say that I felt a gesture was needed to thank you."

"For not killing Kristoff?" I shook my head. "I told you I wouldn't kill anyone."

"I realize now that I was mistaken in attributing motives to you that are not necessarily appropriate," he admitted. "It was not, I admit, an easy thing to do to give up a Zenith to the mortal police, but I trust that your name is now sufficiently cleared."

"Yes. I'm officially released and no longer a suspect."

"That is a good thing, yes?" he asked with a smile.

"Definitely," Magda answered for me, stretching. "You ready to go, Pia? There's a sweet policewoman outside who said she'd

433

take us to our hotel."

"Yes, I will be in a minute." I bit my lip and eyed Christian.

Magda murmured something about visiting the bathroom, moving off to the hallway.

"She is a good friend," Christian said, nodding toward her. "She understands that you have something you wish to say to me."

I nodded, worrying the light material of my blouse as I tried to figure out how to ask what I wanted to know.

His hands stopped mine. "Perhaps I can save you a little grief and tell you that both Alec and Kristoff have left Iceland."

"They did?" My shoulders slumped. I knew they were going to leave now that everything with the Brotherhood group was over, but to leave without saying anything to me . . . that hurt.

Christian's black gaze was oddly compassionate. "It would seem that in addition to being wrong about you, I was incorrect in assuming you were Alec's Beloved. I understand now that it is to Kristoff you are bound."

I turned away and looked out the window. It was early evening. I'd been in the police station for almost twelve hours, and I was just about dropping. "So it would seem."

He was silent for a moment. "It is not my

business to interfere, but if there is a message you would like to pass along to either man, I would see that it reached them."

"Thanks, but I don't have anything to say."

"Pia . . ." I turned around to face him again, too tired to feel much of anything anymore. He took my hand. "I have a Beloved. She is very dear to me. No, that is an understatement — she is everything to me. I would lay down my life for her in a heartbeat. I cannot conceive of it being any other way. I realize that our ways are new to you, but I believe that you would make Kristoff an excellent Beloved."

"Thanks," I said, smiling as I gently pulled my hand back. "I just don't think it was meant to be, that's all."

He said nothing, just bowed, and started to leave when Rowan threw open the doors and rushed in, looking around wildly. "Is he here?"

"Who?" Christian asked.

"The French reaper." Rowan turned to the side. The entire left side of his face and arm were bloodred, covered in blisters. "We were taking all the reapers to the plane when that bastard Frederic tripped me up, and got away while I was trying to get out of the sunlight. I chased him here. He got my gun."

Christian muttered something and bolted out of the door.

A horrible presentiment shook me. I turned on my heel, pausing to tell the woman at the desk, "I left something on Detective Jan's desk," before I hurried back toward the detective's room. By the time I reached it, I was running, skidding to a stop as before me, a drama opened in seeming slow motion.

From a side room, Denise was being escorted, handcuffed and manacled, a policewoman keeping a firm grip on her. To my left, out of a connecting hall, a voice called out, and Frederic appeared, sliding to a stop as he raised a gun.

"No!" I heard myself scream out, but it was too late. Shots reverberated loudly through the station. Denise stared at Frederic for a moment before throwing back her head and laughing, even as her body crumpled to the ground.

"No!" I cried again, clutching the wall for support.

Frederic let the gun drop from his hand as the police swarmed him. His gaze met mine for an instant, and I knew without any doubt that he had sought his own form of justice.

Justice for Anniki.

■ ■ ■ ■

"What are those steps again?"

I looked out of the window of the hotel to the bright, glittering sea. It was almost, but not quite, the color of Kristoff's eyes.

"Does it matter?"

"Well, I'm kind of curious how you could think you were doing the steps with one guy, but really have done them with another. I know you had sex with both, but didn't you say there was something about a blood exchange?

"Yes. Kristoff bit his tongue during one of our more passionate moments. I assume that and the fact that he drank my blood satisfied the exchange requirement." I turned away from the window and summoned up a little smile for my friend. "The steps are unimportant. Christian said that he knew the second I threw myself on top of Kristoff that I was a Beloved. Evidently we smell different, or something. That's why Alec was so taken aback — I didn't smell the same, and he knew something must have happened, and guessed it was Kristoff."

Magda watched me as I fussed with a flower arrangement that sat on a round glass table. "This is going to sound harsh, but I really don't see what you're moping about. Yeah, you didn't get the guy you were interested in, but come on, Pia! Kristoff is gorgeous! He's got those blue eyes, and that chin, and I bet you could talk him into some manly stubble — every man looks better with a smidgen of stubble; it makes them look all ruthless and dangerous — and yet you're walking around looking like life has just kicked you in the gut."

I slumped down onto the couch next to her. "Oh, I'd be doing backflips of joy but for one thing — Kristoff is in love with his girlfriend. His dead girlfriend. And as nice as our couple of romps in the sack were, sooner or later that's going to pale. I want a man in my life, Magda, not someone who swings by every month or so to get his jollies off and scoop up that month's batch of blood, and then leaves without a backward glance."

I was past tears, but the pain remained.

"So he got his soul back, but he doesn't want you?" Magda look thoughtful for a few minutes, then shook her head. "No. I don't believe that. I think you've got the wrong end of the stick here."

"You don't have to take my word for it," I said with a shaky laugh. I waved my hand around the room. "Do you see any vampire here, pledging his undying love to me in gratitude for redemption?"

She couldn't argue with that. In the end, she said simply, "He's a man. Sometimes they need some time to think things through. If he wasn't expecting you to be his Beloved any more than you were, the whole thing probably left him questioning everything in his life." She patted my knee and got up to pour another cup of coffee. "Be patient, Pia. I think with time you guys will work things out. I mean, he can't live without you, can he?"

"We'll see," I said, too heartsick to think about it anymore. I made an effort to pull myself out of a pit of self-pity. "So are you going ahead with the tour?"

"I think I will. We've lost a couple of days in Holland, but now everything is over, the tour is free to go. You . . . er . . . didn't want to come with us, did you? I know that sounds horrible said like that, but I don't think Audrey —"

"Don't worry, I'm going back home. I've had enough of romantic Europe." If there was bitterness in my voice, she ignored it.

"I don't blame you. I still can't believe that Denise was behind it all. I mean, I know it's wrong to speak ill of the dead, but she was just completely wacked out. A total nutter, as Ray says. I just wish I knew why she chose our tour to come on."

I frowned at the cup of coffee that she held out to me.

She watched me for a minute before setting down her cup. "What is it? What's bothering you? Other than the whole business with Kristoff and Alec, that is."

"I don't know for certain. It's just something that keeps nagging at me, something that doesn't feel . . . right." I looked up at her. "Do you really think Denise was nuts?"

Her eyebrows rose in delicate arches. "Are you implying she wasn't?"

"I think . . . yes, I think that's just what I mean," I said slowly. "Detective Jan told me Denise claimed she was on the tour because she wanted a perfect cover for being here without members of her religious group knowing she was checking up on them, and that as a tourist she could nose around without anyone thinking anything of it. But honestly, Magda, doesn't that seem a little thin to you?"

"Maybe," she said, her nose wrinkling as she thought. "I suppose so. But it could just as easily be true."

"And then there's the lies she told at the ruins," I said, blindly staring at the coffee cup. "She was lying through her teeth, I know she was. And Frederic knew it as well — that's why he shot her."

"I don't understand what you're trying to say. So she lied about why she killed Anniki. If she was nuts, maybe she believed her own little fantasy."

"But she didn't. That's how I knew she wasn't telling the truth — she *knew* she was lying, and that's what I picked up on."

"OK." Magda shrugged and set down her empty cup. "So she lied about why she killed Anniki. What does that prove? The only reason she'd lie like that is if she . . ." Magda's gaze jumped to mine.

I nodded. "If she was covering up for someone else, someone for whom she was willing to be convicted of a murder she didn't commit."

"Frederic?" she asked.

"I don't know. Possibly. I don't know if we'll ever really know the truth. Frederic evidently refuses to say anything, and so far as the police are concerned, it's all just part of a weird religious cult filled with wackos."

"Well, I don't see that there's anything to worry about, then. Denise is dead."

I said nothing. Magda hadn't been at Anniki's side when she lay dying in her own blood.

441

"Change of subject. Have you heard from either of your vampires?"

I made a face. "They're not mine, and no. Alec left Iceland before the police were done talking to me."

"That's a weaselly thing to do," she pronounced.

I smiled, amused despite my glum mood. "Evidently Kristoff did the same."

"That's different. He's tortured and tormented and suddenly found himself in possession of a bodacious babe, and hasn't quite come to his senses yet."

"You like him," I said, suddenly realizing the truth.

"Yeah." She grinned. "He's got that bad-boy thing going for him that I love. And his voice — dear god. That Italian accent is so sexy it makes me want to rip off my clothes and throw myself on him."

"He *killed* a man in front of me," I reminded her, my smile fading.

"He *saved* your life," she countered.

"He's a vampire."

"And you're his soul mate. Cheer up, Eeyore. The vamps who wanted you dead a day ago have cleared your name. You got all the ghosts but one to heaven. You cleared out a nest of Brotherhood fanatics, and saw that Anniki had the justice you promised her."

I fingered the moonstone hanging from the chain looped around my wrist.

"And there's one hell of a sexy man out there who I guarantee is thinking about you right this very minute. From where I stand, life is looking pretty good for you."

I wondered if Kristoff was thinking about me. I hadn't seen Alec or him since I'd gone off with Christian to the police, and although I was tempted once or twice to try to mind talk to Kristoff, in the end, I hadn't. It was clear he was upset. I didn't need to make things worse.

"Speaking of ghosts, what are you going to do about this?" Magda touched the moonstone.

"Nothing. I did what Anniki asked of me, and now I'm finished. I'd turn the stone over to one of the Brotherhood people, but they're either in jail or the vampires have them, so I'll just hang on to it until I can find someone to take it off my hands."

Her lips pursed. "You're giving up being a Zorya altogether? Why? I mean, obviously you're not going to go around offing any vampires, but there is the other part of the job that I thought you liked — helping the dead people."

"There are other Zoryas who can do that," I said, fingering the stone. "I did what I promised to do, and now I'm done. This brief but very odd chapter in my life is over."

Which didn't explain why my heart felt like it was made of lead when I considered turning the moonstone over to the rightful authorities.

"I think it's a shame you're giving it up, but I suppose you are justified in not wanting to have anything more to do with the Brotherhood," Madga admitted. "I shudder to think what those vampires'll do to them."

"Me, too."

"Why don't you come to San Francisco? I'd love to have you stay with me for a bit. Eek! Is that the time? I was supposed to have my things packed an hour ago." She leaped to her feet, her face concerned. "You sure you're going to be OK?"

"I'm sure. My plane leaves tonight. Have a wonderful trip, and say hi to everyone for me."

She accepted my hug and gave me a little squeeze. "I'll call you when I get back, OK? Don't think you're going to be rid of me so easily. I want to be there to say I told you so when Kristoff comes crawling back."

I said nothing, just smiled and waved as she dashed out of the room. The sea beckoned me, blue light flashing deep in its depths, reminding me of the last look Kristoff had cast my way.

Perhaps there was hope after all.

ABOUT THE AUTHOR

Katie MacAlister lives in the Pacific Northwest with her husband and dogs, and can often be found lurking around online game sites. To contact Katie, visit www.katie macalister.com.